# A Line Between Friends

# A Line Between Friends

Michele VanOrt Cozzens

**McKenna Publishing Group**
Indian Wells, California

A Line Between Friends

PUBLISHER'S NOTE:
This book is a work of fiction. Names, characters, places, and incidents either are products of the
author's imagination or are used fictitiously, and any resemblance to actual persons, living or dead,
business establishments, events, or locales is entirely coincidental.

ISBN: 1-932172-26-2
LCCN: 2006927632

Cover design by Leslie A. Parker

First Edition
10 9 8 7 6 5 4 3 2 1
Printed in the United States of America

Visit us on the Web at: www.mckennapubgrp.com

*"No love, no friendship can cross the path of our destiny
without leaving some mark on it forever."*
**—Francois Muriac**


*"Platonic Love is a fool's name
for the affection between a disability and a frost."*
**—Ambrose Bierce**

**Also By Michele VanOrt Cozzens**

*I'm Living Your Dream Life:*
*The Story of a Northwoods Resort Owner*

*The Things I Wish I'd Said*

For Mike

# 1.

## Noelle. Present Day.

My father always referred to World War II as "The War." Not W.W. Two, not The Big One or The War To End All Wars. Just The War—as if it were the only one that mattered. Every night at the dinner table, his gray tales ranged from crossing the Atlantic in swelling seas to how Mommy didn't want to date him because he couldn't foxtrot. His shipmates, better known as his war buddies, taught him how to dance, and because of them, he won the heart of my mother, Emily Fournier. They married in 1942, my dad in his formal Naval attire and my mother in a lush, satin gown.

Dad's war stories swayed to Glen Miller rhythms and a gunfire beat, and they are what I remember most about him. I stopped listening when 1960-something caught up with him and his face tightened. Shortly after I was born, the world had stopped measuring up to his expectations. His tone grew as bitter as old olives while he complained of incompetent workers and immoral neighbors.

Dad's war days were his glory days—the best years of his life. It was all downhill from there.

After V-E day, Earl Moncada, tall and sandy-haired, handsome with new creases of worldly experience, returned home from the North Atlantic to the stinking town of Argo, Illinois, the Cornstarch Capital of the Chicago suburbs. At his side was his bride, a sophisticated beauty who worked hard to keep her expression from revealing a distaste of the sour, burning aroma blanketing the blue-collar town. Trained in electronics and wiring aboard ship, Earl took the first, and he assumed best, job

he was offered. He worked as a telephone repairman. The pay
was good, the pension plan acceptable. And like anyone's first
real job, particularly after growing up during the Depression, he
felt lucky. He had a statuesque, redheaded wife at his side and
a paycheck in his pocket.

At first they lived with Earl's parents, but it was not a cozy
honeymoon. For one thing, Emily's new mother-in-law wouldn't
speak to her. Earl thought his mother was intimidated by Emily's
impeccable grammar and East Coast accent; however, when things
didn't get better after a year, Earl purchased their first home
for $16,000 and presented it as an anniversary present to his
young wife. It was a white Cape Cod with a picket fence and
a fireplace, a good twenty-five miles upwind from the skin-pen-
etrating stench of Argo's number one industry.

Throughout the Eisenhower baby boom when my only sister,
Janette, was born, and Kennedy's Camelot when I was born, my
dad climbed telephone poles like a rodeo champion and twisted
wires like an artisan. The company gave him a car—a rusted '58
Olds that we affectionately called the "goo-goo car." My sister
and I were never allowed to ride in it—only sit inside when
it was parked on our blacktopped driveway. Sometimes, when
Janette stole the keys, we listened to top ten hits on 89-WLS.
"CHI-CA-GO!" we yelled in tune with the jingle singers.

Each afternoon Dad came home with a wind-burned face. He
barely looked at Janette or me, but kissed my mom twice—once
on each cheek—and went into his basement. There he hung up
his coveralls, poured himself a shot or two of Jack Daniels, and
then drank half a case of Stroh's beer while whistling along
with scratchy 78-rpm records. As we labored over homework on
the floor above him, sometimes we heard the rhythmic bang of
a punching bag. When he joined us for dinner, the War stories
began, and we weren't allowed to leave the table until he finished his last bite.

Earl Moncada didn't make it till the Nixon administration. He
died while watching black-and-white TV news coverage of the
Viet Nam War. Had a heart attack right in the middle of our
living room.

On the day he died I was eight-years old. A young and quiet
redheaded girl, always standing in the intimidating and perfect
shadow cast by my older sister, I remember clutching her hand
as we watched my father's bloated, lifeless body carried away on
a stretcher. He floated away from me, a puffy cloud on a breezy
day. The front door closed and, still holding Janette's hand, I
turned toward the black-and-white television in the corner of the
room just as the nightly fatality statistics flashed on the screen.

*"543 Killed In Action,"* said the solemn voice of the newscaster. *"To date, it has been Viet Nam's deadliest week."*

"Well, you can add one more to the death toll!" yelled Janette, pushing away my hand and collapsing into violent, convulsive sobs.

Days later, his war buddies served as pallbearers. They folded an American flag and saluted him for the last time. For my dad, it was not World War Two, but the Viet Nam War that was the war to end all wars.

He left me to be raised by two strong and controlling women, my mother and my sister. It was like being pressed between two stone bookends. I couldn't wait to graduate from high school and go to college. Looking back, I barely remember the years at home after my dad died and before I left for school. I was busy looking to my future, to the time when I could break free and taste the sweetness of possibility. My memories fast-forward through my mind like a highlights-only reel: The day my mother let me stay up to watch the late show for the first time and it was about a stripper named Gypsy Rose Lee; the day I made the cheerleading squad; the day I won an Outstanding ribbon at the Science Fair for building a 3-D model of a DNA molecule. Or the day I stole Janette's razor and shaved my long, disgustingly hairy legs and then lied about it to my mother. Another standout was the day my braces finally came off, and for the first time a boy turned his head in my direction.

The day I remember most, however, is the day I left.

Like my father, I, too, believed those first years away from home were the best of my life and was convinced that the friends I made in college would be with me for life—probably carry my casket—and write poignant eulogies when I died.

Two friends I met during my freshman year, both roommates at one point, were Cleo King and Ruby Pappas. They are still the kind of friends I can pick up with where I left off, no matter how much time has passed. While I currently live in Wisconsin, Cleo is in Colorado and Ruby is in Rhode Island. But it doesn't matter. If I'm nervous about something and need to talk it out, all I have to do is call Ruby and she never fails to say something like "Sing Loud Louise!" reminding me that the story of Gypsy Rose Lee was one of her favorites too. And I can count on Cleo to always give an honest and blunt opinion on any subject.

One reason we've maintained such strong, albeit geographically distant friendships, is because we have worked at it. It goes well beyond holiday greeting cards and remembering each other's birthdays. They are people I think to contact when both good and bad things happen. They validate my experiences in a way that even my mother and sister can't quite fulfill.

I haven't had the same experience with all the friends I made when I first left home.

My favorite college buddy was someone named Joel Rolland. He was beautiful. Blond and fair-faced, he had light-blue eyes just like my father's. Joel and I had met briefly during high school, but we didn't become friends until we found ourselves enrolled in the same college course during our freshman year. With this course as a springboard, we developed a friendship that I believed would last forever.

But it didn't.

Just like my dad unexpectedly keeled over and died, Joel turned tail and unexpectedly killed our friendship. He killed it with a letter.

*Dear Noelle,*

*I don't think it's fair that you keep in touch with me. It's not fair to me, and it's not fair to my wife Anita. Please don't write to me or call me anymore.*

*Joel*

It wasn't the eulogy I had in mind.

# 2.
# Joel. Present Day.

Noelle's face looked at me from the morning newspaper. I hadn't seen her picture since the last Christmas card she sent. Had it been five years? Ten? I no longer knew. After I threw away her final card and asked her to stop contacting me, she honored my request and gave up the birthday phone calls and holiday greetings. She had done what I asked and I didn't miss her.

That's what I told myself, anyway, as I read the newspaper ad for the fourth time:

*Noelle Moncada Andersen signs copies of her novel,* A College Affair, *at The House of Books on Manheim Road from 7-9pm on Wednesday evening.*

Noelle knew I was familiar with that bookstore. It was in my old neighborhood, the place I lived when I met her for the first time. But at that time it was a funky shop called "Troves of Treasures," featuring incense and giant feathers, black lights and beaded curtains—classic 1970s décor.

I stared at her photo. The black and white grain of the newspaper hid her faint freckles, but didn't disguise the hint of new and deeper lines around her smile and wispy crows feet sprouting from the corners of her twinkling eyes. She was aging well, just as I knew she would. I wondered, would she say the same thing about me?

Setting down my coffee cup, I looked at my blurred reflection in the window over the kitchen sink. Anita and the boys still slept in the rooms above me. The house was quiet, dark. Soon, the start of my car would serve as their alarm. As I left for the train station, the rooms would burst open like an un-leashed champagne cork. Our boys bubbled and spewed down every hallway, gathering backpacks and lunches, water bottles and after-school gear for the happy day awaiting them. My wife calls it "organized chaos." She amazes me with how she keeps all the schedules straight and gets everyone out the door on time.

I picked up my cup and noticed the ring it left on the newspaper next to Noelle's face. The coffee was lukewarm and bitter. I went for a refill. Blowing on it first before sipping, I set the cup back down on top of her. Steam rose and twisted from the foamy drink, emitting a tantalizing aroma—friendly and familiar—not unlike the sight of Noelle's photograph. It was like the smell of baking cookies drawing me in and teasing me with a two-sided promise: Sweet fantasy and guilty reality.

Noelle and I had unfinished business.

I didn't need to see her picture in the paper to realize this. There was so much I wanted to tell her. I wanted her to know how many times I had thought about picking up the phone and calling her, just to tell her that I was okay. And happy. I wanted to tell her why I wrote that letter asking her to stay out of my life. I almost did it once—actually had the phone in my hand and her phone number scrawled on a piece of scrap paper. It was the first anniversary of September 11, and earlier that day I had watched the memorial service on television, where children read the names of each person killed as a result of the high-jacked airplanes slamming into New York City's World Trade Towers. I thought about all those people—some of them my colleagues in the world of finance—who that morning went to work, rode the elevator, threw down their newspapers, and sipped their coffee. They answered phone messages and e-mail, sighed at the workload cluttering their desks or envied the new suit in the next office. And then at 8:45 a.m., perhaps reading one last report before a meeting down the hall, routine and triviality took on a whole new meaning.

That day I wondered what I might have done had my broker-age firm been in lower Manhattan rather than on LaSalle Street in Chicago, and what I would have done if I faced the decision of jumping out the office window or staying at my desk. Who would I have called besides Anita and the kids?

My mother was dead and as far as I was concerned, so was my father. I had a half brother, Will, whom I hardly knew.

Then, of course, there was Noelle. The memory of her face,

the sound of her laugh, the flash of her catlike eyes all became very clear.

After all these years there was still a place for her in my heart.

I had tried to trivialize my relationship—my friendship—with Noelle. I tried to explain to Anita that we were just friends and that it was possible for a man and a woman to remain friends after they each married other people. But Anita insisted I cut all ties with her.

Writing that letter was both the easiest and the hardest thing I have ever done.

# 3.
# Noelle, 1995.

It's December in Minocqua, Wisconsin, and I feel like an immigrant in my husband's hometown—a city girl dropped into a forest filled with birdcalls instead of car horns, and four-footed critters instead of taxis. Men in monotone business suits have been replaced with men in blaze-orange coveralls, and rather than ignoring me in the grocery store, local women offer advice on everything. Especially on my suddenly visible pregnancy.

My name is Noelle Moncada Andersen. I'm originally from Brook Park, Illinois, a suburban land of curbed streets and stop signs, two-story homes and neighbors who know everything. The houses were so close to one another that we shouted "God Bless You" through our kitchen windows whenever we heard someone sneeze. After four years of college in southern Illinois—a state school as far from the Chicago suburbs as possible—I moved to California to fulfill a Horace Greeley Go West whim and make what I could of my journalism degree.

My California experience can be summed up as follows: One menial job, one good job, and one miserable engagement. Then I met and married Marc Andersen, a Berkeley law student. Two years ago I followed him from San Francisco east into the woods the same way my mother followed my father from New York to Chicago after The War.

It's funny how we follow our men.

Marc and I live in a log cabin ten miles from the heart of Minocqua, "The Island City," deep in the pine, maple, aspen and birch-filled forest known as the "Great Northwoods." Our nearest neighbors are acres away. While I know their names, I

don't know much about them. They, however, seem to know
a lot about me. Once I heard our nearest neighbors—a retired
couple with a last name that has more syllables than I have
fingers—talking about me while on their pontoon boat. "Have
you seen that tall redhead Marc Andersen brought home from
California? She's skinnier than a popple sapling that one—probably won't last through the winter."

You'd think the locals would realize how easily sound car-
ries over the water. They don't. I've heard entire conversations
on quiet mornings while sitting at the end of our dock with
my feet dangling in rippling waves. Mostly it's fishermen telling
lies about the one that got away; however, the pontoon chat
is merely gossip. Lake folk don't like it when boathouse sizes
increase or shore station covers change color. Lord help the
newcomer who decides to put in a new raft or worse, bring
in a jet ski.

Newcomers are feared. They represent change, development.
The only things locals like to see grow in the Northwoods are
the trees. And the fish.

Here there are two seasons: cold and really cold. The snow
begins flying in September and sometimes doesn't stop until
May. During my ten years in California I was accustomed to
stepping barefoot outside the house to collect the mail or the
newspaper at any time of year. Now I traipse around in a pair
of five-pound Lacrosse boots, which are guaranteed to keep my
toes frostbite free to forty-below.

We moved here because my new husband wished to fulfill a
lifelong dream of establishing a law practice in his hometown. He
assured me I'd love the Northwoods and I, believing everything
he said, couldn't object. But I don't think I'll ever love the days
when I step outside and my teeth freeze. I also don't love that
Marc spends every day miles away in Rhinelander, the county
seat, establishing himself as the Atticus Finch of the Northwoods.
It leaves me with too much time alone thinking about my life
and how I, a woman on the business side of thirty-five—where
the biological clock creaks instead of ticks—ended up here. Here
in the Land of Winter.

Winter is a quixotic, Christmas card season in the Northwoods.
The lakes are stilled by ice. A soft, goose-down blanket of snow
protects the land like a cocoon. While I once pressed my ear to
a conch shell and believed it was the sound of the sea, I now
believe it's the sound of the wind swirling through the canopy
of trees guarding my home. Pine boughs wave in slow motion,
while hearty black-capped chickadees pierce the deafening quiet
with sharp whistles. They sound like little kids saying, "ha-ha,"
and during my solitary days, have become my best friends.

My other friends, our huskies Luna and Stella, join me each day on a walk to the mailbox, located on the county road a quarter mile from our front door. Thirty pounds into my pregnancy, walking the dogs is the only exercise I get. Except for when my husband returns from work, it's the highlight of my day.

Back when I read three newspapers each morning, I learned that ninety percent of the population loves getting the mail. I'm in that crowd. Sometimes I rip open an interesting-looking letter and read it on the walk back as the dogs braid trails around me and explore the smells of the woods. When I collected the mail today, however, I didn't allow them to roam freely because one of Luna's recent explorations filled her face with porcupine quills. It cost a small fortune at the vet's office to first sedate her and then bring her back with a second injection after the quills were removed. As much as I fancy becoming a hearty Northwoods woman who uses tried-and-true methods of fending off hostile wildlife and removing quills embedded in my huskies' snouts, I'm an urban girl at heart. I still believe in paying for professional services instead of adapting to the do-it-yourself code of the woods.

Once the dogs were safely returned to their kennel, I went inside where the aroma of burning logs greeted and warmed me. Rays of sun streaked through the wooden blinds, striping the room with late afternoon light. Tiny dust particles danced in the streaks. I kicked off my boots and reached for a tissue to wipe my dripping nose. Without looking in the mirror, I knew my cheeks were as pink as a valentine. I pulled the mail from my pocket and placed the bundle on a small desk. Glancing at the full hall tree, I thought better of adding my coat. It stood in the corner of the room like a Christmas tree decorated by a child. Heavy, woolen scarves hung atop too many jackets like clumps of tinsel—not the delicate icicles hung one at a time like an elegant, properly trimmed tree. My coat would surely send it crashing to the floor.

As I flipped through the mail, an assortment of catalogs and Christmas cards, a letter slipped out and slowly sailed to the floor, hitting the cold tile with a dainty thump. I looked down, turned my head, and saw the return address of my old friend, Joel Rolland.

Seeing his name was instantly uplifting—like hearing the jingle of bells on the ice cream man's truck. I whisked the white envelope from the floor, assuming it was a Christmas greeting containing pictures of his kids—he had three boys—and an update about what sports they played and what vacations they had taken. (How many goals did little Michael score this year? And was it a trip to Disneyland or a visit to the grandparents in New Jersey?) I thought I'd study the boys' pictures and see my friend's face look back at me in triplicate—three sets of clear, blue eyes, sandy tresses—and then I'd place it inside the hanging felt Santa my mother bequeathed to me when she moved to Florida.

I ripped open the envelope and unfolded a single page—a page more like a business letter than a Christmas card.

*"Dear Noelle,"* it read. *"I don't think it's fair that you keep in touch with me. It's not fair to me and it's not fair to my wife Anita. Please don't write to me or call me anymore. Joel."*

"What the. . .?"

I read it again.

"What the hell is this?" My hands began to shake. They trembled like those of an alcoholic on the morning after. It felt nothing like a satisfying treat from the ice cream man. On the contrary, reading this letter—twice—felt like I'd just chased down the Good Humor man on a hot day, only to find him out of my favorite treat.

Instead of a chocolate éclair, I got a bomb pop.

I stared at the page in disbelief. Three terse sentences written in blue ink on lined paper with ragged, spiral edges. He must have torn the page from his son's school notebook. The handwriting, not quite chicken-scratch, was tight, angular, and completely without artistry—certainly without soul. It was pure man.

Or was it?

"Anita," I said, visualizing the woman Joel had married ten years ago.

I remembered her from college. Her name was Anita Dambra. She had rich, dark hair and onyx eyes—the exact opposite of Joel. We all lived in the same dorm complex during our freshman year. I thought Joel considered me a friend; however, from the day we met, Anita's black eyes bore into me like a hawk sizing up its prey.

*Please don't write to me or call me anymore.*

"Why not?" I felt the heat of injustice. A self-righteous scent filled my senses and my thoughts started spinning—churning and grinding like a washing machine. I paced the room.

*Is he accusing me of something? Doesn't he realize I'm happily married? Of course he does. I love Marc so much I gave up my career to raise a child in a land with more birds than people, and a local newspaper that considers bowling league scores major news. It's a fucking fairy tale for God's sake! A clear case of happily-ever-after! Anyone who knows me knows this. This letter makes me out to be the other woman—like*

*Glenn Close in* Fatal Attraction—*or someone poised to make stew out of his kid's pet rabbit. What's he thinking?*

"I'm not anyone's other woman," I said, crumbling the paper into the size of a popcorn ball. I stomped toward the kitchen and threw it in the trashcan under the sink. Kicking the cabinet drawer closed, I placed my hands on my stomach—a niche my palms have found from the moment I discovered I was pregnant. "Friends don't write letters like that," I said as though instructing my unborn child.

I marched into the living room and stoked the fire in the Franklin stove. With the iron poker in my hand, I scoffed at the term "letter." I had notes passed to me in sixth grade—notes folded into neat triangles meant to kill time and make me laugh—which were longer than what Joel had sent.

With each jab, the yellow flames grew angrier. As they sparked, popped, and licked the hot interior of the stove, I tried to forget those terse sentences, wipe them away as though lifting the plastic page on a Magic Slate.

But anger overcomes hope the way paper covers rock. Thoughts of Joel—his face, his smile, his brilliant blue eyes—our history—flooded my mind.

I set down the poker and looked out toward the lake through the giant picture window. The sun was gone and a cantaloupe, alpenglow reflection spread across the room. Focusing on animal tracks in the snow marking a path on the lake the way a motorboat leaves a wake, I sighed. I wished Marc were home.

A crib quilt lay strewn across a rocking chair next to the blazing fire. I'd been working on it for months. Filled with pastels, flowers, and bunnies, it was like a fabric poem or a lullaby, lovingly constructed with bits and pieces of colors and patterns. For hundreds of years, American women filled their hours by stitching their hopes, dreams, and histories into quilts. Like the woman who created it, each textile rendition had a story to tell.

I sat in the rocker, leaned back, and searched for the needle and the place I'd left off. Poking the needle in and out of the fabric and creating tight, neat stitches, I couldn't help but piece together my history with Joel Rolland, including the past ten years when we'd had an uneventful friendship. Nothing exciting. Nothing threatening.

It began in college.

Ah, college, I thought, and laughed. What a breezy time. I used to sigh whenever I thought of those years when my life was in a constant state of run. How I managed full-time classes, part-time work, a house full of roommates, and the constant party

I'll never know. It was a time when every idea seemed new and around every corner was the chance for a fresh start.

Joel was there from the beginning. He sat next to me in my first college class, Oral Interpretation of Literature—SPEECH 201. I remember the professor, what was his name? Long hair, a beard, John Lennon glasses. He made us all take nicknames. We were Noble Noelle and Soulful Joel. There was someone named Daphne Duck. It was an eight a.m. class, far too early for eighteen-year-olds to function properly. And yet that class was among my favorites.

It was because of Joel.

Stitching around the letter 'C' of an ABC block, it was as though Joel were once again seated right next to me, watching me with those bright eyes and wearing his perpetually bemused expression. I think it was that expression that made me think of him as a brother—or someone with whom I shared an un-spoken understanding.

He was like the cute boy next-door. You know that boy. He's the one who taught you how to throw a ball without a girl-elbow or drive a stick-shift, even after you put his yellow Volkswagen on someone's precious patch of lawn. He's the one who was willing to pick you as the only girl on his touch football team, and when he sent you out for the long pass, he actually threw the ball to you. And you caught it. When you scored the touchdown, he ran to you, picked you up, and twirled you around until you felt like you'd just been elected MVP of the neighborhood.

And yet he's not the one you dreamed about. He's not the one who made your stomach flip-flop at the mere mention of his name or the one who made you want to tear off your clothes the moment he walked in the door. He's merely the one who made you smile. In your memories, he reminds you of who you are and where you came from. He, in a unique way, is as much a part of you as your own childhood. Ultimately, as time passes and memories fade, he's simply another college buddy—just an-other name on your ever-expanding Christmas card list.

Very simply, he is your friend.

Last week I mailed my Christmas cards, which included a card to Joel. One of a hundred cards I prepared in an after-noon, it didn't carry much value beyond the cost of the stamp. Christmas cards are a chore I perform each year out of habit. I'm afraid if I fail to send them, friends might think I got di-vorced or something. At least that's what *I* think when I don't receive a Christmas card from someone who usually goes to great lengths to enclose family photos or one of those deadly, rambling greetings.

I don't send letters. I pick out a photo and have our name embossed on reprints under whatever kitschy Christmas art icon the town photo shop offers. This year's image featured the mountainous snowdrifts in front of our cabin, our huskies, Luna and Stella, Marc and me. Marc's hair is too long and hangs between his thick eyebrows like a misplaced comma. His skin looks tan, as though he just returned from either the ski slopes or the islands. Even though he squints into the sun, carefully watching for the timed shutter to snap, the blue in his eyes is captured. My red hair is loose and wavy, and my smile is as large as a brick of Colby cheese. It reflects the sun like a flash bulb, and the more I looked at it, the more I felt I looked like Bozo the Clown. A red holiday sweater bulges as if to say "look at me, I'm pregnant," and while my hand rests atop Luna's head as she exhibits a perfect canine smile for the camera, Stella looks up at Marc adoringly. *"Merry Christmas from the Andersens,"* it reads. I stuck a mailing label on each envelope and with a rubber band around the outgoing stack, walked to the mailbox and put up the flag. As far as 1995's Christmas card was concerned, Joel was just another Chicago address on the 'R' page of my address book.

Of course, I noticed he had never given me his home address, but didn't care if he kept our correspondence a secret from Anita. I had nothing to be ashamed of and it wasn't a secret on my end. I didn't and don't have secret friends. My husband knows about Joel the same way, I assume, most husbands and wives know about their spouses' platonic relationships with the opposite sex. In fact, just last spring the three of us had had lunch together. Marc and Joel greeted each other like old friends with a firm handshake and one or two of those patented guy-motions where they slapped each other on the back. "Do you two know each other?" I had asked.

Joel said he recognized Marc from the Christmas cards.

Still stitching, I accidentally poked my finger with the needle and barely felt the jab due to the callus built up from years of quilt making. And while insignificant jabs hurt less when no one is around to hear you say "ouch," I still let out an audible complaint and examined the puncture. Squeezing my finger, a crimson drop the size of a seed bead appeared and I brought it to my mouth to taste the bitter blood.

Joel and I had a pact. While we didn't prick our fingers and exchange blood, it was a verbal agreement made in California when he came to visit me years earlier. I didn't know it then, but figured out later that he came to determine whether or not he was going to marry Anita. During that brief visit, Joel only mentioned that he was seeing "a woman." He didn't say it was his on-again, off-again girlfriend, Anita Dambra, and never mentioned he was on verge of proposing to her.

Anita was someone we had learned *not* to talk about.

"Ha!" I scoffed. "Some pact." Those three sentences sat on the page in my garbage can like snot on a tissue and made a complete mockery of our friendship. There was no way Joel could have forgotten that trip to California and our pact. How many pacts does one make in a lifetime? Furthermore, Midwesterners don't forget trips to the Golden State. For one reason, it's a four-hour flight. Secondly, San Francisco is completely different from Chicago. It smells different, tastes different, and leaves a little tattoo on your brain the way Chicago only wishes it could. Joel even talked about that visit when he called on my last birthday.

"I had a dream you came to me on your bicycle," he had said.

"That wasn't a dream, Joel," I said. "That was a memory."

It was a clear memory for me. As clear as the day my father died or the day I went off to college. Joel and I hadn't seen each other in three years. He had come from Chicago to Oakland and called me at work to arrange a visit. At the time I was unhappily engaged to a man named Nick Austin, and I worked for a small publishing company in North Berkeley—a job that Nick disapproved of with all his being. As far as he, the heir to the Austintini Vineyards was concerned, I worked on the *wrong* side of the Bay.

I didn't tell Nick my old friend was in town. From work that afternoon I rode my bicycle four blocks to the BART station, where I first saw Joel from a distance. He stood alone, leaning against the building and looking over the top of the green pages of *San Francisco Chronicle's* sports section. As soon as he spotted me he smiled, and his smile froze upon his face as though he were posing for a photograph. It was the expression I remembered very well.

He didn't say a word. Not even hello. I followed his lead and simply smiled back. "I'm starving," he finally said.

"Well then. Let's get a latté."

"Latté? Is that a California thing?"

"No, it's a coffee thing," I said. "C'mon. There's a shop right around the corner."

When I brought the full, frothy ale glasses to our table, his eyes popped open with surprise. He sipped tentatively and the foam formed a mustache above his full, pink lip. "Order me another at once!" he said.

With the caffeine of two lattes apiece pumping through our veins, from the coffee shop we headed uphill through the residential neighborhood of North Berkeley. Surrounded by colorful Victorian houses and funky bungalows, the air smelled of eucalyptus and pine. We climbed and climbed, each taking a turn at pushing my bicycle up the steep hill, and finally we reached the Rose Garden, a public park overlooking San Francisco Bay. There, among countless varieties of colorful and sweet-smelling roses, we sat on the grass and talked.

We talked about everything. His job. My job. The world of books. The world of stocks. His mother. My mother. The Chicago Cubs, the San Francisco Giants. I talked about my fiancé, Nick. He mentioned he was seeing "a woman."

"You're very tempting," he said suddenly.

"Tempting?" I shook my head, not knowing—or wanting to know—what he meant. I scrambled, wanting to change the subject. "Joel," I said, putting my hand atop his. "Let's make a pact. Let's promise to stay friends for the rest of our lives."

"You mean call each other on our birthdays and send Christmas cards? Is that what we're destined to be to one another?"

"Don't you want to be friends with me?"

"Of course I want to be friends with you," he said. "I can live with that. But can your fiancé live with that?"

I didn't answer. I didn't know. But what I also didn't know was whether or not I could live with the fiancé.

A month later, Joel once again called me at work. I had a sneaking suspicion his call was about "the woman" he said he was seeing, and sensed through the phone line that Joel felt he owed me something—some information.

"Hi Joel," I said. "It's funny you should call me today. I've been thinking of you."

"Why's that?"

"I broke up with Nick. I'm not getting married."

"Then this is a bittersweet phone call. Because I *am* getting married," he said. "I'm marrying Anita."

My finger continued bleeding. I must have poked it deeper than I thought. Not wanting to stain the quilt, I set it aside and walked to the bathroom to get a bandage. Relieved to find one remaining on the top shelf of the medicine cabinet, I located the thin, red string—the ripcord—and peeled away the tissue. As I tried to wrap my finger, again my hands shook. I hadn't thought about my relationship with Joel in years. Now I was obsessed with trying to figure out how I felt about him.

Was he just my friend or was he a former lover of whom I couldn't let go?

Then it dawned on me. I realized why he had come to California all those years ago, and it had nothing to do with making a friendship pact with me. No way. Joel Rolland didn't look upon me as merely a friend. Instead, he looked at me as the girl behind door number two.

I looked at my blotched face in the mirror. "I'm *not* the guilty party," I said to my reflection. Turning away quickly, I carried the bandage scraps to the kitchen and pulled open the cabinet door with too much force. It banged against the neighboring oak panel with a startling shot. Before me was the letter—the evidence—sitting amid the rest of the day's trash. I grabbed it, smoothed it on my stomach, and noticed a small grease stain had penetrated the page. Turning and walking to the kitchen table, I placed the damaged letter in the center and stepped back as though examining the placement of a freshly hung photograph. Then I turned my back and returned to my baby's quilt. Resuming the methodical stitching, I leaned back in the chair and let it rock forward, knowing that my husband, the man I truly loved, would soon be home.

# 4.
# Joel. 1977.

At some point nearly every day, I find myself wondering whether or not all seventeen year-old boys hate their fathers. This morning while lying in bed with my head surrounded by smelly pillowcases, I realized I hadn't seen my father in three days. Once again it was the first question on my mind.

I took a sip of water from the full glass perched on my nightstand, set it down too hard, and knew that one thing in my life was perfectly clear.

My father ignored me.

I don't know what his problem is. It wasn't always like this. When I was little he was cool. Walter Rolland, Walt, was a black-leather-jacket beatnik, with slicked-back hair and a rippled, James Dean forehead. He referred to his friends as 'cats' and listened to jazz in the basement, always making sure I developed a fine appreciation of his music. While I walked around humming tunes by Charlie Parker and Thelonius Monk, the hippest songs my friends liked were by the Beatles and Paul Revere and the Raiders.

They might have been groovy, but I was *cool*.

Walt, and I call him by his first name instead of calling him "Dad," is a social studies teacher at the local junior college. He's always treated me like one of his students. I mean, what dad has his kid read Jack Kerouac at the age of nine? He actually gave me a test on it. When I passed, thank God, instead of giving me an 'A', he bequeathed his favorite book of poetry by Alan Ginsberg with as much ceremony as a father handing over his class ring to his first and only son. He called me "Soulful Joel."

Soulful Joel. It was a moniker I took to heart. I liked the sound of it and from that point forward, read everything he gave me without grumbling. Plato's *The Republic,* Skinner's *Walden Two, Black Elk Speaks.* The list was endless. Books were my candy—my reward for being a good, bright scion—the fruit of his loins.

But then something happened. After Jane Fonda went to Viet Nam he began angry tirades about Hanoi Jane being responsible for the wave of women's lib ruining the social structure of our society. Don't even get me started on Gloria Steinem. When Jimmy Carter was elected president, each night my mother and I faced lectures on how the Peanut Farmer was fucking up the country. After spewing his angry opinions, he left the table, stormed out of the house, and often didn't come back.

Mom called it a "mid-life crisis." I'd heard the term. It had a familiar, jingly ring to it like midriff bulge or Grecian Formula. But witnessing it in action wasn't anywhere near as benign as watching it on television. I didn't know what to make of the change. Was he disappointed and did he suddenly need to re-evaluate his life? To relive his glory days or lament he'd never had any? "Some men go out and get tattoos or buy sports cars," said Mom. "Your father is just a little lost right now." She tried to sound casual, but the distracted look in her eyes and a new, sad slant to her head made me realize there was more to it.

I rolled over and faced the wall. It was Friday morning. TGIF. With fifteen minutes left until my alarm, I rubbed my fingertips along the smooth surface of the Corvette poster next to my bed and then picked at the yellowing cellophane tape. Hung when I was ten, the poster now seemed juvenile and silly.

I would never own a Corvette.

I drive a beat up, yellow Volkswagen, which my mother bought from a coworker for three hundred bucks. And she, not my father, taught me how to drive it. Took me to a parking lot and didn't laugh when I ground the gears. It sounded like the worst kind of belch. One you let out on purpose after a big swig of Coke. "Find 'em. Don't grind 'em," she said with a laugh.

Mom's always patient. Ask her a question and she doesn't give an immediate response. She just sort of looks at you, cocks her head like a dog hearing a high-pitched noise, and a deep perforation appears between her eyebrows—kind of like an exclamation point. She's a teacher like my dad, but instead of turning everything into some kind of lesson, she focuses on giving the correct answer.

Leaning over, I peered out the window of my attic bedroom and was greeted by the same gray street, same big trees. Only the late autumn oaks had remaining leaves, a deep, burnt brown. I spied the closed curtains on the window next door. It was Maria's room. Maria Aniballi—a girl I can safely call my first girlfriend. Her room was once connected to my own by a chain of blackened newspaper rubber bands and a Dixie cup communications center. When the Dixie cups failed to work, we resorted to flashlights and sometimes used Morse code.

.- -. .-.. .- -.-- ..- -.. (Translation: Play?)

A couple years ago she busted me looking at her in her underwear. That night she closed the communications center with a final message.

..-. ..- -.-. -.- --- ..-. ..-. (Translation: Fuck off)

Even though we've stayed friends, she never again opened the curtains.

The Aniballi family moved into the neighborhood when Maria and I were in kindergarten. Her parents were little Italian people with thick accents, and sometimes on summer nights, I heard them shouting at each other with lots of rolling R's. Our mothers were delighted that we were in the same grade and each day as we walked together to school, brown bag lunches swinging at our sides, they stood at the foot of our adjoining driveways, waving like we were off to war.

Our neighborhood had tons of kids. After school we all hung out together at the baseball diamond two blocks away. And while I was always stationed at first, Maria played third base. Her arm was better than half our little league team and when we played catch, my palm was sore from the wicked throws she fired at me. I felt sorry for any guy who told her she threw hard "for a girl," because first she whipped off her cap letting thick, brown curls spring from her head, and then she'd wind up and bean him.

Sometimes we stayed at the park, sat on a bench, and made-out. But Maria never let me get to second base. The farthest I could get with her was French kissing.

By sophomore year she was a head taller than I, heavier too, and come summer she said she wasn't comfortable going out with a shorter guy. She told me we'd always be friends. And I think we were pretty good friends. At least we were until three weeks ago when I got a new girlfriend.

I don't know what it is about girls that makes it impossible to have a girlfriend and a friend that's a girl at the same time.

I leaned away from the window, falling back into the pillows and pictured my new girlfriend, Lara Romano. Just the thought of her made me hard. It was like a butterfly had suddenly flown into the room and landed on my dick. Within seconds I was as solid and smooth as the white walls of the Corvette. But there was no time to indulge. I hit the switch on the alarm before it could ring and swung my legs around to the green shag carpet. The matted strands surrounded my feet like overgrown grass.

Lara was still on my mind.

She goes to another high school, West Suburban High, and it's so close that if we lived three blocks to the east, I would have gone there too. I guess you might say it's our sister school and for whatever reason, the girls over there seem more interesting. It's a small school by suburban Chicago standards, like mine. We play each other in the same sports conference. Well, others play. I don't anymore.

Walt doesn't know it, but I gave up sports. I played baseball since the time I could walk and was pretty good at first base. But when I got to high school, I couldn't stand the baseball coach. His name was Mr. Engebretson and he was like a drill sergeant who made us call him "sir." He walked like something was jammed up his ass.

As I tiptoed toward my robe, imitating his high-assed walk, my tighty whiteys were like his tight, snow-white shorts and matching sneakers. Grabbing my robe I squeezed my eyes shut and crunched my face into a grimace, trying to erase the thought.

Quitting the baseball team led me to a reporting job at the school newspaper, the *Trumaine Trumpet*. I cover baseball and golf in the spring, swimming in the fall, and wrestling in the winter. And after I wrote a piece about Title IX and our school's attempt to comply by introducing co-ed P.E., they made me the sports editor. I'm not sure why, though, as it wasn't a good piece. I couldn't get the male P.E. teachers to quote anything on the record. They either grunted at my questions or said "no comment." Engebretson even called me a pansy for quitting the team and becoming a "journalist." He used air-quotes when he said the word journalist and shook his head in disgust—like I was the enemy.

Tying my robe, I descended the stairs toward the bathroom, passing my mom, who was alone in her room. Her face was pressed to the screen and a cloud of smoke poured from her lips like she was some kind of dragon sending a warning to the neighbors. I cleared my throat to let her know she was busted, and she quickly stubbed out her cigarette, wound shut the window, and pushed the ashtray on the windowsill behind the curtain.

"Don't tell Walt," she said with a wink. "And your jeans are on top of the dryer. I didn't have time to get them to your room last night."

"Thanks," I said. "Your secret's safe with me, Smoker. When would I see him anyway?"

"Smoker," she said mockingly. "Look who's talking, Mr. Pot Head."

"Don't tell Walt," I said, closing the bathroom door.

So, yeah. I smoke pot. I smoke it nearly every morning in the science wing john with my buddies Keith and Joe. They're from my neighborhood, and like Maria, I've known them since kindergarten. Keith Greenwald just finished his fourth year of football quarterbacking for the Trumaine Trojans, and says he might go out for a college team. He's got the build, but with the way he dopes up these days, I don't think he'll last long on the college gridiron. He's already decided to give up wrestling this season and I can't say I blame him. I never understood why guys chose to dress in tights and roll around in each other's sweat. The back acne—or *bacne,* as we called it—was turnoff enough.

Keith is as blind as Ray Charles and except when he's around girls, wears aviator-frame glasses held together with duct tape. We keep telling him to get contacts but he says he can't stand the way they feel in his eyes. He says it's like having an eyelash in the way. And he should know. He's got these really long, Bambi lashes that the girls love.

The water in the shower ran cold. It felt freezing on my hand and I held it under the faucet and waited for it to warm before pulling up the shower switch. I stepped inside the tub and let my feet get used to the temperature.

My other buddy, Joe Blum, is a total burnout and proud of it. He's never without his red flannel shirt and torn, grease-stained Levi's. He's kind of like a 1970s version of the *Peanuts* character Pigpen, with a cloud of pot-tainted dust always wafting around him. Joe's eyes are swollen shut from sunrise to bedtime because he's always stoned. He'll be lucky to graduate.

I can say one thing for Joe, though, and that is he's a smack auto mechanic. He can fix just about anything on a car. He drives a souped-up Mustang fastback that he practically built from scratch, and every time I go to his house he's washing or waxing it, rubbing it like it's his girlfriend. He works at the local Petrolo gas station along with a bunch of other shop guys, and they run quite the little drug ring out of that place. Anyone can go there, fill the tank, wash the car, and then buy an ounce of weed.

Joe likes to get stoned before first period because he says it's best when "your mind is so fresh." It gets him through Consumer Education, where he has the sad misfortune of being married to Carol Wright. Carol is an awkward girl—the one who's been the last choice since first grade for everything from dodge ball to debate. We used to call her Carol Wrong, but now we tease Joe and call her Carol Blum. Keith and I think he's secretly sweet on her and know she's probably responsible for getting him through that stupid class.

The school board or the state or some decision body with the power of deeming what's important for us to learn before releasing us into the real word made Consumer Ed a requirement for high school graduation starting with our class. I thought it was a waste of time and embarrassing when the teacher played matchmaker and wed you to a girl whose name you drew out of a hat. As a married couple we had to plan a household budget and make decisions about kids and all that crap.

I took Consumer Ed sophomore year just to get it over with and was lucky to marry a girl named Stephanie Jezik, who was a total babe. I wanted five kids with that girl, but she told me she was "celibate." I had to look up that word in *Webster's*.

At last the water temperature was perfect and I let the penetrating force hit me in the face. It was the only way to truly wake up. "Wake up," I said. "Waken. Rouse. Revive. Stimulate. *Stop!*" Words spun through my head like some kind of out-of-control thesaurus. I couldn't help it. My mother had turned me into a word freak.

I look up words in the dictionary the way Joe looks up auto parts in his gearhead magazines. At Mom's suggestion, I put a checkmark next to each word I look up and have pretty much destroyed her old book. I remember when I learned that celibacy had to do with giving up sex for religious reasons, I bought my Consumer Ed wife, Stephanie, a glow-in-the-dark Virgin Mary at the Troves of Treasures over on Manheim Road. It's a store that reeks of incense, but where you can always find the greatest gag gifts like fake vomit and whoopee cushions. I gave it to her and said it was a wedding present. She rolled her eyes and never again spoke to me outside of class.

If that class was supposed to teach me something about marriage, it only confirmed the idea my parents had already given me. When it comes to relationships, one person always seems to be more interested or committed than the other.

I rinsed the soap from my hair and shook like a dog.

Hot cereal and orange juice waited for me at the kitchen table.

It was the same breakfast my mom served me every morning. "Hey there, Sweetie," she said. "You look nice. Have any plans for the weekend?"

"Sure do." I poured milk into my bowl. "Lara's coming over Saturday night and she's bringing a friend for Keith."

"You like this girl, huh?"

"She's okay. Reminds me a little bit of Maria. You know, the Italian part."

"You rarely talk about Maria anymore. Are you two still friends after she did that to your hair?"

"I thought you liked my hair!" I said with a mouth full of oatmeal. Some of it drooled onto my chin and I wiped it away with my hand.

"Use your napkin!"

I shook my head the way I did in the shower, and my still wet hair sprinkled water onto my mother's arm. "You said you liked it."

"You don't have to act like a poodle. I do like your hair, Honey. I particularly like that you had the balls to perm it. Bravo."

"Thanks a lot. And yes, I'm still friends with Maria. Of course, we're still friends. These days she's just like one of the guys to me."

"Still," she said, "you never forget your first love." She sighed heavily, grabbed a cigarette and put it between her lips without lighting it. "I've got to get to work. You okay?"

"Of course. Geez, Mom. What's with you and the smokes?"

"Don't tell Walt," she said while slinking out the door.

I put away my dishes and ran upstairs to get my books. Stopping in the bathroom I combed through my springy curls with a pick instead of a comb. I studied myself in the mirror, turning my face from side to side.

After she gave me the perm, Maria said I looked like Roger Daltry from the Who. I suppose I do look a little like him, and that's not a bad thing. I brushed my teeth, smiled in the mirror, and decided not to shave.

*"Tommy can you hear me?"* I sang as I grabbed my keys.

My Volkswagen was reluctant to start. Each time I turned the key it sounded like an old woman clearing her throat. "Start, Mrs. Beetle," I said, pumping the gas pedal as Phil Collins's voice on WXRT pumped through the speakers. Finally it blubbered into action and I wasted no time backing out of the driveway. When I got to the street, I put it in neutral and moved the seat back. Had I grown overnight? Maybe, I thought, I was finally taller than Maria. But it was too late to get her back. Besides, she started seeing some college guy.

"Friends, right?" she said to me each time we passed in the hallway or saw each other over the bushes separating our back-yards. "Friends," I'd respond with a lame thumbs up.

Fine with me. It led me to Lara.

Lara and I met at a party at my buddy Jon's house. It was after the last football game when the Trojans finally won. After a painful losing season, the unexpected win added a certain charge to the air—a burnt-orange charge made up of pure Midwestern football season. Keith was the hero of the game. Sick of running backs who fumbled and wide receivers who couldn't catch, he ignored his coach's call and ran forty-three yards at the buzzer. It was the last touchdown of his high school career and as the crowd roared, he was as high as I'd ever seen him. "I should've f'n blown off coach's calls all season," he had said while the team swamped him with praise and congratulations. When the celebratory huddle finally broke up, he threw his hands up in the air and yelled, "PARTY!"

"Party hardy!" cried the team.

We all piled into the available cars—my Beetle, Jon's Firebird, Joe's Mustang, the wide receiver's mom's station wagon with the fake wood-paneled sides—and headed to Jon's. His parents were out of town—the main reason for anyone to throw a party—and he said his cousin from the next town planned to be there and would be bringing some of the girls from his school, West Suburban.

I spied Lara Romano the second I stepped through the door. It was her hair. Honey-colored, it hung to her waist in a straight, thick Wella Balsam commercial kind of way. She was pretty, but not unapproachably pretty, and she had a certain confidence about her as she spoke to a small group of girls I didn't rec-ognize. She used pointed movements, kind of like a teacher, and seemed to have a semaphore relationship with the other girls at the party. They all had an eye on her, waiting for direction.

I was sure she was going to go for Keith. But that didn't hap-pen. Keith focused on Joe's cousin, a tall drink of water named Jane. The moment I caught Lara turning one of her big brown eyes in my direction, I felt it was okay to make a move.

"Great hair," she said when I sidled up next to her. She reached up and uncoiled a newly permed strand above my forehead. When she let go, it coiled like a Slinky. "I'm Lara," she said in a breathy voice, and tossed her hair off one shoulder. Her eyes, as large as marbles, penetrated my skin and I saw her contact lenses. They rested on her protruding eyeballs like a suction cup on a window. As I narrowed my eyes and focused on her lenses, she smiled. "You should see me in my glasses," she said. "They're as thick as the bottoms of Coke bottles."

"What?"

"Oh, nothing," she said. "So, what kind of music do you listen to?"

"Jazz, mostly," I said.

"Oh yeah? Me, too!"

I instantly fell in love with her.

\* \* \* \* \* \* \* \*

On Saturday night, my dad was out as usual. "He spent all week teaching at the college and now he's working a second job at the prison teaching the GED," Mom said. "It's an hour in good traffic to Cook County, you know."

"On Saturday night?" I asked, suspiciously.

"You should be proud of him, Dear."

"Oh right. I'm proud. I'm so proud that he can take the time to teach social studies to incarcerated purse-snatchers and guys who got busted for selling weed. So that's why he's never home anymore? Because he's taken a second job?"

"Someone has to pay for your college, young man." She raised her reading glasses and wrapped a crocheted afghan over her legs. A stack of papers with raw, spiral notebook edges lay on the coffee table in front of her, and a paperback novel lay open across her chest.

"Whatever. What are you reading tonight?" I asked.

"Tonight?" She laughed. "Well tonight I have a choice. It's either trash or more trash. Can't decide."

All at once we heard the unmistakable sound of Led Zeppelin rise from the floor. Keith had let himself in through the basement door and helped himself to the stereo. When I got downstairs, he was sorting through albums. "You have a pitiful supply of Zeppelin," he said.

"Well, you managed to find something." I turned down the volume.

The doorbell rang and we heard Mom greet the girls. High-pitched voices channeled through the ductwork of our house and into the basement. "Would you like a Coke?"

"Sure," chirped Lara. "I'd love a Coke. What are you reading?"

"Sidney Sheldon," said Mom. "But don't tell anyone. The boys are in the den. We used to call it the basement, but since my husband hung dark paneling and moved the TV down there so it could project some kind of sports program into the room at all hours, we call it 'the den.' "

The girls ambled down the stairs, Cokes in hand like bright red flashlights. Jane looked past me like I wasn't in the room and smiled at Keith. She kissed him and they fell into the sofa and started making out like it was a seventh-grade party. Lara looked at them and rolled her eyes. She pulled out a baggie from her oversized leather purse and tossed it on the coffee table. "Want to get high?" she asked.

"Why not?"

"I need an album cover to clean this."

I handed her Elton John's *Goodbye Yellow Brick Road,* and as she pulled the weed from the bag, the aroma of skunk filled the air. She busily separated seeds and stems from the good stuff. "Columbian," she said. "I bought a lid last night from the Petrolo boys."

"You know the Petrolo Boys?"

"Who doesn't?"

"Then you must know Joe."

"Who?"

"Joe Blum. He's my buddy who works at that gas station."

"Maybe. What does he look like?"

"I don't know. A regular guy, I guess. Listen, my mom is pretty cool about pot, but we should probably smoke in the bathroom with the fan on just in case."

Keith and Jane didn't notice us get up and move to the bathroom. I closed the door and grabbed a towel off the rack to roll up and seal the room. "I can't believe Jane just threw herself onto him like that. They barely know each other," said Lara as she licked the joint into a neat, spiral package. She flicked a black, BIC lighter, lit the end, and inhaled deeply. Holding her breath so that her eyes bulged from her head, she pursed her lips and then finally blew out a thick cloud of blue smoke. "I personally need to get to know a guy better before I, well, you know." She smiled, hopped on the sink, and crossed her legs.

"What do you need to know?" I took the joint from her, inhaled, and at once felt the familiar bite in my throat. Lara responded in babble. Her voice sounded like running water.

"I've got honors English this year, and I think I'm developing a thing for Jane Austen. Then there's physics—full of nerds—and calculus—the same nerds, and my absolute favorite class, Western Civ. It has cool people in it. Not just these calculator-on-belt types that still think of me as the cheerleader I was during sophomore year. I was captain."

"Get out," I said, coughing out the smoke. "You were a cheerleader?"

"I was good, too. I can still do my school song." She jumped off the sink, and in the small space between the shower and the toilet, danced around with imaginary pom-poms, singing of loyalty and praise.

I watched with a gaping mouth as she punched her fist into the air and yelled, "fight, fight, fight!"

"Wow," I managed. "That *was* good. Why'd you quit?"

"I decided that jumping up in the air and forcing my legs apart wasn't what I wanted to do with my life."

As I watched her suck in the last of the joint, I got stuck on the image of Lara forcing her legs apart.

We left the fan rattling in the bathroom and returned to the room. Jane and Keith had moved to the fireplace hearth where Keith, with his back to us, arranged twigs in a teepee formation like a boy scout preparing a campfire. Jane watched him with a skeptical expression as Lara and I settled on the sofa. "I only went out for cheerleading because all my friends were doing it. The girls' swim and field hockey teams didn't interest me," said Lara.

"I totally know about girls with potential to be great athletes but who don't have any real sports to play in high school," I said, trying to keep the conversation going. "My friend Maria is a kick-ass ball player and she didn't want to go out for field hockey."

"Those women are built like men," said Jane, handing Keith a match.

"Who's Maria?" Lara asked.

"The girl next door," offered Keith. "She's the one who did that to his hair." He lowered his voice and put his hand over his mouth. "Talk about being built like a man. . . ."

"Like the East German swimmers," Jane said laughing. "That's what we all look like when they make us take swimming in P.E. Have you seen those nasty blue tank suits? I swear they're from the Depression!"

"At least they let the girls wear suits," Keith said. "We can't graduate without going through naked swim class and being sized up by the fag P.E. teachers."

"They do that at our school too. I can't believe you guys don't start a petition against required public nudity," said Lara.

"It's a guy thing," I said. "Like girls need to be cheerleaders."

"Well *I* was never a cheerleader," said Jane.

"Oh please. There's nothing wrong with cheerleading. I've got friends who are cheerleaders," Lara said. "One of my good friends is still wearing the skirt. I'm not sure why, since she says she hates it. But I think it's because her mother won't let her quit. At least that's what she says when she's blowing a joint with the rest of us."

"Your cheerleaders smoke pot?"

"Who doesn't these days?"

"The jocks," I offered, looking past her toward Keith who, having given up on the fire, used his latest match to light a bong hit. "Then again, maybe you're right. Keith, can you take that in the bathroom?"

Keith stood, snorted through his nose while trying to hold in his hit, and then leaned into the bathroom and let go of the smoke. "There goes the quarterback," I said.

"See what I mean?" said Lara.

"I know people who don't smoke," Keith choked out through a series of short coughs.

"Yeah? Who?" asked Lara.

"Two words," he continued. "Pep band."

"At our school we've got the freaks—you know, the real burnouts, the jocks and the burnt jocks. They sort of cross over between the two groups," said Lara. "I'd say my friend Noelle is a burnt jock."

"Noelle?"

"Yup. Noelle Moncada. Mother's French, father was . . . I don't know. Something. But he died when she was like really little. Heart attack," she said nonchalantly.

"Moncada? Was he Italian?"

"Maybe," she said, closing one of her big, marble eyes. "Actually, I think his family was from Argentina. But you know those South American countries. They're as much a melting pot of European culture as the States."

"If you say so," I said. "Do all your friends smoke dope?"

"What friends?" snorted Jane.

"Shut up Jane," Lara said without looking at her. "You've probably already seen Noelle, especially if you cover the basketball games for the newspaper. Can't miss her. She's really tall. And she's not like the other cheerleaders."

"Because she gets high?"

"Partly," she said evasively. "Because her dad died, her mom is really strict. She has this incessant need to ask permission for everything. Don't you think, Jane?"

"Are you asking my permission to be right?" asked Jane.

"She tries to act like her older sister, Janette, who is really cool," continued Lara, "but she doesn't really pull it off."

"She's okay, I guess," said Jane, using the bellows on the small flame. "But why are we talking about her?" Satisfied with the fire, she set down the bellows and took Keith's face in her hands and kissed him on the mouth. The fire was now fully ablaze.

I moved closer to Lara and wanted to kiss her, but she kept talking.

"I think Neil Young will return to Crosby, Stills and Nash,"

she said unexpectedly. It was like a diversion—an excuse not
to kiss me, or her version of the book we passed around in
grade school called *My Darling, My Hamburger.* It taught girls
to suggest to guys who were about to make a move that they
instead go out and buy hamburgers. She slipped through my
hands like a fish not ready to be caught, sprang to her feet,
and swam to the album crate. Squatting, she flipped through
the selections. "Have this. Have this. Don't have this," she said.
Finally, she pulled out Bob Dylan's *Blood on the Tracks,* and
squealed so loudly that both Jane and Keith looked up. "This is
my favorite album of all time," she sang. "Can we listen to it?"

"Why not?" I put it on the stereo and then flipped on the
television, turning down the sound. We sank back into the sofa
while the TV, muted and cascading blue reflections into the
room, acted like a guest in the corner begging for attention. Lara
asked if we could change the channel at ten-thirty and watch
*Saturday Night Live,* saying that's what she and her friends
usually did on Saturdays when they were relegated to someone's
basement and the "parental units" slept two floors up. Granting
her request, I turned the channel at ten-thirty and held her hand
as we watched Ray Charles host the show.

# 5.
## Noelle. 1977.

A Saturday without plans lay ahead. Staring out my bedroom window I felt mired in Suburban boredom. Everything was surrounded by the cold fog of a late autumn day. I saw tall, leafless trees with gnarled, black trunks and twisted limbs. An amber haze billowed from the city and penetrated the neighborhood.

My hometown was not a pretty place. At least not at this time of year.

Holding my stomach and swallowing bitter, mid-morning breath, I felt like I had gained five pounds from eating a bucket of buttered popcorn after last night's basketball game. It had been the highlight of the evening. With nothing going on, no parties since no one's parents were out of town, I came home early, got into a pair of sweats, and read forty pages of Virginia Woolfe's essay *A Room of One's Own*. It was the first thing I've read by Woolfe that I could understand.

I've had my own room for my entire life. And in the light of day, it was a mess. Everything seemed dusty and out of place. Open drawers, too many pairs of shoes. My cheerleading sweater lay in a heap next to the dresser, and the smell of sweat wafted from the yellowed wool and permeated my nostrils. No dry cleaner in all of Cook County could get rid of the odor of a long line of West Suburban cheerleaders. And tonight there was another game. How was I going to get through another night in that sickening, stinky uniform?

Being a cheerleader just wasn't what I thought it would be.

When I was in grammar school, I spent hours pouring through my older sister's high school yearbooks hunting for names in the photo index with a string of numbers as long as a kite tail. While there was only one page number listed after Janette Moncada's name, and I was only too familiar with the snide smile of my brilliant and bookish sister, I looked for the true stars—the elite group belonging to the cheerleaders, the Key Club and National Honor Society, the Synchronized Swimmers called "Sabrina," and the Dance Club called "Orchesis." The VIPS, however, were the cheerleaders. I memorized their names and their smiles in the same way I had committed my times tables to rote memory. I knew I was destined for those pages in my future high school yearbooks.

To improve my skills, I begged my mother to let me take jazz dancing and gymnastics lessons; however, her mind was always on other things. Like raising Janette and me without a father. I think she spent more time worrying about raising us, than actually raising us. Especially me.

My mother, Emily Moncada, can be summed up in two words: "Tall" and "taut." And if there were a street named after her, it wouldn't be Emily Lane, but One Way. She works at a bank where she started shortly after my dad died. First she was a teller, then a group leader. Now she's a loan officer. Her hours have steadily increased over the years as she climbs the management ladder and now with my sister off in graduate school, no one is around after school when I come home. No mother, no sister, no father.

I hardly knew my father, but the World War II photographs I have of him depict pale eyes and chiseled features. He was blond and wore his hair slicked back like Elvis. I thought he kind of looked like the early photos of Elvis. I spent many hours pouring through Dad's high school yearbooks too. Narrow and sepia in tone, they were called "Argolites," named for his town, Argo, and Jason's adventurous ship. I traveled through them as they silently showed me my father's modest and humble beginnings. In my hands they seemed as ancient as mythology.

I don't know for sure, but I have the feeling my mother married beneath her. Her French Canadian relatives who migrated to New York had important titles like District Attorney and prosecuted historical cases like the Rosenbergs. Another cousin was an NHL hockey player. But my dad, a child of the Depression, was a working class pedestrian from Chicago, whom my mom said was so handsome in his sailor's uniform that every girl's head turned when he walked into the room. Family lore had it he robbed the cradle when he stole Emily Fournier from her New York City girl's school and took her back to the blue collar side of his hometown.

He worked as a telephone repairman climbing poles in oppressive weather, and my mom, who didn't get pregnant for six years, worked as a telephone operator by day and took classes in management by night. She said it was a good thing she had had that training and work experience, otherwise she wouldn't have been able to support us after dad died so unexpectedly.

Management was the perfect occupation for my mother. She was great at running other people's lives. It irked me no end that she wasn't the least bit supportive of my early cheerleading endeavors. While National Honor Society and Key Club earned her approval and I wasn't invited to join either group, cheerleading was a little too provincial for her.

What did she know? She couldn't even turn a cartwheel.

As for Janette, well, she rolled her eyes anytime she saw me turning flips in the backyard. The first time she witnessed me perform a flying split, she was home from college on summer break. I jumped into the air with my legs outstretched and landed with a thud into a perfect split, shooting my arms into the air with great fanfare. She was horrified. After opening her eyes she grabbed her crotch and made the pained expression of a woman experiencing a menstrual cramp. "Don't ever do that in front of me again," she said.

In spite of Janette's aversion to any kind of athletic activity, she did talk our mother into finally letting me take dance lessons from Miss Rose, the woman who lived next door. Janette found me with my face pressed up against the glass of her studio window watching swirling pink ballerinas as though I were in some kind of trance. When she looked into the window to see what had me so fascinated, she stepped back and flatly said, "It looks like an acid trip."

My sister was a hippie. In today's language, she'd be called a freak. She smoked cigarettes in the bathroom and always had her nose shoved in a Philip Roth or J.R.R. Tolkien book. She had long, red hair, just like mine, but we were eight years apart and a lot can happen to hairstyles in eight years. In high school she wore hers like she had just stepped off a stage production of *Hair.* I wore mine like one of *Charlie's Angels.*

I hung up the cheerleading uniform on a wire hanger and carried it downstairs. A day swinging in the suburban breeze might air it enough to be tolerable by six o'clock.

"Where are you going with that thing?" my mother asked, her teacup held to her painted, coral lips.

"It stinks and I don't have time to get it cleaned. Mom, can I quit cheerleading?"

"Quit cheerleading? You must be joking."

"Here," I said, shoving the sweater toward her. "Smell this. You'd want to quit, too, if you had to wear this thing."

"My darling Noelle, you tried out and you made it. You owe it to everyone to stick with it," she said. "Think about all those girls who wanted to be cheerleaders and didn't get to because you took a spot."

"No one cares anymore," I said. "Girls have all kinds of sports."

"No daughter of mine is quitting anything," she said. "Even if it is cheerleading. What if I came home from the bank one day and said I was going to quit? Could you imagine what that would do to us? Hmm?"

"It's not the same"

"Regardless," she said. "You stick with it and do your best."

I seriously doubt my quitting cheerleading would have had any effect on the livelihood of our family or on the world in general. I don't even like the girls on the squad anymore. My best friend, Lara Romano, quit after sophomore year, cleverly proclaiming cheerleading as "sophomoric," and my other best friend, Rebecca Smyth, didn't make the varsity squad this year. And since the Smyth family was to West Suburban cheerleading what the Kennedys were to Massachusetts politics, it was the end of a world.

On the morning the varsity tryout results were posted on the dean's office window last spring, I had an orthodontist appointment to have my retainer adjusted, so I missed the initial commotion stirred up by a Smyth not being on the list. If I had had an appointment on the days the results were posted during my first two years of tryouts, I would have made other plans since those were practically the biggest moments of my life; however, by the last year my braces had come off and I was a well-established West Suburban cheerleader. Morning ortho appointments were too valuable to pass up. They got me out of first hour P.E. and enabled me to sleep an extra half hour. Plus, they meant I didn't have to drive to school with our next-door neighbor, Mr. Novak, and his boring daughter, Debbie. I've been a passenger in his pale yellow, boat of a Cadillac since freshman year and endure a haze of Winston cigarette smoke each morning after my orange juice and Cheerios while he blasts Wally Phillips on the tinny AM radio. I'm sure I walk into school reeking like the freaks who smoke in the bathrooms. I guess he thinks he's doing the poor widow a favor by taking her daughter to school, but truthfully, I would rather walk three miles in the snow. At least I'd have something to tell my grandchildren.

Still, I wish I'd been there for Rebecca. When she found out she didn't make the senior varsity squad, her whole world fell to the ground like a missed baton in a major competition. She actually called me at the orthodontist's office to tell me the news. It was as though she had to say it out loud to believe it.

"Noelle?" she had said in a small voice. "I didn't make it."

"Didn't make what?" I asked, still surprised there was a call for me in that office.

"My name wasn't on the list," she said with a sniffle. "I'm not going to be a cheerleader."

"It must be a mistake. There's no way you couldn't make it. For God's sake, you're a Smyth!"

"Obviously it didn't make any difference to the judges. You won't believe who they picked."

"Who?"

"Sally fucking Thomson," she said. "Can you believe that? She's like a robot. And she's FAT!"

"Who else?" I asked selfishly. After all, these were the girls I'd be spending the next year with.

"Claudia Ryder."

"You're shitting me. Claudia Ryder and Sally Thomson?" I looked around the office to see if any of the assistants in their starched, white uniforms had heard me swear. (The one who answered the phone and never missed a thing was staring right at me.) I lowered my voice. "That's like Laurel and Hardy! Do you think those two spastics making it has anything to do with Claudia's sister being one of the judges?"

"I thought they liked me!" said Rebecca, sobbing.

"Of course they like you. They're probably just jealous of who you are and where you come from. They've probably wanted to stick it to you and your sisters for years."

"My mom is so upset I think she's going to call the school. I'll die if she calls the school."

Her mom *did* call the school. Mrs. Smyth was more upset than Rebecca. She informed the cheerleading sponsor, the school's Russian teacher, Mrs. Zanda, that she was going to write a letter to the school board.

Sweet Rebecca with yellow hair and a beautiful smile, bounced back quickly. She took a deep breath and moved ahead. She decided to try out for the wrestling cheerleading squad, a group considered second rank by some imagined standards. Rebecca didn't know the first thing about wrestling; however, for the love of the skirt, she tried out, made it, and was elected captain.

I hung the sweater on the backyard clothesline and looked at the blue and white, woolen uniform dancing in the breeze. The letters "W" and "S," linked together and sewn on with a blanket stitch, were jabbed with a collection of stickpins once meaning everything, now meaning nothing. I would gladly turn over my varsity rank and another long basketball season to Rebecca Smyth. She deserves it a lot more than I.

"Honey," called my mother. "You have a phone call. It's Lara."

Delighted, I rushed inside. I hadn't heard from Lara in what seemed like ages. Not since she got a new boyfriend. Lara had always been one of those girls who dumped her girlfriends as soon as a guy came into the picture. I vowed never to do that. It was an easy vow to make, seeing that I never had a boyfriend.

"Hi Lara," I said after taking the receiver from my mother. I instantly wound up the coiled telephone cord around my legs, wearing it like a white, see-through skirt.

"What's up?" she asked.

"Nothing. I've got hours to kill before tonight's basketball game. I can't believe we're starting the season with back-to-back games."

"Why don't you come by? I'm making grilled cheese."

"I'll be there in twenty."

Jumping on my bicycle, I rode through the quiet streets of the neighborhood. It was colder than I thought it would be, and I lamented not wearing a warmer jacket. Peddling my way toward the forest preserve that separated our neighborhoods, I believed it was going to be a long winter. I wished I lived some place tropical. Or at least warmer. Like Florida or California—even Tennessee, where my sister was, had to be a better place than Brook Park, Illinois. How, I wondered, did people wind up in places like this? Places completely devoid of dramatic landscape and excitement.

Lara was home alone and didn't bother to dress up for me. She wore her thick glasses and a Wellesley sweatshirt, and her uncombed hair hung in ropy, blonde clumps around her shoulders. After letting me inside, she immediately handed me a book entitled *Western Civilization.* "I want you to take this class with me next semester," she said.

"Hello to you, too!"

"I mean it," she said. "It's got the coolest teacher ever. I have him now for the intro course. He actually asks our opinion."

I followed Lara to her room and watched as she flopped on

her bed. A pile of books was stacked next to a ceramic lamp and was nearly as tall. The walls were covered with coffee-colored wallpaper with silver foil designs—Lara's choice when redecorating her room two years earlier. Bob Dylan stared at me from one corner, the tongue of the Rolling Stones stuck out at me from another. In front of the solitary window, plants hung in tied-jute hangers made during her fascination with macramé last summer. A collection of Chianti bottles cluttered the top of her dresser. Some were covered with candle wax, another supported a bouquet of peacock feathers. Between the bottles were pot pipes, a bong, and blown glass joint holders painted with flowers and butterflies. They were cleverly disguised as vases holding dried flowers from various homecoming dances and last year's junior prom. Lara had a string of boyfriends who had taken her to every dance since freshman homecoming.

"The other day our Western Civ teacher showed us a movie about Cromwell, who was a total fox," she said.

"Who's Cromwell?"

"Oliver Cromwell," said Lara flatly, "is a key figure in Seventeenth Century British history. He's very controversial."

"Are you talking about a knight in shining armor? Someone devastatingly handsome?"

"I don't know what Cromwell really looked like, but the actor portraying him in this film foxed me out! In fact, he looked a lot like my boyfriend Joel."

"Here we go again. Joel, Joel, Joel," I said, kicking off my shoes. I sat on the edge of her bed. "Joel for President already!"

"Maybe," laughed Lara. "He's fairly smart. Great vocabulary. And I like that he goes to another school. The guys at Trumaine are much cooler than the guys we know."

"How so?"

"Well for one, he listens to jazz. And he has a perm. How many guys can you name from West Suburban who would have the guts to let an old girlfriend give him a perm?"

"Yikes. I hate perms. Does it look like a perm—you know, tight, kinky curls like a poodle?"

"Not at all. I didn't know it wasn't natural at first. I think he's going to write a story about it for the school newspaper. He wants to be a journalist."

"So do I," I said. I sat up, a little more interested in this new boyfriend. "I've wanted to be a journalist ever since I saw *All The President's Men*."

"You should start working at the paper then. At the very least you've got to take Western Civ with me next term. It's your final semester of high school. Take something interesting for a change." Her eyes bugged out as she took the book from my hands and paged through it. "If you sign up for anything to do with Home Ec, I'll put my hands around your neck."

"I've *never* taken a Home Ec course and I don't intend to start now. I already know how to sew. What else is there? Cooking? I don't think so."

"I could stand to learn to cook. Lately I've been living on nothing but cheese sandwiches. I'm thinking about going vegetarian."

"You'll be happy to know I'm taking an Asian area studies class for sure, because I just loved Mr. King for sociology and he teaches it."

"Well that's good, Noelle. I'm glad to see you're broadening your horizons beyond vocational typing and the rah-rah world of cheerleading."

"You bitch!" I snorted and flicked her shoulder.

"Why don't you just quit?"

"Can't. Mom says no," I said. "In fact, we were just talking about it. I think she's trying to teach me about commitment and responsibility or something."

Lara dropped her glasses down her nose. "It's a good thing you only have one unreasonable parent to deal with. Have you ever thought about it that way?"

"No. Can't say that I have. By the way, you shouldn't knock vocational typing. That class taught me how to type like a secretary on speed. If I'm going to be a famous journalist like Bob Woodward, I need to be able to type that fast!"

"Who gives a crap about Bob Woodward? Now Robert Redford is someone I wouldn't push out of my bed. You know, I think Joel looks a little like Robert Redford. With curly hair."

"Again with this Joel guy. What's he doing today? I mean, he's obviously tied up since you called me."

"I'm seeing him tonight. You have a basketball game at Trumaine High tonight, right?"

"I don't know where the game is," I said, thinking of my uniform left hanging in the backyard breeze. "All I know is that I have to be at school by six o'clock to catch the bus."

"Joel and I are going to come. I want you to meet him."

"Perm boy? You want me to meet the future president perm boy?"

"Mention the perm," she said, "and you're dead."

# 6.
# Joel. 1978.

Lara and I entered my high school gymnasium during the first half of the basketball game, and the noise hit me with the same surprise as a car stereo coming on at full crank on a quiet morning. Cheerleaders yelled on each side of court, the pep band blew horns and beat drums, and excited fans kicked the bleachers in a low rumble registering at least three on my personal Richter scale. Echoes of bouncing balls and squeaking sneakers ricocheted between the lacquered gym floor and a high ceiling filled with exercise equipment.

I scratched my head, lamenting that joint we smoked in the parking lot ten minutes earlier.

With my senses at full alert, I inhaled the essence of varnish and sweat, and then looked directly into one of the florescent, overhead lights. *"Don't look into the sun!"* It was my mother's voice reverberating in my head. Dutifully, I squeezed shut my eyes and as I tried to regain my focus, a surreal haze blanketed everything with rainbows. I had to sit down.

Lara stood beside me, searching. A silent grin spread across her face as big, chihuahua eyes bulged from her face. Was she feeling the same stoned detachment as I?

Blinking away the black floaters hindering my eyesight, I focused on the shine of fifteen coats of shellac. It covered everything. The floor. The bleachers. My brain. I needed to adjust—level out my buzz and try to feel normal, but found it impossible in this myriad of echoing activity. I combed through my hair, the curls feeling coarse and foreign, and felt a powerful urge to dash out of the gym and go sit under the bleachers at the baseball field. Lara sat down next to me and put her hand on my knee, momentarily taking me outside of my head. I was about to ask her if she wanted to leave. But before I could open my mouth, something—someone—grabbed my attention.

She was as thin as a cattail in a golf course swamp and *very* tall. She may have been over six feet, which meant taller than I. Shining red hair tumbled down her shoulders, bouncing like coils in slow motion. And as abruptly as an unexpected power outage, the cacophony of the gym muffled.

It was a frozen moment. A snapshot.

Without regard to anyone or anything around me, I stared at the copper-headed cheerleader—a girl with skin as translucent as tissue paper. She wore a royal blue sweater that hung from her shoulders like a football jersey without shoulder pads. She jumped and swayed, keeping time to a rhythm, as hints of white escaped from the pleats of her matching blue skirt. As she twirled around, a perfect three-sixty, my head spun with her movement. I looked above her head and expected to see a hole in the ceiling with a moonbeam breaking through and causing her hair to shine, but instead saw only the gymnasium light providing this halo—this aura—surrounding her. The same light that had only moments earlier blinded me.

Lara didn't have to tell me who she was.

I had never before been interested in cheerleaders. Thought they were in a class all to themselves—a class that uttered a language I didn't understand, where words were spelled and shouted instead of spoken: "R-E-B-O-U-N-D; F-I-G-H-T; S-U-C-C-E-S-S, that's the way we spell success!" *Clap-clap-clap. Stamp-stamp-stamp.* But as I watched this girl, this smiling bouncing girl, she intrigued me right down to my new Nikes.

I took a deep breath and, as I exhaled, the bouncing ball, the vibrating rim of the basketball hoop, the referee's shrill whistles, the mocking trombone and squeaking sneakers burst back into my realm. I shook my head as though waking up and thought what I always thought when I saw a beautiful girl for the first time.

*I didn't stand a chance.*

"There she is," said Lara. "There's Noelle."

I had momentarily forgotten I was with Lara. "Huh?"

"My friend. She's right there." She stood and pointed.

"Which one?" I asked.

"Right *there*. Let's cross over." She grabbed my arm, pulling me from my perch. "You're going into enemy territory with me Mr. Rolland."

We walked toward Noelle, and I watched as she moved away from the bleachers and bent into a white porcelain drinking fountain. The arching flow of the water hit her in the nose and she used the back of her hand to wipe her face.

"Hey Moncada!" cried Lara. "I want you to meet my boyfriend."

Noelle straightened, wiped her mouth again and then ran her fingers through her hair. She looked at me, squinted and pursed her lips. It was the exact face my editor made when pasting up the school paper, checking to see if the copy was straight.

I couldn't think of anything to do or say, so I squinted back, aping her. She snapped to attention and grew even taller. I couldn't see the top of her head and rocked forward, suppressing the urge to lift up on my toes. That's when her eyes—two laser beams—shot through me.

"Wow," I said. "Your eyes are very green."

"And yours are blue," she said with a laugh. "I've heard a lot about you, Jo-el. Hey, how do you like that? Jo-el, No-elle. Our names rhyme."

Her sing-songy rendition of my name reverberated through my head. I smiled and felt my face redden. "Lara's talked about you, too, Noelle."

"Oh really?" she said skeptically. She brightened and her cat-like eyes shrank to a normal size. Then she smiled. It was an enormous, perfect smile, and I'm not kidding, it made my heart beat a little faster.

"We're not really staying," I heard Lara say as I looked around Noelle and toward the bleachers for a seat. "I think we're going to do a movie or something. Right, Joel?"

"Su-re," I said, focusing back on Noelle. "What? Oh yeah, sure Noelle. I mean, Lara."

"C'mon, Joel," Lara said. "Are you coming or what?" She sounded a lot like the way my mom talks to my dad.

"See you later," said Noelle. "Nice to finally meet you. See ya, Lara."

I nodded and shuffled sideways, moving away from her. Following my heartbeat, I trailed after Lara.

We worked our way between the rest of the West Suburban cheerleaders and the bleachers and found seats at half-court, about four rows up. It was far from where Noelle stood clapping her hands and dancing around like cheerleaders do; but I could still see her while watching the game.

I had never before sat on the visitor's side in my high school gymnasium. It was like being in another country. I turned my head left and right as the players shot and missed and shot and scored. Basketball wasn't one of my favorite sports. From time to time I'd catch the Harlem Globetrotters playing on TV, spinning their red, white, and blue ball and clowning around with their patsy opponents, but high school basketball wasn't the least bit exciting.

I chose to watch Noelle instead, and she saw me looking at her—gave me a double take and once again showed me that magnificent smile. She stopped clapping and dropped her hands to her sides. Her green gaze felt warm and familiar. It was like we were the only two people in the gym.

I'm not sure, but I think she mouthed the words, "nice perm."

\* \* \* \* \* \* \* \*

My eighteenth year loomed over my head as a milestone destination. The same way my sixteenth birthday meant driver's license, my upcoming birthday meant the right to vote. I invited Lara to welcome in 1978, the year that would forever be known as our graduation year. We went to a party at Keith's house.

She arrived with a tribe of girls and, showing off for them, kissed me deeply and turned to make sure they were watching. She smelled of garlic and wine. "I want you to meet my friends. They're over by the door."

"I'm sure my friends would like to meet them too."

"Of course you know Jane. And you probably remember Noelle. But I. . . ."

As soon as she said Noelle's name I stopped listening. So much taller than the rest of the girls, Noelle was impossible to miss. She stuck out like a periscope keeping watch for the clan. Her hair curled around her face, spilling onto the shoulders of a tweed jacket. Very preppy. She wore a ruffled shirt with two, maybe even three buttons open, and a brown suede vest. I followed her long legs all the way to the floor and saw a pair of three-inch heels. Did she really need the heels? I backed off and fell into a chair.

"Who is *that?*" asked Keith from behind me. Not waiting for my answer, he stumbled toward her and I felt a territorial urge well up inside me. It felt like he was barging in on a pickup softball game and disregarding the rules.

I chugged the last of my warm beer from an even warmer bottle.

"Brought you another," said Lara, handing me a beer. I hadn't noticed she'd left my side.

"Thanks," I said. I felt her hand grab my chin as she sat on the arm of my chair. She turned my face to her and she was so close, it took me a minute to focus. And when I did focus, I saw mascara smeared below her left eye like grease paint on a football player. It looked like she'd been hit. "How many drinks have you had?"

"It's New Year's Eve," she said. "Who's counting?"

"You think Jane's going to get pissed if Keith goes after Noelle?"

"Jane dumped him. Said he had a small dick."

"Ha!" I practically snorted beer out my nose. "I thought he dumped her."

"Whatever. But Noelle won't have anything to do with him. Not her type."

"What is her type?"

"How should I know? She doesn't go out with anyone. At least not that I know of."

At some point after midnight—after the countdown and the annual show of guys trying to kiss as many girls as possible—we moved into the basement. The only girl I had kissed was Lara, and she sat with me like an appendage, laughing one minute and zoning out the next.

Keith provided the entertainment. Like a DJ he spun Jethro Tull and Steely Dan, then played Clapton's "After Midnight" before resorting to his endless collection of Led Zeppelin. Keith was as proud of that collection as Joe was of his car. Making a great a show of cleaning the vinyl and putting the stylus in place, he cranked the volume and mimed his trademark air guitar.

*Eyes that shine burning red. Dreams of you all through my head.*

Shrieking lyrics pierced the smoky air until one of the speakers blew, and then at regular drumbeat intervals, the music buzzed like airbrakes on a semi. Keith raced to turn down the volume amid the ruins of the evening stacked up around us. Beer bottles covered the tables and ashtrays overflowed. Jackets and scarves were draped about the furniture and stray shoes littered the floor.

You could always tell how well the party was going by surveying the mess.

Lara had stopped making sense. And just when she looked like she was about to either hurl or pass out, all at once this yellow-haired girl I'd never seen before grabbed her by crooking an elbow around her neck—as though she were a lifeguard and Lara was drowning. Lara resisted and sat back down on me with a thud.

"Time to go," said her friend in an authoritative voice. She sounded like someone's angry mother. Or a P.E. teacher. "Looks like I'll have to drive your car."

"I'm fine, Robyn!" slurred Lara. "Really. I can drive."

"Oh no you're not," I said. "I can be sure she makes it home. Tomorrow. Wait, it *is* tomorrow."

"I don't think so," said Robyn. "Where are your keys, Lara?"

"I've got my keys," said Lara, grabbing them from the belt loop of her Levi's, where she had hung them with a purple carabiner clip. I thought one of her eyes was going to pop out and roll across the floor.

"Now *I* have them," Robyn said, snatching the clip with a quick motion. The next thing I knew, she hoisted Lara off my lap and the entire posse of girls was gone so fast it was like a vacuum had sucked them out the front door.

I didn't speak to Noelle that evening and it left me with a great sense of disappointment.

I continued seeing Lara through much of the second term, and waited patiently for her to go all the way. Each time I built up the nerve to ask, she gave me a hard time, saying she intended to lose her virginity to "just the right man." But she was perfectly willing to make out with me in my Volkswagen until our lips were chapped and our pants were around our ankles. Finally, I told her I couldn't stand it any longer and that we should break up. That's when she gave in.

And it was as we put our clothes back on that I realized I was relieved we planned to go away to different colleges.

She decided on Mills College in Oakland, California, while I set my sights on a state school. It was the most my entry exams and my budget afforded. I did well on the verbal section of my SAT tests, but my math was in the toilet. I suppose I took after my mother, the English teacher.

I didn't want to think about what I might have inherited from my father.

While both my parents went to Northern Illinois University in DeKalb because it was the closest four-year college to home, I took the road less traveled and chose the opposite end of the state. Southern Illinois University at Carbondale—Illinois's party school—or I should say *one* of Illinois's party schools. I had heard the same label given to Western Illinois in Macomb and Illinois State in Normal. During the spring term, I visited all the state schools including U of I in Champaign (too big, too Greek), and liked Southern the best. It was in the Shawnee National Forest, and the dorm I picked was on a lake. Most importantly, it was nothing like the Chicago suburbs. People even spoke with southern accents. (I soon learned that anyone from south of Kankakee spoke with a southern accent.) And Carbondale, six hours south of Chicago and a train stop on the City of New Orleans Amtrak line, was Illinois's own heart of Dixie.

Southern Illinois is also known as Little Egypt. There are several theories as to how it attained this moniker, but the first I heard was a Biblical reference made by a Baptist minister while teaching Bible stories to French settlers and Illini Indians. From the bluffs of Edwardsville he viewed the Mississippi and Missouri Rivers conjoined at the southern tip of Illinois and likened the mighty Mississippi, the longest river on the North American continent, to the Nile. He identified the fertile land within the riverbeds as the "Land of Goshen," and compared the land outcroppings, or mounds, to the Egyptian pyramids. The towns of Cairo and Thebes soon followed.

The way I looked at it, Southern Illinois was the farthest I could get away without leaving the state and still have the benefit of paying in-state tuition. My mom told me that we couldn't afford much on the income of two teachers and only promised to pay for the first year. If I didn't pull off decent grades, she had said, "you're on your own!"

In August she accompanied me on the six-hour drive south. We took her car, a Volvo station wagon, since my Bug couldn't hold all my clothes and books, not to mention the stereo and record collection. Walt said he was "too busy" to make the trip, and said goodbye with a firm handshake—the handshake of a business associate rather than a father. I hadn't seen much of him over the summer, and when he was around he was aloof and angry. When I asked my mom questions trying to figure out what was wrong, she waved her hand like she was erasing something on a chalkboard, and refused to talk about him.

I drove while my mom sat tucked into the passenger side with the seat pulled all the way forward. My mother is not tall. She's small enough to fit her head under my armpit. Her light brown hair is cropped short, and like half the girls in my graduating class, styled like Dorothy Hamil. Unlike most of the ladies in our neighborhood, she doesn't dye it, and I think the gray streaks fit her personality, which is sharp, intellectual, and always volatile. I never know what might come out of her mouth.

On this trip, it was mostly smoke. And she kept tossing out her cigarette butts onto the highway.

"Mom," I scolded, "will you stop sending tobacco bombs into unsuspecting traffic?"

"I don't want your father to know how many cigarettes I've smoked on this trip," she said. "And you had better not say anything to him."

"Look at those dried up cornfields. You could start a fire. Cut it out!"

"Stop giving me a hard time or I'll tell Dad you smoke grass!"

"When would you see him long enough to have an actual conversation anyway?"

"Never you mind. How fast are you going anyway?" she asked. "Stop passing everything. Getting a speeding ticket is not the way to inaugurate your college education."

"Mo-om! I'm doing fifty-six. Get off my back, okay?"

"Okay, okay." She lit another cigarette. "Shame about Maria, don't you think?"

"What do you mean it's a shame about Maria?"

"Junior college? She could have had higher aspirations. Maybe even a scholarship."

"I don't know one person who won a sports scholarship, Mom. The only scouts who showed up were looking for football players. The girls teams didn't have a chance."

"It's because our school is too small. Maybe if *you* stayed in baseball you'd have a chance at a better school."

"There's nothing wrong with the school I chose," I said sighing. "Correct me if I'm wrong, but wasn't it you who always said that school is what you make it?"

"That's what I'm worried about." She looked out the passenger window and into the cab of a Peterbuilt semi in the parallel lane. "What are you lookin' at, Mister?" she said to the driver.

Four hours later we followed the signs through town to the campus and she helped move my things into the third floor of Baker Hall. It was one of a dozen dorm buildings in an area called The Point. As dorms go, it was a nice setup—woodsy, rural. Inside, however, it was a pretty typical dorm room. About the size of a shoebox.

Mom made up my bed with a set of standard issue, sea-foam green sheets. "We paid for the sheet exchange service," she said. "So be sure to change your sheets once a week."

"Yes, mother," I said dutifully.

"Wish I could have met your new roommate. What was his name again?"

"Sam. A pig farmer from Watsonville. I can't believe I actually have to share this space with another person."

"Look at it this way," she said. "He could be the brother you never had. Do you want me to wait with you through orientation?"

"I'll be fine," I decided. "Just walk me down there. It's right where you parked your car."

We walked downstairs and stood in a short line at the orientation table near The Point cafeteria. I tried to say goodbye, but she clearly didn't want to leave. She held me around the waist, tucked her head into my chest and I felt her welling up.

"I mean it about those sheets. I also paid for the full meal ticket, so don't skip breakfast. Do you hear me?"

Tears flowed down her cheeks like rapidly melting icicles.

"Mom, please. Are you going to make a scene?"

"I'm losing my only child," she sobbed. "You're my baby boy."

"Oh my God," I said and put my arms around her. No wonder she'd been so nervous on the drive. I squeezed her a little tighter and she held on, not ready to let go. Her body hiccoughed like a little kid on a crying jag.

"I'll be at the Holiday Inn overnight in case you need anything," she whispered.

"I'll be fine, Mom. It's just college. Not the Army."

"The Army? Good Christ," she spit, digging her nails into my back. "No son of mine is ever going to join the Army. Don't even think about it. You hear me?"

"I hear you. Everyone can hear you."

Finally she pulled away. She used the back of her hand to wipe her cheeks and sniffled. Then she hesitated for a second and without warning, walloped me right across the face. "Stay out of the playpen," she yelled.

Stunned, I watched as she turned her back and walked away. She climbed inside the Volvo, lit a cigarette, and drove off.

I missed her immediately.

My first class was on Monday at eight o'clock, a time slot only freshmen are dumb enough to fill. Armed with my new leather backpack, a few notebooks and BIC pens, and a brand-spanking new *Webster's Dictionary* that my mom gave to me as a graduation gift, I was ready for action. The class was in a building a mere two hundred and thirty two steps from my dorm and I was the first one there. Entering the bright, empty room I first double-checked the room number before choosing one of the chairs arranged in a circle. I hung my pack on the back of a chair facing the door so I could monitor the students coming inside, sat down, and raised the desktop from the armrest. The soft wood was dirty—full of pencil lead—and scratched with the initials of a hundred students who had chosen the seat before I.

My classmates trickled in one at a time, like somber droplets from a slow-dripping faucet, and we exchanged self-conscious nods and pursed-lipped smiles. There were as many guys as girls and most of them carried Styrofoam coffee cups. Some had hot-pink cans of TAB. It was a room full of strangers from different parts of the state—cities and suburbs, cow towns and farms. Some nervously tapped pencils; others stared up at the buzzing fluorescent lights or the large wall clock audibly ticking toward eight o'clock. I reached into my backpack for a spiral notebook, thinking I should take notes.

Then all of a sudden, *she* walked into the room.

It was a mass of red hair—a tall and reedy figure—an ethereal beauty that took over the otherwise drab and expectant room. My God, I thought, could it really be she?

"Noelle," I heard myself say too loudly, and all heads turned toward her as she looked at me. She narrowed her eyes and momentarily considered me, the same way she had on the night of the basketball game when we first met.

"Joel?" she said. "Jo-el? You . . . remember . . . me?"

"Of course I remember you," I said, motioning to the chair next to me. "Here. Sit here."

She hesitantly moved in my direction, still not sure of something. "What?" I asked.

"It's your hair," she said. "It's different." She hung her Army green backpack on the chair.

"Perm grew out," I whispered, as she sat down.

"Oh, yeah. The perm. Hey, wait a minute. Did I know you were coming to this school?"

"I'm not sure, Noelle. But I guess it's pretty clear that yes, I *am* here. And here we are at an eight-o'clock class. Who the hell advised us to do this?" I ran my fingers through my now straight hair as she reached behind her and without looking, pulled out a spiral notebook. All eyes in the room were upon us.

"Eight o'clock. I should have my head examined," she said in a softer voice, "but I really wanted to take something other than General Studies courses."

"I hear that."

"My God, Joel. I can't believe I have you in my very first class. It's great to see you," she said, putting her hand on top of mine.

Her touch was slightly cool. I looked down and saw translucent fingers with a smattering of faint freckles on the knuckles and long but unpolished fingernails. Her skin had the slightest hint of a blue tint. Then I looked up and her green gaze was warm and instantly familiar.

"You, too," I said.

"This is such a coincidence," she said. "Where do you live? DON'T say The Point or I'll fall right off this chair."

"Baker Hall."

"Ha! I'm in Montgomery. We're neighbors!"

Our instructor, Professor Hamm, walked in and enthusiastically greeted his new class. But I hardly paid attention. I was too busy recording this moment.

Because it was at this moment—with her hand still on top of mine in a small college classroom in Carbondale, Illinois—that Noelle Moncada and I first became friends.

# 7.
# Noelle. 1978.

The initial lessons I learned in the seductive setting of my freshman year were about two things: Beer and weight gain. As a college co-ed I learned that even skinny girls gained the prerequisite Freshmen Fifteen during the first semester.

And in my case, fifteen more soon followed.

I blamed a complete lack of self-control. I was once one of those girls who could eat anything and not gain an ounce, and stupidly believed I'd have that kind of metabolism for the rest of my life. Secondly, I blamed the cafeteria starch smorgasbord at the dorm dining hall and the quarter beers at BJ's Biker Bar, where my roommate Cleo and I went every Thursday, Friday, and Saturday night.

BJ's would not have been my first choice in hangouts if the game of roommate roulette hadn't landed me in room 213 of Montgomery Hall with Cleo King. Featuring two pool tables; a foosball table; and Jack Daniel's-drinking, longhaired, and hairy-chested Harley men with lots of black leather and chains, it was exactly Cleo's kind of Kiddyland and a replica of the bar "up north" where she had hung out since the age of twelve.

Cleo had arrived at our dorm room the day before I and helped herself to the bed and desk near the window. Her half of the room was already decorated, as though she'd been there for months. The light blue cinderblock walls were covered with posters of bands, which I reviewed to see if we'd be compatible in the very important area of music. I recognized Jerry Garcia from the Grateful Dead, Crosby, Stills, Nash and Young, the Doobie Brothers, and Willie Nelson—all acceptable. Blue Oyster

61

Cult and REO Speedwagon weren't among my favorites, but I
was relieved they weren't Debbie Boone, The Partridge Family,
or Donny and Marie.

"Expensive stereo," said my sister Janette. She had chauffeured
me to school on her way south to Memphis, where she worked
as a sign language interpreter. "You can always tell if your roommate has money by the stereo equipment and the shampoo."
She proceeded to check out the shower stall, located inside a
bathroom we shared with an adjoining room occupied by two
women known as suitemates. "Just as I suspected, it's Vidal Sas-
soon," she called from the shower. "Shampoo *and* conditioner.
Must be from the North Shore."

I examined my roommate's stereo, stationed at the halfway
point of the room and directly across from the sink and medicine
cabinet (already filled with enough toiletries for four people), and
saw that my new roommate had a top-of-the-line Harman-Kardan
receiver, compact Bose speakers, and a Technics turntable. They
were all arranged on top of two fruit crates placed side by side.
There must have been two hundred albums in her collection
compared to my meager sixteen.

Next to the stereo on her desk was a color photograph in
a purple frame. Pictured were two people, a blond man with
long hair and a handlebar mustache with his arm around an
equally flaxen-haired girl holding a three-foot bong in her hand as
though it were a trophy. *"Remember the Midnight Rider,"* read
a file-folder label stuck onto the frame.

"Look at this," I said to Janette. "Another mediocre
dope smoker."

"Yeah, but she can afford it. You better concentrate on saving
your money for next year so you can get the hell out of these
dorms and get into your own apartment. Damn, I don't know
how I lived in a room this small for two years."

"Your dorm room didn't seem as small."

"Believe me. It was. But mine wasn't so filled with plants.
It appears this chick likes her bongs *and* her plants. It's like
a terrarium in here."

Brass, floor-to-ceiling plant stands were positioned like sen-
tries on each side of her bed. I recognized the philodendron,
English ivy and purplish-wandering Jew plants on one side. On
the other were green and white-striped spider plants and waxy-
leaved Swedish ivy. African violets with pale pink flowers in
foil-wrapped terra cotta pots lined the windowsill. A furry, zebra-
striped blanket and a leopard-print backrest covered her bed. It
looked like Elvis's Jungle Room at Graceland, where Janette had
taken me on my first visit to Memphis.

"Did we get everything out of the car?" I asked.

"I think so," said Janette. "You should go to that orientation meeting, kid. It may feel hokey at first, but I met my best friends at that first meeting, and you might as well go ahead and get started."

I felt like crying. "You think Mom's not going to be too lonely on her own?"

"Don't worry about Mom. That's one lady who can take care of herself. And so can you. You'll see."

I put my arms around my sister's waist and my head fell upon her shoulder. She smelled like lemons. "Have fun, kid," she said. "Make sure you study, but make sure you have a good time too. Remember I'm only a few hours drive away if you need me. Just call and I'll jump in my Saab and head north."

And then she was gone. My *summa cum laude* sister, who breezed through six years of school without seeing a 'B,' was off to a land where people no longer called her "Janette," but Jan, and cars were no longer called "beaters" but Saabs. As she walked out of my life once again, I watched her red curls sway in sync with her hips. She strode confidently down the wide hallway of my new home and I sighed.

Jan-don't-call-me-Janette was a tough act to follow.

Aware that I watched from behind, she raised her hand and wiggled her fingers without turning. When she disappeared around the corner, I sighed again and felt my aloneness. I took a step forward, thinking I might run after her, and all at once the door behind me slammed shut. "Shit!" I swore. I didn't have my key.

The silver numbers, 2-1-3, hung silently on the door, mocking me, while I stood there, a stupid freshman locked out of her room.

With no other choice, I headed from the second floor and through the chilly, dark stairwell around the corner. And as I trotted down the stairs to the first floor, my footsteps echoing noisily, I noticed someone had spray-painted "Fe" on the wall in blue paint. "Fe," I said aloud. "Iron." It was, perhaps, one thing I had retained from high school chemistry class. Opening the door to the first floor corridor, I tentatively looked left and right, trying to determine where the room for the orientation meeting was located. Surely someone there would tell me where to get an extra key to my room.

"Looking for the meeting?" asked a cheerful woman in a maroon shirt with a white SIU circle.

"Uh, sure. Orientation?"

"It's this way. They've just started."

I entered a bright room where about thirty co-eds gathered

in loose clusters. A few turned from their conversations and stared at me, giving me the once-over. No one smiled, but two women craned their necks, as though they were fresh off the train from the country and spied a tall building for the first time. That often happened to me when I walked into a room. I was always intensely visible. And then another maroon-shirt clad woman wearing a large white button proclaiming her *"Head Resident, Montgomery Hall,"* asked us to get in a circle and take a seat on the floor. Her Shirley Temple curls bounced as she spoke in a sugary voice, and she had a dimple in her left cheek that was so deep I wanted to stick my finger in it and say, "goo."

"Come on, peoples," she said, clapping. "Let's circle around and get this orientation going. Come, come! Don't be shy!" Her direction felt awkward—like we big peoples were being asked to sit in little peoples' format.

We did not comply. We raised our eyebrows, crossed our arms, and didn't move. "Okay," she tried again. "Please?"

Finally, we formed an amoeba of a circle on the tiled floor and she clapped her hands in approval. "Aren't you going to join us?" she said to one straggler still chattering to no one.

This was the first time I saw Cleo King. Identifying her from the picture I saw on the desk in my dorm room—and recognizing her ensuing *shtick* as one of a hundred class clowns before her—I watched as she shuffled toward the amoeba where we sat with our legs in crisscross, applesauce formation. She was tall, not as tall as I, but probably about five-eight or five-nine, and she had a perfectly round face. Her forehead was low and she had thin blonde hair parted down the middle and hanging to her belt. She wore a custom-issue, teenager-from-the-city black tee-shirt advertising the band RUSH, and a suede vest with a pale yellow *"Question Authority"* button on it. Her worn blue jeans were blanketed with red, orange, and brown leather patches accented with black embroidery thread in a rough blanket stitch.

I'd never seen anyone like her.

Digesting the idea that this person was my new roommate, I stared as she chattered and babbled. I wasn't the only one fixated on Cleo King. She offered running commentary out of the side of her mouth after just about everything the soft-spoken and polite Head Resident, H-R, said.

H-R: "Hi, I'm Rebecca Swift."

Cleo: "Better known as Fast Becky among the men of SIU."

H-R: "For a lot of you, I know this is your first home away from home. We want to help it be just that."

Cleo: "How do you like that? Our very own Welcome Wagon!"

H-R: "I just want you to know that each of our three floors here at Montgomery Hall has its own Resident Assistant. They're called the 'R-A.' If you haven't met her yet, you will shortly. As for me, I live on the first floor and my door is always open."

Cleo: "I'll bet it is. They don't call her Fast Becky for nothin'!"

H-R: (Maintaining her poise in spite of the Cleo's commentary) "When we're finished here, we're going to head to Old Campus to meet the guys from one of the other dorms here at The Point for a sort-of Watermelon Fest."

Cleo: "Yippee! Do we get to play spin the bottle and then slow dance?"

H-R: (Finally addressing Cleo) "If you like. Did you remember your Bobby Sherman records?"

One would think that Rebecca's comment, which she uttered with fluttering Betty Boop eyes, might shut up the class clown; however, for Cleo it was like the invitation to a duel. She kept up the commentary until Rebecca completed her spiel. Rebecca's curls stopped bouncing and we saw less of the dimple by the time she simply gave up.

Cleo had won and self-satisfaction plastered across her round face like a yellow smiley-face sticker.

Since three or four new residents—all anxious freshmen who probably didn't dare ask questions with the likes of Cleo the Commentator in the room—instantly surrounded her, there were a lot more questions to be answered. And because I needed another key to my room, I approached her too.

On second thought, however, I veered toward my new roommate. Why not ask her to let me into our room?

I neared Cleo and noticed blue eye shadow caking up in the lid creases above her gray eyes and black eyeliner outlining her lids like parenthesis. I looked at her plump, milky hands and saw fingernails painted black—my mother's worst nightmare. Any time I wore anything bolder than clear or pastel pink she grabbed the nail polish remover and a cotton ball and wiped off the color. My mother had very strict rules regarding personal grooming. I was lucky she didn't skin me alive the day I snuck my sister's razor and shaved my legs for the first time. "Now you'll have to do this for the rest of your life," she wailed. And heaven help me if I tried to wear make-up or dangling earrings. No daughter of Emily Moncada was going to look like a whore.

But Cleo didn't look like a whore. She looked like experience. And she saw me coming. Watching me approach, she fingered a big hoop earring while rings on every finger sparkled in the light. One ring was a pot leaf made of turquoise.

"Nice ring," I said.

"Thanks," she said, somehow knowing I referred to the pot leaf. "What do you say we blow this pop stand and go smoke a joint?"

"Sure," I said. "I'm Noelle."

"Noelle Moncada by chance?"

I nodded and smiled and Cleo instantly squeezed her eyes shut and put her hand to her forehead like a shield. Without looking at me she said in a low monotone, "I think I'm your roommate." She opened her eyes and squinted at me, her eyes growing rounder as she looked me over from head to foot and back up to head. She frowned. "Figures I'd get a preppy-looking roommate with brand new jeans and a high-amp smile. Are you sure you want to get high?"

"Lead the way."

"Jesus! Did you just get your braces off or do you always smile that much? I never wore braces although I probably should have. See?" she bared her teeth to reveal a small set with a minor gap in front and canines protruding from her upper gums. "I didn't have the patience and certainly didn't want to be caught dead with a bunch of rubber bands in my mouth. Braces just didn't play in my world. My boyfriend, Dennis—at least he was my boyfriend until the cocksucker broke it off with me five weeks ago—would have broken up with me a lot sooner if I had shown up at The Bar with railroad tracks on my teeth. Say, I know the perfect place to go, which is right near the Ag building where most of my classes are. I've already gone around campus and mapped out my route. Have you done that yet? Because you really should. It's that low-rise building right over there near the woods. See?"

"You think it's okay to smoke out in the open?" I asked, finally managing to get in a word.

"Of course it's okay," she growled, punching me (hard) in the shoulder. "Damn, you're a skinny bitch. Don't you eat? Look, it's better to smoke in the woods than it is in our room, although we can always use the old towel under the door trick. Are you moved in yet? I don't imagine you are because I was there just before the getting-to-know-you meeting. . . ." She momentarily broke into a soft-shoe routine and sang, *"Getting to know you. Getting to know all about you. . . ."* And then she abruptly stopped singing and without taking a break continued, "and there was no sign of your stuff. Do you intend to move in anytime soon? I already took the window side. I can't sleep in a room without the window open. And I'll never sit in the middle of anything. At the movies. On a plane. Whatever. I always have to be on the aisle. I like to have a quick escape route if you know what I mean."

I didn't know what she meant. "I've been to the room," I said. "I just dropped off my stuff and said goodbye to my sister. Then. . . ."

"I have six sisters. I'll bet you can't beat that. Even worse is that I'm smack dab in the middle of all of them. I've got three older—all of them psychotic—and three younger, all of them jocks. I'll bet you were a high school jock. I can smell it on you. But then again, you say you smoke weed so you can't be all bad. And speaking of weed," she sang as she produced a large joint from a Marlboro pack stashed in an inside vest pocket. She placed it under her nose, and sniffed it like it was a fine, Cuban cigar. We continued walking down a path in the forest and Cleo stopped near a large boulder and perched against it as though it were a throne made just for her. As I looked to see if anyone was around, she pulled out a silver butane lighter decorated with a skull and crossbones and fired up. "Don't be paranoid," she said. "We're not going to get busted."

Between inhaling and exhaling and occasionally passing me the loosely rolled stogie, Cleo King never stopped talking. Within minutes I had heard the short version of her relationship with Dennis, the cocksucker, that she had run away from home twice, and that she worked the midway with a traveling carnival. She chose SIU because she wanted to be a "Naturalist Park Ranger" and it was "the best forestry school in the state." Even though she claimed an IQ high enough to qualify for MENSA membership, she had a lousy grade point average in high school (since she skipped class so much), and her strict parents relegated her choices to state schools only. So, while her older sisters had gone off to Wellesley, Princeton, and Boston College, she was stuck in Illinois—which she pronounced "ill noise."

I spent the rest of the day wandering campus with a wide-eyed buzz and looking for my class locations. I whittled away the better part of an hour in one building alone, searching for my Spanish classroom. The building, Faner Hall, which was as large as the Titanic and a confusing maze of colorless concrete hallways, was the biggest building on campus. It divided the quaint, old section of campus and the newer buildings on the west side. With half my classes on either side of the Faner monolith, and my schedule showing a Monday morning zigzag pattern—from the Communications Building over to a building called "Wham," then back to Life Sciences and finally Faner—I was glad I brought my bicycle to school. Janette had said it was a good idea. As always, Janette was right.

In spite of having to get up too early, my first morning of classes went well. I couldn't wait to tell Cleo about the incredible coincidence I experienced by running into Lara's former boyfriend, Joel Rolland. I had no idea he planned to attend school at the same place as I. And then to have him—or anyone I knew—show up in my very first class was crazy.

I suppose you have to move away from home to understand the meaning of the oft-used phrase "it's a small world."

It took me a moment to recognize Joel without his curls. It had been months since I last saw him—wherever that was. Lara told me she broke up with him because she wanted to go to California without a long-distance boyfriend. But Lara told Jane they went all the way and Jane said he dumped her after that. Lara never mentioned anything about having had sex with Joel. She probably thought I either wouldn't approve or couldn't handle the news.

It hurt that she didn't tell me. Isn't first sex something you're supposed to report to your best friend?

After morning classes I returned to our dorm room and planned to eat lunch and finally unpack my boxes. With the key still attached to a leather strap on my belt loop, I unlocked the door and found Cleo lying on top of her furry zebra blanket, face down. "Guess what!" I said, as the door slammed.

She didn't roll over. "Are you planning to be this loud every morning?" she grumbled into her pillow.

"It's not morning," I said. "Don't you have any classes?"

"Are you cracked? Classes before two in the afternoon?" She rolled over displaying a labyrinth of pillow creases on her face. Her eyes were slits. "Fill me a bong, will you? And while you're at it, unpack your shit. Are you waiting for the maid service to do it or something?"

"You did such a good job decorating your half of the room, I thought you'd take it upon yourself to do it for me," I said, reaching for the bong, The Midnight Rider. She said she had stolen it from Dennis after he broke up with her. "Where's the pot?" I asked.

"Didn't you bring any?"

I shook my head.

"It's in the top drawer of my desk," she said. "Oh my CHRISTS, I have a headache. I knew I should have gone home with you last night, but that guy was so fucking luscious I couldn't stand it. I swear he looked just like Dennis and I was about to go off on the back of his Harley and have ten kids with him." She greedily grabbed the bong from my hands like a toddler grabbing a bottle and drew a long, bubbly hit. As her lungs filled with smoke, her face turned pink and she coughed through her nose. She spoke as she exhaled a cloud of thick intoxication. "I LOVE hairy men," she sang, the gravel rumbling in her throat.

I thought she might start beating her chest.

"Well, speaking of hair," I said sitting down on her bed. "I ran into someone in my first class this morning. He dated one of my friends."

"Is he hairy?"

"Well, that's just it. He used to have a head full of curls, but I almost didn't recognize him because his hair looked like a food service worker with a hairnet. Then it dawned on me. He had a perm when I met him."

"Gay guy?"

"No!" I said laughing. "Not at all. At least I don't think he is. I don't know him very well. Like I said, he used to date my friend."

"Your girlfriend or boyfriend?"

"Girlfriend!" I said, frowning. "She lost her virginity to him." Cleo rolled her eyes.

"Anyway, he looked completely different and I had no idea he was at this school."

"So," said Cleo, pinching another dose of reefer between her fingers. "Are you going to fuck him, or what?"

"What?"

"Fuck!" she shouted. "You know, screw? Bang? Have sex? Do the dirty deed? You have heard of it, haven't you?"

"Uh," I stammered. I didn't know what to say.

I didn't have the nerve to tell Cleo I was a virgin. Given the résumé of sexual exploitations she had outlined for me on the previous day—without once asking about my own experience or noticing that I was cringing—she might think I was some kind of leper.

"Well then, maybe I'll fuck him!" she said with a great burst of laughter. "Let's call him. Here, have a hit."

"No thanks," I said waving off the bong. "I'm applying for a student job this afternoon and it requires a typing test. I set up my class schedule with an afternoon work block. I need the money."

"Man, did I ever get the wrong roommate. No doubt you're a virgin and I knew you were straight. Listen, I mean it about unpacking your shit. You do plan to stay, don't you?"

"Yes, Cleo," I said, rising from her bed. "I plan to stay."

For that entire first semester I was a fly wrapped in Cleo's web. I was like a wide-eyed innocent sitting open-mouthed at story hour, as Cleo recounted tale after tale. The stories of her life were like a series of *ABC After School Special* subjects or *Go Ask Alice* movies. Chronologically Cleo King and I were only six weeks apart; however, when it came to experience, she had already lived about five lifetimes. "Like a cat," she had said. "I still have four lifetimes to go before calling it quits and have no intention of slowing down."

She invited me to join her on the roller coaster ride she called day-to-day living and I got over worrying that she would not find me interesting enough to be friends. I, after all, had no exotic stories. But Cleo was happy to have me as an audience. I listened intently, believing that I was somehow a part of her more interesting world—or at least I would be in the future.

Cleo King and college life made me infatuated with possibility.

# 8.
# Joel. 1979.

Professor Joshua Hamm, our instructor for Oral Interpretation, set the tone for my college education. He was theatrical and animated, wore an Elizabethan beard and John Lennon glasses. Each week he had a new accent.

Dr. Josh, as we called him, taught us how to create ourselves. He said our goal as individuals was to interpret ourselves orally.

During the first week of class, he spoke as though channeling Sigmund Freud, and asked us to name the last book we read. Mine was *Winning Through Intimidation* by Robert Ringer. Noelle's was *The Bell Jar* by Sylvia Plath. During the second week, in the voice of a southern plantation owner, he required us to pick out nicknames for ourselves. It was a light exercise meant not only to tell the class how we felt about ourselves, but also to help make our names more memorable. By the end of class, we had Daphne, who called herself Daphne Duck, Moonlight Melissa, and Gorgeous George—to name a few.

I was Soulful Joel. It took me no time to come up with the name.

*"Don't tell Walt,"* I heard myself say in my mother's voice.

Going around the circle, everyone clapped and laughed as the names were announced and almost all seemed appropriate—at least until it was Noelle's turn.

"I can't come up with anything other than Needle-nose Noelle," she said, blushing.

"Needle nose!" said a bald-headed black man, Gorgeous George. "You don't have a needle nose."

"Well my body is shaped like a needle," she said. "How about just Noelle the Needle?"

"You can do better than that," said Dr. Josh, rising from his chair. His accent headed across the pond. He became a Shakespearean actor. "Far better, I'm sure."

"I could call myself Coppertop," Noelle said, looking down. "Like a Duracel battery? How about Duracel Noelle? That kinda rhymes."

"Nonsense," said Dr. Josh, walking toward her. I saw the intent gleam in his eyes as he approached her like an arrow on its way to a target. He picked up her hand and pulled it to his mouth. "Class? Let's help out Noelle, shall we?" He bowed and lowered himself on one knee like he was about to propose.

"Oh my God!" she said. "What are you doing?"

"Kissing your exquisite hand, my dear," he said, lightly touching her reedy fingers with his lips. Then he rose and pressed his hand firmly upon her head. Her thick red tresses swallowed his hand and her face, now as red as her hair, looked like it might explode. She closed her eyes. "I dub thee Noble Noelle." He looked over his shoulder. "Class? Do you approve?"

Everyone clapped and nodded. "That fits," shouted Daphne Duck. Someone else yelled, "Perfect!"

I thought so too, but was mired in jealousy. I could only wonder what it might feel like to make Noelle Moncada blush like that!

Other than our class with the ever-changing atmosphere created by Dr. Josh, during the first semester I didn't see as much of Noelle as I would have liked. Sometimes we sat together at breakfast, the only diners in the large hall before our eight o'clock class. I never saw her at lunch, and rarely at dinner.

The dining hall was a much different place at dinnertime. It was dorm life happy hour with all kinds of positioning and the establishment of social hierarchies between bites of roast chicken and Salisbury steak. It wasn't exactly like high school where only the cool seniors sat at the head table and the geeks sat in the corners, but people definitely formed social strata and chose their tables the way people in large families assigned themselves seats at the family dinner table.

The first time I saw Noelle at dinner I raised my tray as though tipping my hat. She smiled and waved me over. There was one seat open at the table and it was next to a blonde I'd seen walking on campus. This blonde was hard to miss. She was the kind of girl who walked on the sidewalk like she owned it.

"This is my roommate, Cleo King," said Noelle gesturing toward the blonde. "She's a volunteer. I mean she helps people who need assistance with meals. Cleo, this is Joel Rolland."

"So this is cute, cute Mr. Rolland you've been telling me so much about Miss No-elle," Cleo said, patting the chair next to her as though beckoning a puppy to come sit. Her thin eyebrows danced up and down like Groucho Marx and she smiled, exposing a mouth full of small Chicklet-like teeth. I set down my tray, sat to her right, and smelled cigarette smoke wafting from her denim vest. "Noelle calls you 'Soulful Joel,' but I hear you had a perm in high school."

"Yup," I said, suddenly a little embarrassed about the nickname. I suppressed the urge to comb my fingers through my now straight hair. "What else has Noelle told you?"

"That you popped the cherry of her best friend and then dumped her."

"I DIDN'T say that," protested Noelle. She shot Cleo a piercing look. "Honestly, Joel. I didn't say that. I don't know why you and Lara broke up. She never said."

I didn't know why either. It just ran its course, I guess. Noelle blushed and whispered the words, "I'm sorry," at me. But I didn't really care. Lara and I were ancient history.

"This, by the way, is the guy I sometimes feed," said Cleo leaning back and pointing a spoon full of potatoes at a man in a wheelchair seated to her left. "His name's Bill but everyone calls him Little Billy."

I was about to reach in front of Cleo to shake his hand, but before I could, I noticed that Little Billy didn't have any hands. I spied the short sleeves of his white tee-shirt, which hung from his shoulders like limp flags on a windless day, and tried to mask my shock. I allowed my eyes to travel down his abbreviated torso where he sat slumped into one corner of his chair. Cut off blue jeans were covered with iron-on patches of peace signs and pot leaves. They covered sausage-like legs not more than twenty inches long. Protruding from the fringed edges of his pants were bare feet and gangly toes, which danced around as though waving to me.

"I'm just your basic, run-of-the-mill-wheelie," he said, only briefly looking me in the eye. He added a punctuation mark by opening his mouth to receive the potatoes.

"He's a Thalidomide baby," said Cleo.

"I don't know what that means," I said, certain I didn't feel comfortable discussing it in front of Little Billy. But his stone-faced expression, tight lips, and unemotional eyes—all part of a perfectly normal-sized and good-looking face—didn't indicate any kind of embarrassment or discomfort. Robotically, he opened his mouth and took in another spoonful.

"Thalidomide was a drug, a sleeping pill I think. His mother used it to combat morning sickness. A lot of women took it back in the fifties before they knew it caused severe birth defects," Cleo explained. "You've never heard of it?"

"Well, I have now."

"Besides the arms and the fact that my legs are half the size of yours, I'm a perfectly normal guy," said Little Billy, still chewing. A piece of chalky potato oozed onto his chin.

"That's a matter of opinion," laughed Cleo. "Just wait until he asks you to help him take a piss."

"Cleo!" said Noelle. "Honestly."

"This dude is one of the few who can claim that he's gotten half the girls in Montgomery Hall to hold his dick."

"My face please? You know I can't wipe it myself," said Little Billy. "Am I going to have to get a new volunteer?"

"Chill out little man," said Cleo. "A lot of these guys have to pay to get this kind of help. Half of them are loaded you know, due to big financial settlements from whatever accident landed them in their chairs. Here, have some more carrots. Hey Joel, I'll bet you never met a guy who could write an entire essay with his toes. I made Billy autograph one of his compositions and sent it to my mom."

Billy rolled his eyes as Cleo cleaned the potatoes from his chin.

Further down the table sat a man with a hairnet and a full beard. He fed another guy in a wheelchair, whose spastic movements made him look like he was protesting something.

I took a bite of sour chicken salad and felt like protesting it.

Cleo talked through the rest of the meal. She used Thalidomide babies as a springboard to launch into a myriad of reasons for birth defects, citing the toxic chemicals recently discovered at Love Canal, and how when she was a little kid they sprayed DDT in their neighborhood to control mosquitoes and she and her friends used to dance in it. "I'm never going to have kids," she said. "Because of that and all the LSD I did in high school, they'd likely come out in worse shape than Little Billy over here."

Noelle watched her, chewing softly and drinking several glasses of milk. She was rapt, like a first grader listening to her teacher tell a story.

Most things Cleo said horrified me, primarily because she didn't care who heard her or who might be offended. Even Noelle, who seemed to be such a fan, nearly spit out her milk when Cleo pointed to a man at the next table and claimed she wanted to thrust her hands into his hairy chest and 'fuck him silly.'

By the time I finished eating, I had a headache. I picked up my tray, nodded toward Noelle and Little Billy and thanked Cleo for an interesting meal. "You know something Cleo?" I said, "I really think you ought to form an opinion."

"Ha!" she laughed. "I like this guy, Noelle. He's not really my type, but I can see the two of you together."

Noelle shook her head. I couldn't tell if she was embarrassed or put off by the thought.

As I dropped off my tray, my mind swimming with uncertainty regarding my feelings for Noelle and the various forms of toxic chemicals and birth defects discussed during dinner, I heard Cleo's gravely voice droning on like background music. I opened the door for a shorthaired woman in a wheelchair, who steered the device with her mouth, and she temporarily removed the clear steering tube from her lips and grunted what I assumed was "thank you very much."

"You're welcome," I said, hoping that was the right thing to say.

Our dorm complex was teeming with wheelies. It was the one residence area on campus that made everything handicapped accessible. The buildings, all situated on a small lake, were only three stories high, and the first floors of each were the wheelie's domain. Prior to my life in the dorm, I had never been around anyone with any kind of disability. Where I came from we were separated. *We* took the regular bus while *they* took the short bus. I grew up thinking that handicapped kids were dumb or somehow less.

Boy, was I wrong.

By mid-October I was tight with a wheelie who lived on the first floor of my dorm. His name was Kim Harper and he was from Chicago. The north side. 'Kim-the-Cubs-fan,' as he was known, even wore his blue Cubs cap to bed. He explained that "wheelie" was an accepted term in his world. "Like blacks who now call themselves African-Americans and homos who have embraced the term 'gay,' " he had said, "our world is a wheelie world."

Kim and I were in the same Contemporary American History class, a lecture group of about fifty who met on Monday,

Wednesday, and Friday afternoons in the Tech building. He sat in the front and was the most vocal guy in the class—always challenging the young professor and causing him to stammer. Kim was a few years older than most freshmen because he had joined the Army right out of high school. And it was while he was in the Army that he broke his back and wound up a quadriplegic. According to Kim, he suffered the injury while trying to break up a fight.

Although he was a quad, he still had use of his arms and was a good athlete. He played wheelchair basketball, lifted weights, and had upper arms as big as my thighs. I think he was in better shape than most of the guys in Baker Hall, and I'm certain he was the most serious student on all three floors.

Kim Harper amazed me. He had spent twenty years as a regular guy and even an athlete, and then had to say goodbye to his legs the way someone might say goodbye to a dying friend. And yet, he wasn't bitter. I never once heard him complain or feel sorry for himself.

He only complained about his roommate. "That asshole took one look at my chair and decided not to like me," he had said. "I've seen the look a hundred times."

We had that in common. My roommate didn't like me either.

Sam the pig farmer was a total recluse. Except to go to class, he never left the room. And he certainly never talked to me. All I knew about Sam was what I could figure out through his scant possessions. Only half of his side of the closet was filled. He had three shirts hung there, which I never once saw him wear. His daily uniform consisted of a series of SIU tee-shirts, which his mother probably bought for him thinking it was the required uniform, and a pair of Wrangler blue jeans with iron-on patches over the knees. Like an old man, he wore them too high on his waist and belted with a thick, brown leather strap that looked like the switch my grandpa used to sharpen knives. There was a big, brass belt buckle, too, but I never got close enough to see what was on it. Actually, I didn't want to know. (I figured it had something to do with either John Deere or hog feed.) He was an Ag major—agricultural economics or something like that—and he must have been a decent student because he always had his nose in a textbook. Yet Sam looked at these books while wearing a pair of headphones that were plugged into a tape recorder, which he was rarely without. He carried it in his backpack and wore the headphones as he walked to and from class, looking like he was consistently recharging his skull.

Two cassette tapes and one empty case for another remained on his nightstand. From what I could tell, he listened to those same three tapes over and over.

I grew very curious as to what he was listening to so intently, and would have come right out and asked him, but I was sure he'd ignore me like he ignored everything else I said. So, one day while he was at class, I investigated. Picking up the tapes, I felt conspicuous, like I was venturing into his diary or something. I hoped he wouldn't walk in and catch me. The labels read "From Julie" in fat, backhanded cursive. A heart dotted the "i." Next to the tapes was a wallet-sized photo of Sam in a powder blue tuxedo with his arm around a small, pretty girl in an equally blue prom dress. I guessed that this was Julie-with-a-heart and wondered how a bona fide nerd like my roommate Sam could score with a sweet thing like that.

I couldn't resist. I loaded one of the tapes into my cassette deck.

"HI HONEY," screamed a woman's voice. I had the volume up too high. Quickly, I pressed the stop lever, rewound the tape and turned down the volume.

"*Hi honey,*" cooed the now soft voice of Julie. It was high-pitched with a slight drawl—just like her picture, I thought. *"It's sunny here today and I still miss you. The sky may be clear but I'm surely cloudy. Josie dumped her second litter last night and was in some distress. You might remember the trouble she had last spring. So Pop and I stayed out back with her pretty late. The runt didn't make it through the night. Isn't that sad? I'm so sad right now I can't stand it. Are you coming home again this weekend? I think you should look into taking classes with me over at the J-C so we can be together. I mean, if you hate it there as much as you say you do. . . ."*

It came as no surprise when I learned through Doug, our Resident Assistant, that Sam wasn't coming back in January for the second semester.

This gave me a new roommate. His name's Don Carver and he's a good guy. He talks to me more than Sam, but not much more. He's pretty quiet and not completely serious about school. He reminds me a little of my buddy Keith—that is if Keith had grown a beard. Like Keith, he has sandy-colored hair and a big build. And also like Keith, the girls swoon around him. Actually, I should rephrase that and say that women swoon around him. In college, we no longer call girls, "girls." The same way the girls I knew at the *Trumaine Trumpet* started calling their diaries "journals" during senior year, I've discovered that once girls step outside their mother's homes and onto college campuses, they're called "women."

Much to his annoyance, after his first week at The Point, my new roommate earned the nickname "Don Juan," courtesy of the women who lived at Montgomery Hall.

We became quite the pair. Don Juan and Soulful Joel.

For a while, every time we walked past Montgomery on the way to the dining hall, someone whistled and sang our nicknames. Someone once even threw out her dorm key to Don from the third floor window. It was wrapped in a pair of silky, red underpants.

They're worse than construction workers in downtown Chicago.

I knew Noelle was responsible for telling everyone my nickname, however, it never occurred to me that she was one of those girls shouting and whistling. I found out she was, though, on the day I introduced her to Don.

It was a damp January day at the beginning of the second semester, and as Don and I headed toward the cafeteria for an early dinner, I saw Noelle by the bike rack, struggling with her lock.

"Hey, Noelle," I called to her. "Having trouble?"

"Oh, hi Joel. No. I mean, yes. A little trouble. My fingers are so cold I can't seem to get this stupid cable coiled up the way I want it."

"Let me help," I said, grabbing the brittle plastic cable. "Have you met my new roommate?"

"This is your *roommate?*" she asked flashing her laser eye beams at Don. "Why didn't you tell me you had a new roommate?"

"I *did* tell you!" I said. "I told you the same day you said you got a new roommate too."

"Oh, yeah," said Noelle. "I just didn't realize that it was him. I mean you. You're Don Juan."

"It's Don Carver, actually. Nice meeting you." Noelle bent over to pick up her backpack and Don's eyes focused on her ass. As I watched him do it, I felt a churning inside my stomach. When she stood up, he looked her over from head to toe and she blushed. He smiled and stretched out his hand for her to shake. But instead of shaking Don's hand, she studied it for a moment and slowly turned it over and pulled it to her face. Then like a hen pecking at a piece of corn, she quickly kissed her *own* hand.

"The pleasure is all mine," she said, flashing that brilliant smile. She winked at me, threw her backpack over her shoulder, and wandered off toward her dorm building, leaving me holding her bike lock. Don and I both stared after her.

"Wow," exhaled Don. "Is she going out with anyone?"

"I don't know if she's ever gone out with anyone."

"Why? What's wrong with her."

"Not a thing."

Noelle was looking *fine*. She let her hair grow out of the Farrah Fawcett look and put on a few pounds. Because she was so tall and fragile-looking, I always thought she'd tip over and break if the wind ever blew too strongly. But during the first semester she developed a new sturdiness. I noticed a certain confidence build in her, too, especially during our Oral Interp class. In fact, everyone in the class had noticed it.

I missed having that class with her. It was as though I had spent the entire semester studying her and watching her metamorphosis from a shy, soft-spoken girl to a strong and self-possessed woman. During her first two presentations, she was awkward and nervous behind the black music stand we used as a podium. And while I thought she'd have the robust voice of a cheerleader, she spoke softly—too softly for the material—and Dr. Josh made her read again. It's not that she didn't express feeling; it was more like she didn't express confidence in the feeling.

I locked Noelle's bike to the rack and we headed toward the dining hall.

"Hey, Don Juan!" called a voice from the second floor as we crossed the street. "Noelle likes. . . ."

Looking up at the windows, we heard muffled giggling. Someone put a hand over someone else's mouth. "And Soulful Joel, you're not so bad yourself."

And then another voice: "Hey, baby. How 'bout it?"

More giggles. Don raised his eyebrows and let out a small laugh. I punched him in the shoulder and opened the door for him.

One of the voices I didn't recognize belonged to Noelle's new roommate, Ruby Pappas. Noelle said she spun the wheel of roommate roulette and out went Cleo King and in came Ruby Pappas.

Ruby looked a little like Maria with dark hair, dark skin, and deep-set eyes. She had a funny way of talking through a crooked smile, and a vocabulary all her own. Every time I saw her and Noelle together, they were laughing. Sometimes they even skipped and held hands like a couple of kindergartners. Not long into the semester, they were inseparable.

"You and Ruby are inseparable" I said one morning after breakfast as Noelle and I walked from the dining room back to the dorms. "You're red and she's ruby. Ruby red."

"Gee Joel," she laughed. "Did you just make that up or have you been working on it?"

"You like her, don't you."

"I love her!" shot back Noelle. "It's YOU who likes her!"

"Better than Cleo. Where'd she go anyway?"

"She's got an apartment on the East Side of town. She's a vegetarian and won't get near anything processed."

"A vegetarian? I thought I saw her ripping apart a steak more than once."

"It was a new development. Or maybe just an excuse to get out of the dorms. You know she's really smart, Joel, and we're still good friends. So if you say anything bad about her, I'm going to have to punch you."

"I know," I said. "I guess I just didn't like the way she took over all the time. But never mind her, tell me more about Ruby."

"I knew you liked her. She's pretty funny, right? But I'm not sure how serious she is about school. She doesn't have a major yet."

"Sounds like Don."

"Yeah?" Noelle stooped down to unlock her bicycle from the rack. "He doesn't say much so I can't tell if he's shy or, well, stupid. Honestly, with his looks I don't care."

"Sure you want to ride your bike in this slush?"

"I'm late," she said. "I have no choice."

"It sounds like you've got it for my roommate."

"Well, he sure is cute! In fact, he's almost as cute as you."

I wondered if I had heard her correctly. Did she just tell me I was cute? "Hey, why don't you guys, you and Ruby, come by our room tonight? Do you have any plans?"

"No plans," she said while wrapping the thin, silver cable below her bike seat. "I'll check with Ruby. I happen to know she thinks you're pretty cute too."

"She does? She thinks I'm cute?"

"Get over yourself, Rudolph," she said. "I told her you were *soulful!*"

I held my hands to my heart and staggered backward while she rode off to her first morning class. As I watched loose red strands of hair cascade over her shoulders, she maneuvered her bicycle down the wheelie ramp and onto the street toward campus. Within moments she was out of sight.

I checked my watch and saw I only had five minutes to get to my room to brush my teeth and grab my backpack before making it to my Moral Decision small group in the nearby Ag building. Jogging toward Baker Hall I didn't think about being late. I didn't think about Ruby or even about Maria. Instead I thought about Noelle.

I wondered how I could I tell her that it wasn't her new roommate that interested me.

# 9.
# Noelle. 1979.

I was convinced I was the only virgin on campus.

Everyone was having sex. Everyone. And it was all so . . . so . . . NORMAL! The women in our dorm talked about sexual encounters as easily as they talked about group projects or term papers, and I felt left out like the nerd who wasn't invited to the birthday party. I was as conspicuous as Hawthorne's Hester Prynne—destined to wear a scarlet "A" on her bosom labeling her secret sin. But I was more like Hester Prig, with an invisible "V" for Virgin stitched onto my shirt.

It didn't help that my former roommate, Cleo, made a point of telling everyone about my unusual sexual status. "Meet my roommate the virgin," she'd say any time I walked into the room. She was like a stage actor giving the audience an aside, while I stood exposed, watching her audiences' eyes grow to the size of October full moons.

Sexual status clearly separated the girls from the women. I wasn't just a girl. I was an anomaly. A freak. I had taken all the prerequisite courses required for college admission, but skipped class when high school offered the rudiments for dorm life and campus living. And by the bemused faces of those in the cell-like rooms around us, fellow dorm residents thought so too. They thought I didn't get the dirty jokes they told, and often made a point to unnecessarily explain.

Why didn't my sister tell me about this aspect of college?

At first when Cleo told me she was moving out of the dorm, I was hurt and took it personally. Sensing my hurt, she quickly explained that dorm life wasn't for her because of her need to

83

eat purely vegetarian, unprocessed foods and to bring home hairy men and screw their lights out without an audience. And since I'd spent many a night pretending to sleep while listening to the grunting and moaning of Cleo's active sex life, I was ultimately relieved when shortly before the holiday break she made plans to move into an efficiency apartment across town.

"It's almost as small as this hole," she had said, "but it's only a hundred bucks a month and it'll be worth every red cent." Her small, round eyes glared back at me like the red pennies she had described.

The second time around in the roommate sweepstakes, I got lucky. My new roommate's name is Ruby Pappas. At first glance we didn't have much in common. While we came from the same end of the state, "the land without accents," as she called it, Ruby had an exotic ethnicity about her and a repertoire of accents rivaling Rich Little. Like the professor I had for Oral Interpretation last semester, she often changed her tone to fit the scene. The first day she entered our dorm room, she called me *"daahling,"* and curtseyed. Then she reached for my hand, drew it to her lips, and kissed her own hand. "I'd kiss you, but I just washed my hair," she said.

I was a fly caught in a new web.

Ruby's short, stout, and very loud. Proud of it, she makes no secret of her Greek heritage. Her parents own a grocery store in Greek Town on the west side of Chicago, and once the business obtained a certain level of success, she said they moved from the city to the Northwest suburbs. Ruby claimed it gave her dad a reason to buy a new Lincoln Continental so he could enjoy the commute.

She isn't beautiful—by Miss America or supermodel stan-dards—but I think she's cute and she has gorgeous hair. A deep chestnut brown, it hangs to her waist and is as thick as a wool blanket. Unlike my perpetually outgrowing layers, which are finally long enough to wear in a ponytail and not have strands falling in my face, she's never feathered or layered her hair. She has olive skin and small but deep-set features, and a crooked smile. When she laughs—she always laughs—she exposes dimples on each cheek as well as one prominent Kirk Douglas dent in her chin.

Ruby had spent her first semester in temporary housing, a room in the basement of our building that she shared with four others. They were lost souls down in the land of concrete block walls and no windows, waiting for dropouts or people like Cleo, the way prisoners await parole. Fortunately for them, the first semester of college was like boot camp. Not everyone was cut out for it. There were so many vacancies in January that each wayward co-ed found a room by the second semester.

By February we were best friends.

Ruby burst into our dorm room with plastic shopping bags in each hand and proclaimed February her least favorite month. "What's good about February?" she asked. "Valentines Day stopped being fun after second grade and the weather is so totally sow."

"I've never given it much thought," I said over the top of my algebra book.

"Each February I make a point of spending as much time as I can shopping." She threw the colorful bags with mall store names on her bed. She then reached inside one and unveiled her latest purchase, the new Grateful Dead album, *Shakedown Street.* Slitting the cellophane wrapper with a red thumbnail, she flashed her crooked smile and then carefully pulled the vinyl disc from its paper sleeve, holding it by the edges between her hands. After squirting a few drops of cleaning fluid on her disk washer and then rubbing it around the album, she placed it on the turntable, lowered the stylus in place, and cranked the volume.

The concrete room instantly filled with a steady beat, and I watched as Ruby bobbed her head and jutted her jaw in syncopated approval. When I mimicked her movements, she flung the cardboard album cover at me like a Frisbee and then bounced on my bed and sent my algebra book to the floor. I took that as a cue to cast aside the notebook filled with penciled calculations and studied the freaky cartoons on the Grateful Dead album cover instead.

They made about as much sense as the quadratic equations.

As I stared at little fleshy men riding choppers and grinning like Cheshire cats while spaghetti hair flew in their wakes, Ruby yelled something over the music.

"What?" I asked. She tried again and I shook my head. "Can't hear you," I mouthed.

"My younger sister has never slept with a guy and neither have I," she shouted over the music.

I set down the album cover and squinted at her. Did she just say what I thought she said? I shook my head. "*Where* did that come from?" I asked.

"What?"

"Wait a minute," I said and got up, walked to the stereo and turned down the volume. The room went quiet and my ears rang as though a crowd around me still murmured. "Ruby," I said, "your sister is fourteen years old!"

"What does that have to do with the price of tea in China?"

"What?"

"Please, Noelle. Are you kidding me?" she scoffed. "The way these chicks around here talk, they've all been doing it since they were twelve. I'm a frickin' freak."

Putting thoughts of my own sexual status aside, I crossed the room and reached for the pale yellow container of birth control pills next to the sink. I picked it up and shook it like a percussion instrument. "What are these for then? Huh? Each morning I watch you put a tiny pill on the end of your tongue like it's a religious experience. It's as much a ritual as unveiling the week's newest record."

"I had to tell *someone*," said Ruby. "I've lied to everyone else—especially those *kargiolas* I lived with in temp housing last semester and the nasty sluts next door to us. Do you know they bring home different guys from the bars every night?"

"Apparently they're not afraid of getting herpes." I sat back on the bed.

"They've probably got it," said Ruby. "We should call them sowmates instead of suitemates. I can't imagine what's growing in our bathroom."

I was relieved to know I wasn't the only virgin within a twenty-mile radius, but instead of telling Ruby that I, too, was a virgin, I couldn't get past wondering why she took birth control if she wasn't having sex. I reached down and picked up my algebra book and tossed it on my bed. "Ruby," I said looking up at her, "why are you on the pill if you haven't had sex?"

"I intend to very soon," she said, smiling. "Don't you? I mean, you do have your sights set on *Dondo Juando,* don't you?"

"He hates being called Don Juan."

"You should find out if he deserves the title."

"Maybe I should," I said with a small giggle. Something made me throw the algebra book back to the floor. "I gotta tell ya, Ruby, I admire your preparedness. You're like a teenage boy with a packaged rubber in his wallet while waiting for the big night."

"What I want to know is when you're going to get me together with that cute roommate of Don's. I think Joel Rolland is a perfect candidate for me. Don't you?"

My eyebrows shot up. Joel Rolland? Ruby actually wanted Joel? *My* Joel?

"Well?" she asked. "What do you think?"

I didn't know what to think.

Was that why girls had guys as friends? To set them up with their roommates?

"Joel actually asked me about getting us all together," I said, reaching for the phone. "You game?"

\* \* \* \* \* \* \* \*

"Three-one-two," Ruby said, reading the number on Joel and Don's door. "Hey, our room number is two-one-three. Three-one-two, two-one-three. See? This is meant to be," she sang, and pounded her fist against the door. "Open up! We're here and the fun can start!"

The door creaked open and Ruby burst through like a party favor. Both Joel, flattened against the wall, and Don, sitting on his bed, looked stunned. And stoned.

I sniffed the air. Pot. Always pot. We couldn't go anywhere these days without weed as a main focus. It was the Southern icebreaker. Instead of "what's your major?" the standard opening line at any typical college gathering was "want to smoke a joint?"

And lately my answer was "no." Especially because as I got to know Don, I believed that weed was just what he *didn't* need. He was naturally quiet and a case of pot paranoia further tied his tongue.

Mixed with the smell of reefer was the unmistakable odor of dirty towels. Their room was a mess. Aside from the unmade beds, clothing poked out of drawers and books and papers were strewn everywhere like confetti after a parade. I suppressed the urge to plug my nose, closed the bathroom door, and sat down on the only space open, Don's bed.

The moment I sat down, a striped, gray kitten jumped on my leg.

"Holy shit!" I yelped. "Where did this thing come from?"

"Ooh, kitty!" squealed Ruby, reaching out to grab it. She held it to her face and at once, curled her lip with sheer distaste. "This has got to be the *ugliest* kitten I've ever seen," she said. "What's its name?"

"Kitty, I guess," said Don.

"Der!" said Ruby, "Can't you come up with something better than that?" She pinched the scruff of the kitten's neck and set it down on Don's chest.

"Der?" asked Joel. "Did she say 'Der'?"

"Yeah, DER, as in Duh or Dumb Der?" Ruby stuck her finger in her chin dimple.

"I guess you guys don't care about the no pets rule in the dorms," I said.

"Neither do the five other guys on our floor who have kittens," said Joel. "He's okay, don't you think? And I think we should call him Der in honor of Ruby. That's a good name."

"What, Der?" chuckled Ruby. "Hell yeah! Why don't you name it Der? That's a darling name, Jo-el" She plopped onto his lap.

"Oomph!" grunted Joel. His eyes popped open. "Have a seat, Ruby."

"Okay," she sang. "Hello." She sounded like a little bell going "ding-dong, ding-dong." Ruby put her arms around Joel's neck and he spread his legs a little, allowing her to share his lap with the bed beneath him. She smiled in his face and he looked back at her as if he were studying her dimples.

"You're kinda cute," he said, poking a finger in her chin.

"Did you hear that, Noelle?" said Ruby. "He said I'm *kinda* cute! Good GOD that's the kiss of death. I am sick of being called 'cute.'"

"Think how Dumb Der the kitty feels over there," said Joel. "You called him ugly."

"Good point," said Ruby. And then she sighed—the kind of verbal sigh that my sister called a "leaky air bag," and burst out laughing. "I didn't mean to make that noise. Kind of a girl noise, don't you think?"

Ruby was on stage, performing for all of us. Her voice, ascending an octave as she talked about her child development class, made me feel we were like a group of preschoolers whom she meant to entertain. Joel watched her with a bemused expression.

Did he like her? Did I care?

It was often hard to tell how Joel felt about anything. It was as though he had an inner conversation going on that he dared you to be a part of.

While Ruby was clearly having a good time, I felt a cat allergy coming on and grew tired of watching Don caress his feet. We'd only been there for half an hour, but I suggested we leave.

"I'm staying put," said Ruby, winking at Joel. "Why don't the two of you go for a walk?"

"Don, are you up for it?" I asked.

"Sure," he said. "Let me grab some shoes."

Don was better one-on-one. With no cat or no Ruby to distract him, he looked me in the eye and we walked with an easy gait around the lake.

"Someone told me this used to be a vacation lake," he said. "There are still some cabin sites around it. Want to try and find some?"

"Okay," I said.

It was warm for February and my hand felt comfortable inside his. Smelling a distant campfire, I thought of childhood nights when I had just been allowed to be out after dark.

"Joel told me your dad died when you were pretty young," said Don as we rounded the bend by Kellogg Hall. "How come you never talk about it?"

"I don't talk about it?" I laughed nervously. I didn't expect to talk about my father. "It happened so long ago I guess it's just a fact of my life."

"My dad just died," he said. "Heart attack at the end of last summer."

"Oh, Don. I had no idea. I'm so sorry." I stopped and took his other hand in mine.

"It's probably a good thing that my parents were divorced," he said. "I don't know if I would have left for school if they were still together and my mom was actually torn up about losing him. I mean, she was sad and all that, but not heartbroken."

"Is that why you didn't start school until January?"

"Yeah." Don looked out at the lake. "I couldn't get my act together, so I stayed home and worked at a camping equipment store. My dad was really into camping—rock climbing and rappelling and stuff like that—and I went with him on weekend trips after the divorce." He dropped my hands and started walking again, while I trotted at his side keeping up. His hair blew into his face and he tossed his head to get it out of the way. "You know, Noelle, I've got gear. I should take you to Giant City State Park where they have a great rappelling wall. Have you been rappelling?"

"Is that where you maneuver down a cliff by bouncing like a SWAT guy on a raid?"

"Huh?"

"Never mind. Sure, I'll go with you."

"Good. How about next weekend? We can ask Joel and Ruby to come too. They seem to be hitting it off. Don't you think?"

"We can ask them. But I'm not sure Ruby would want to swing on ropes."

"Yeah, but she wouldn't be afraid to try, would she?"

"She's not exactly an outdoor girl."

On Saturday, Ruby flat out refused to go rappelling at Giant City. "No hang gliding, free falling, rock climbing, or rappelling," she said as though citing lyrics to a bad country song. She and Joel spent the day together instead, while Don showed me how to properly connect myself to a harness and use my legs to push off the face of an eighty-foot, sandstone cliff.

That evening when we returned from the park we found Ruby and Joel leaving our room together.

"Noelle," said Ruby, "you got way too much sun."

"You look good," said Joel. "Both of you. Healthy. Was it fun?"

"Oh yeah!" I said. "I loved it. Ruby, you should really try it sometime."

"Maybe in my next life," she said. "We're going to the Student Center to see a movie. See ya."

I watched them make their way down the hall, Joel looking straight ahead, Ruby skipping at his side. Watching them leave together made me feel lonely. I wanted to go with them.

"Hey, Babe," said Don stepping into the hall after depositing my backpack inside the room. "I'm going to go shower and I'll be back. Okay? We can order a pizza if you like."

"Okay, sure," I said absently. "Why not?

When Don came to my room, he turned it into the landmark time and place I knew I'd remember for the rest of my life.

We kept the room dark and when I played Ruby's Joni Mitchell album, *Miles of Aisles,* Don swept me into his arms. *"You turn me on, I'm a radio,"* he whispered, half-singing. Standing together in the center of the small room, we swayed to the music and then he put both hands on my face and kissed me. His beard was soft and warm and he was gentle, gingerly licking my lips. Soon, however, his kisses grew more passionate and forceful, and as his tongue explored the roof of my mouth and each of my teeth, I had the distinct feeling of being the recipient of his kisses instead of the administrator. I felt lost.

I'd kissed guys before on a few dates in high school—that is, after I got my braces off and guys started looking in my direction—but I knew that right there in the middle of my tiny dorm room, I had stepped into a new arena.

Don Juan was the professor, and I was his student.

He lowered his hands to my waist and pulled me close. Moving backward in a slow step, as though we were still dancing, he pulled us toward my bed and lowered us down on top of it. I let him pull off my tee-shirt and unhook my bra, and he groaned as he took handfuls of my breasts into his hands, caressing and fiddling as though playing in the sand. Then he rolled me off of him, sat up and took off his own shirt and threw it to the floor.

I heard his breathing and saw his heart pump through his hairy chest. I tried not to think of Cleo and her penchant for hairy-chested men as I lay with my head on the pillow looking up at him.

Don centered his body over mine and, pressing against me, reached for my pants.

"Stop." It was more of an exhale than a word. "I... Don, I...."

"What, Babe?"

"I...."

"Hey, it's okay. Tell me. Is this your first time?"

"No," I lied, sitting up. "No, it's not my first time."

"Okay. Okay." He extended his elbows and I focused on the coiling dark hairs covering his chest. He reached for my face and I turned away.

"What is it, Noelle?"

"I don't know." I drew in my breath. "I'm sorry. Sorry. I just... I don't know."

"It'll be okay." His voice was a warm whisper. "Trust me."

I sat up as though hearing an alarm. *Trust me?* Did he really just say that?

The last time I had heard those words they were uttered by my father on the day he insisted I learn to ride a two-wheeler. "Stop being such a baby and trust me!" His baritone voice was both soothing and frightening as he ran behind me holding the seat of my mom's spray-painted pink bicycle. The bike was too big and I couldn't reach the pedals from the seat. It took all my strength to balance my frame on this oversized, absurd bicycle by straddling it and pedaling up and down as we wheeled past our house and half way past the Parker's. My dad, panting, jogged behind me and labored to keep me upright.

I remember the breeze in my face was exhilarating. It was like a boat ride on Lake Michigan where the horizon was undefined and the possibilities unlimited. A surge of excitement rose in my stomach while a tingle of fear stimulated my toes. I begged him not to let go.

"I won't let go," he said. "I promise."

But of course, by the time we got past the Parker place and approached the Gorgons', he let go. Instantly, I wobbled and zigzagged like a kite without a tail and found myself veering off the sidewalk. Before I knew it I had smashed against the Gorgons' last remaining elm—the giant beauty still unaffected by the Dutch elm disease otherwise plaguing Chicago's western suburbs.

Momentarily splayed against it, I felt the rough bark chafe my face. It was the harsh kiss of an unshaven man. I fell to the grass atop craggy, exposed roots, and lay in a heap with my mother's bike next to me looking like spilled Pepto Bismol.

I felt like a complete failure. Not only was I disappointed in my father for letting go, but also in myself for trusting him.

Losing my virginity to Don in my dorm room bed felt exactly like that.

The next day I found out that my lover was of the kiss and tell variety. He went straight to Joel and told him of his accomplishment.

That's when Joel stopped looking me in the face.

# 10.
# Joel. 1979.

I shouldn't have gotten so drunk. I should have stopped after the first bottle of Tanqueray and I certainly shouldn't have left my room. The consequences were high on many levels and my hangover lasted for days. And as I tried to piece together my escapades of that afternoon and evening, the only positive thing I could think of was that at least Noelle found out how I felt about her.

But I'm getting ahead of myself.

I think I fell in love with Noelle the moment I first saw her in my high school gymnasium. I don't know why I didn't ask her out when I had the chance. Like when we discovered we had chosen the same college and had the same class together. She lived next door to me, for god's sakes. Before I knew it, she got all kissy-faced with my roommate and it was too late. When she slept with him it felt like I'd been shot.

Don came home the morning after the big event and didn't say anything, of course. The guy just didn't like to talk. But I knew what had happened before I asked him.

"Well?" I had asked.

"Well what?"

"Come on, man! Did you do it with her, or what?" He nodded his head and then laughed. It was the laugh of a satisfied man. "Shit," I said sighing. "Now you're married."

"Yeah, I guess I am," he said.

Although I was pretty sure he wouldn't tell me anyway, I didn't want to hear the details. While he was in the shower, I grabbed my backpack and left for the library, purposefully

93

avoiding the sidewalk in front of Noelle's dorm. She was the last person I wanted to see.

I didn't see anyone as I walked to the library with my head down. Usually walking on campus was all about the people you saw—everyone greeted one another as though it were Main Street in a family movie. But on a dead Sunday morning I was alone, walking it off while others remained indoors, nursing their hangovers or sleeping away the last hours of their teen-aged lives.

The library was cavernous, filled only with dust mites and bound pages of silent knowledge. Not even the main floor librarian, no doubt a weary grad student, looked up from her book to greet me. I adjusted my eyes to the cruel florescent lights and darted into a stairwell, climbing to the fifth floor. There I found a table in the corner, a serious workspace hidden from anyone who might amble by. Throwing down my backpack, I pulled out a yellow folder labeled "Philosophy," and paged through dog-eared sheets of purple, mimeographed type. It was my current burden: A reprinted essay by Nietzsche I had read days ago. I had to write a five-page paper, due on Tuesday, and had yet to come up with a topic sentence. I couldn't remember a single word of what I'd read.

I sat down, propped up my feet on the chair next to me and gave Friederich Nietzsche another shot. Blurry, purple type met my eyes as heady ink vapors emanated from the pages. I couldn't concentrate. The only solution was to hold my hand over my nose and mouth like a surgical mask and get to it. I knew I could ace this class because I was probably the only freshman whose father introduced Nietzche instead of a baseball bat. "If you gaze for long into an abyss, the abyss gazes also into you," he had said while handing me a book of his work.

This essay focused on the burden of memory in relation to history, comparing man and beast. It was typical Nietzche stuff with what I deemed to be a good translation. As I turned the pages, folding them one atop of the other over the staple, the words fed into me like an IV drip. The noise of my hurt and confusion over Noelle dissipated and this time, Nietzsche was interesting. He wrote about trying to describe a feeling that he found tormenting and taking "revenge on this feeling" by exposing it.

I set down the packet and returned my feet to the floor. Leaning back in my chair, I looked up at the abyss of the dirty, dotted ceiling. My stomach growled. It audibly confirmed that I was filled with nothing *but* a tormenting feeling.

I picked up a blue Bic pen and flipped to a clean page in my notebook; however, before I wrote a word, I set down the pen. Could I base a paper on the torment I felt at believing Noelle and I could have been together if only I'd acted on it? Was it the only feeling strong enough inside me to expose? It would no doubt mean I'd face condescending commentary from the pompous grad student who graded my papers in small group. After all, two weeks earlier he condemned me for using the phrase "cop out" in a paper about the moral decision of assisting handicapped students. He circled the phrase in red and wrote: "Passé." As far as I could tell, he took off a whole grade because of it.

"To hell with subjective grading," I said to the abyss. My father graded me subjectively for years and what did I ultimately learn from him? Mostly that I was better off with the calculus class I took last semester, in which I barely pulled off a 'C.' At least I knew that what I got wrong was actually wrong.

Until college, school had been about classrooms and teachers, homework assignments and after school activities. All the things that interested me revolved around my school. Home was an insignificant satellite. I never considered mortgage payments, utilities, or grocery bills. Mom made Quaker Oats for me each morning and had it ready and waiting on the kitchen table, next to a glass of orange juice and a vitamin. I hardly noticed when she switched from Flintstones chewables to One-a-Day. I never once operated the washer or dryer. I put dirty blue jeans and tee-shirts in a bathroom hamper and miraculously they reappeared in my drawers, cleaned and folded. When I lived at home my parent's voices were merely background noise, like a television left on in a room where no one was watching. After my father stopped handing me books and spent less time at home, my mom constantly issued instructions and advice. And while I heard her, I wasn't really listening.

I thought of my mom's sister, Aunt Sue. When she was pregnant she constantly talked to her bulging stomach. She insisted on reading Shakespeare and playing Mozart to her unborn child, saying he'd soak in all that culture through osmosis. I guess mothers never stop talking at their children and eventually some of it manages to penetrate. It took moving hundreds of miles away from my mother to finally hear her voice echoing inside my head. "Change your sheets each week!" And, of course, the now infamous, "Stay out of the playpen!"

Half the guys in Baker Hall were in that proverbial playpen and the other half took college seriously. The good students went to class, studied in their rooms, and talked about the work they were doing. The rest—the non-students—were just there to party and clearly had no respect for their parents' money. As for me, well, I liked to party, but I also knew that I had to keep up my grades or my mom would pull me out of school so fast that I'd be stuck taking classes with Maria at the junior college where my parents taught. There was no way I wanted that to happen. As much as I didn't mind the idea of driving to and from school with Maria, I liked being away from home so much more. I knew it was time to hunker down and try to pull off some decent grades. I owed that much to my mother.

I didn't leave the library until my Nietzche paper was complete and later that week, received it back with an "A." There were no condescending remarks. The pompous grad student liked that I wrote from the heart.

Sometimes, I guess, the abyss *does* gaze into you.

During the remainder of the semester, I spent a lot of time with Kim Harper and learned to practice his study habits. He made a great impression on me during our first semester history class, and I felt like I learned something from him during every conversation.

Kim was in the school of engineering and he dove into his trigonometry and physics books and scribbled numbers and problems in his notebooks that went on for pages and pages. I marveled at his ability to concentrate and to make all those pencil scratches actually mean something. He was a natural teacher and taught me about thermodynamics and kinetics. He knew a lot about motion because of his wheelchair.

One time we were on campus together and worked our way up a small but steep hill where there's a funky grouping of freeform sculptures. Just as we reached the peak he explained the concept of  "second derivative." It had something to do with a trig function, a slope and a tangent, and he sounded a little like Charlie Brown's teacher when he spoke; however, I understood that we hit the second derivative when suddenly the pressure of the uphill climb eased on my legs (and apparently on his wheels). I had noticed that feeling as a kid when riding my bike uphill and loved knowing it had a name.

Kim was full of bits and pieces of knowledge like that. Like Lara Romano had been the smartest girl, Kim was clearly the smartest guy I had ever met. I was starting to collect smart people the same way I collected the words I had looked up first in my mother's dictionary and now my own. I was amazed at the amount of knowledge available in the world.

I knew I had it in me to be a good student. As long as I could avoid the distractions. Especially at The Point. It was like a small town and often full of drama. In fact, we called it Peyton Point.

Spring fever hit with early warm temperatures and people were outside more. The good students read books and wrote papers while splayed upon towels and blankets, and the non-students played Frisbee and partied. Music from a hundred dorm room stereos pumped into the air through open windows. Impromptu picnics sprung up on the lawns and pickup basketball and volleyball games added competition and laughter. The air smelled like sweet flowers—jasmine—and marijuana. Always marijuana. The whole world was stoned.

It had been a while since I had run into Noelle. I stopped calling Ruby after Don and Noelle spent the night together, and since I hung out with Kim and took up residence at the library, I wasn't around the dorms as much. But Noelle stopped coming to our room in search of Don, too, and she either stopped eating at the dining hall or was taking her meals before or after prime time. Regardless, I still should have seen her around the grounds—at the bike rack, the laundry, or the mailboxes. To just stop seeing her was nothing less than suspicious.

I wasn't the only one who noticed Noelle's seeming disappearance. While Don never said a word about her, Kim, who was the only one who knew I had a thing for Noelle, asked where she'd been. And then Anita Dambra, a woman from our first semester study group, said something about Noelle one day too. I hadn't seen much of Anita since the group disbanded at the end of last term, but she came up to Don and me in the dining hall one day and asked about Noelle and Ruby.

"So where are your sidekicks, Fatty and Skinny?" she had asked.

"Who?"

"I haven't seen *that* Noelle and her loudmouth roommate in a while. They're usually all over the two of you. What gives?"

"Ruby's right over there," said Don. "She's with the wheelies."

"Oh," she said, unimpressed. "So, are you and *that* Noelle over, or what?" she asked Don while looking at me. I shrugged my shoulders and wondered why she kept calling her *"that* Noelle."

"Whatever," said Don. "Who wants to know?"

"Plenty of people want to know," said Anita. And then she winked at me and smiled. "Those two have been hogging the two best looking guys on The Point."

I set down my fork and looked up at her, interested. It was the first time I really looked at Anita Dambra. And, well, she was a babe—a babe with dark skin and dark hair and an Italian way about her. She looked like Maria with straight hair. (God! Was I destined to compare every single girl with Maria?) Her eyes were deep-set and almond-shaped and she had an intense, almost sinister gaze. Yet there was an obvious sparkle—which perhaps she turned on for me. I could tell she liked me. And clearly, she didn't care for *that* Noelle *or* Ruby.

Ruby didn't seem to notice or care that I'd stopped calling. She stopped calling me too. Meanwhile, she had taken up with a new group and was no longer inseparable from her roommate. While nothing serious had happened between us, I still enjoyed her company and looked for her in the dining hall, thinking that if I saw Ruby, I'd see Noelle.

Finally, shortly after spring break, I spotted Ruby at a late dinner. She sat with Little Billy and a guy named Pete who took over feeding him after Cleo moved out of the dorms. I debated with myself for a minute, but then thought what the hell? I picked up my tray and walked to their table. Billy saw me first.

"Hey Joel," he had said. "What's up?"

"Hi Bill. Hi Ruby. Mind if I sit down?"

"Why Jo-el Rolland," she said, turning around and flashing her crooked smile. "Long time, no me-ow."

"What's the news?"

"News?" she asked, laughing.

"Yeah. Like what's going on with your roommate and Don?"

"Like I'm supposed to know about that," she said. "Ask *him!*"

"I did," I said. "But he's, well, he's Don." I placed my tray on the table and sat down next to her.

"Don's a moax!" she said. "Noelle got sick of him."

"Does she eat anymore?"

"Not much," said Ruby. "She's spending a lot of time studying, if you can believe it. She's totally into her Spanish conversation class and last weekend, I never heard a word of English come out of her. I'm going to have to take Spanish next year just so I know what she's saying about me!"

The next day as Don and I walked out of the dining hall together and toward our building, we heard the distinct sing-songy voice of Ruby call out: "Hi Jo-el! Hi Don, you MOAX!" We looked toward the voice and saw both Ruby and Noelle next to

Montgomery Hall. They giggled like second graders and Noelle grabbed Ruby by the arm and pulled her inside their building.

"I don't know what her fucking problem is," said Don, shaking his head.

"Whose problem?" I asked. "Ruby or Noelle?"

"They're both idiots," said Don. "It's over between me and Noelle."

Within two weeks, Don was all hot and heavy with another girl from Brokaw Hall, where Anita lived. Her name was Susan and she was as tall as Noelle. Don was totally into her and basically stopped going to class. I was back to dining alone. That is, until Anita started taking late meals as well.

Anita Dambra is a plant and soil science major from New Jersey, and she has a grandmother who lives just west of Carbondale in the town of Murphysboro. She spent a lot of time with her grandmother as a kid and loved Southern Illinois enough to choose it for college, and used her grandmother's address for in-state tuition. Admirably dedicated to her grandmother, Nana, Anita spends most weekends with her working in the garden or green house. "Nana's specialty is geraniums," she had said. "But my passion lies within the soil in which they grow. I love mud. There's nothing better than plunging my hands into pure, rich soil and watching the particles fill the cracks in my knuckles and the lines of my hands."

I expected to see dirt under her fingernails, but that wasn't the case. Her hands and nails were impeccably clean. In fact, her hands are beautiful. She has smooth skin and long fingers and her fingernails are always unpainted and filed short. She wears two black onyx rings—the same color as her eyes—on her right hand and said they were from her grandmother. "I only take them off to wash my hands," she said. She also said she wears them on her right hand because like me, she's a lefty.

Anita intends to own or operate a nursery when she finishes school. She's a good student and knows the names of every tree on campus. She collects things like sweet gum pods and ginkgo leaves to decorate her dorm room, which looks like a terrarium. She even dragged in an enormous tree branch on which she has hung potted plants and flowers. It looks like it's growing out of the tiled floor.

Anita dresses plainly, has a dry sense of humor and is actually pretty sarcastic. Her voice is deep and sexy, and always sure of herself, she speaks emphatically.

Each night that we ate together felt like a date. But I had a problem. My problem was that I couldn't shake Noelle from my dreams. While both she and Anita were tall and even regal in appearance, they were visual opposites. I was attracted to Anita—there was no doubt—especially because she was right there—available. Noelle, on the other hand, was distant and un-attainable. She was like a helium balloon tethered to my wrist and floating above my head. But I let go and she sailed away.

I thought of the times as a child I had let a balloon slip from my hands and the helpless feeling of self-pity that con-sumed me as I stood watching the bold red circle fade into oblivion. "Don't cry over balloons," my mom had said. "Balloons will always pop or float away. You can get another."

But could you get the same balloon?

* * * * * * * *

During finals week in May everyone partied like it was a graduation. Each afternoon, dorm residents already finished with the day's exams gathered on blankets on the grassy lawns between Montgomery and Baker Halls, an area we called "the veranda," and welcomed home fellow residents like they were soldiers returning from the front. Backpacks were dumped and guys took off their shirts. The women wore sundresses and suntan lotion. Everyone openly drank and smoked and no one cared about getting caught. Most of the Resident Assistants had long since given up their narc duties, and we were as out of control as a first grade class with a substitute teacher.

My last final ended at noon on Wednesday, and to celebrate I started drinking gin in my room and cranked Dire Straits. There were so many stereos going it was like a battle of the bands. The longhairs down the hall had Rush playing loudly as usual, and I heard The Cars and 801 Live.

By mid-afternoon I was feeling no pain, and I heard a call to party from the hallway. "We're here and the fun can start!"

It was Ruby. I knew her voice. I opened my door and looked down the hall; however, instead of seeing Ruby, I saw Noelle. And she was nothing less than a vision—a goddamn goddess.

Her red hair had grown to her waist and it was so thick it covered her shoulders like a Mexican serape. She was barefoot and wore a white gauzy dress with thin shoulder straps that drooped down her shoulders. Mesmerized and definitely drunk, I stepped into the hallway and watched her walk toward me. She brightened when she saw me and smiled. It was as bright as an old-fashioned camera bulb.

"Hey, Joel Rolland," she said softly, "where have you been all my life?"

I grabbed her hand and yanked her into my room. She laughed and happily came with me. Once inside, she looked at my tee-shirt and mouthed the one word printed on it in green capital letters: "NO!" She threw back her head and burst out laughing. "NO!" she shouted to the ceiling. Then she looked back at me and stretched out her arms as if to say "YES!" and I couldn't help myself. Something burst inside me and I put my hands around her thin frame and forcefully pulled her against me.

She felt small, thin. I couldn't believe how small she felt. I tightened my grasp on her, sensing her sharp hipbones against my stomach, and looked into her eyes—her impossibly green eyes. She had long, white eyelashes as fine as cilia, and pale freckles on her eyelids.

I ingested her like I was taking a long slow sip of a drink.

We stood in the middle of my dorm room, amid books and papers recklessly strewn. The beds were unmade. Drawers were open and dirty laundry lay in piles near the closet. Unpacked duffel bags and boxes covered the floor. I didn't care. I just wanted to memorize her face.

I had her back within reach and didn't want to let go.

She returned my gaze until her nearly invisible eyebrows knit together and a small, vertical line appeared and divided her eyes into a look of confusion. "Joel," she said. "What are you. . . ."

I kissed her. I pressed my lips to hers and felt the soft hairs of her face against my skin. Without taking air I moved one hand from her waist and reached up through her hair to the back of her head and grabbed a handful as I plunged my tongue into her mouth. I kissed her deeply and she let me. She didn't pull away.

"I love you, Noelle," I said. "I've loved you all semester."

"You do?" she asked. "Wait a minute. You *do*?"

She pulled away and I stepped toward her again and placed both hands on her delicate shoulders. Then one at a time, I raised the fallen straps of her dress, glancing my fingers against her prominent collarbones. Instantly, the straps fell off her shoulders again and she laughed a little through her nose. Then she closed her eyes and I saw wispy purple veins, like eye shadow, coloring her lids. I kissed each of her eyes. "I don't even know how long I've loved you, but I do," I said. "And I just had to tell you."

"I love you too," she said, kissing me lightly on the cheek. She stepped backwards and turned her ankle against the spiral-bound notebook lying on the floor next to my desk. "Damn," she swore. "I can't go a day without turning my stupid ankle on something."

"Are you okay?" I asked reaching for her again. But she put up her hand.

"Wait a minute, Joel," she said. "You're drunk and you don't know what you're saying right now. I better go."

"Don't go!" I said. "Please, Noelle. Sure, I'm a little drunk but so what?"

"You're *a lot* drunk," she said. "And look . . . I just started seeing someone else."

"Someone else? Someone *else?* Who is it now?"

"Now?" she asked. "What's that supposed to mean?"

"Well, how serious is it? I mean you finally go to bed with Don and then you dump him. I'm just wondering if that's your *modus operandi?* Your M.O?"

"My M.O? I don't have an M.O."

"Sure you do," I said. "Fuck 'em and dump 'em. Just like you did with Don."

"Jesus, Joel," she said. "One minute you tell me you love me and the next you act like I'm some kind of whore. I'm *not* like that."

"I'm sorry," I said. "I'm. . . ."

"I'm *out* of here!" she said, hobbling slightly toward the door. Her hand slipped once on the handle and then she managed to open the door and she was gone.

I stood still for a moment trying to remember what I had just said and how it went from good to bad so quickly. "What did I say?" I asked the air. I reached for the gin bottle and stepped into the noisy hallway. First I looked left and then right, but Noelle was nowhere in sight. She must have taken the middle staircase. "Fuck it," I said. "Fuck her."

"I'd fuck her," yelled someone from down the hall.

"Shut up," I called back, and then finished the bottle of Tanqueray. I threw my head back and polished it off.

Down the hall Ruby and a group of guys sat in an arc of colorful, plastic chairs openly drinking bottled beer. They were as rowdy as a group of football fans during a playoff game. Someone threw a bottle against the door of the room at the end of the hall and the rest of the group laughed manically when it smashed into a fireworks spray of glass. Others followed suit, throwing bottle after bottle. Soon, the sound of smashing glass competed with the music.

I shuffled over to the group and found Doug, who was probably happier than anyone because his thankless R.A. babysitting responsibilities were over, winding up for another shot at the door. "Ready, aim, fire!" he yelled. As the bottle exploded against the door, Doug hooted like he'd just witnessed a touchdown.

"Your turn, Joel," said Ruby. "Is that bottle empty?"

I again put it to my lips and tasted the last drops of gin on my tongue. Then without another thought, I wound up like a major league pitcher and sent the fat green bottle toward home plate. It didn't make it as far as the door and smashed into a thousand shards in the middle of the hallway.

That's the last thing I remember about that day.

# 11.
## Noelle. 1979.

I stood naked in the shower, letting the cool water fall over me. Squeezing my eyes closed I hoped to wash away the ugly things Joel had said to me.

There was banging on my door. Loud and insistent, it echoed off the concrete walls.

"Noelle," cried an angry voice. "For crying out loud, get out here and get rid of this drunk."

"What?"

Turning off the water, I looked down into the stall and momentarily panicked. The draining water at my feet was a sick shade of crimson. It pooled and swirled and washed down the drain like shame. I bent down and examined the gash on my foot. In my hurry to get out of Joel's dorm, I had stepped on a piece of broken glass. The green and brown shards of discarded liquor were impossible to step around. They carpeted the slick tile floors, shining like confetti as everyone who could, celebrated the end of the semester.

"No-ELLE!" yelled the voice again.

"Just a minute," I called, annoyed.

"There's a drunk out here with a bottle of Tanqueray who's screaming your name. I think it's Joel Rolland. But *he* thinks he's Marlon Brando."

"Marlon Brando?" I grabbed a towel. I held it to my face and it smelled moldy. Those rotten sow suitemates were using our towels again!

"It's like *Streetcar Named Desire* out here . . . *Stella . . . Noelle!*"

It was Kathie Hausman from down the hall. I recognized the tone. She didn't care much for Ruby and me and often knocked on our door and told us to turn down the Joni Mitchell records. Every time she passed us in the hall she rolled her eyes and started singing something like: *"My analyst told me that I was right out of my head. . . ."* She was a year older than we, a sophomore, and treated us like bratty little sisters. From the day I started dating Don Juan, Kathie made it her business not to like me. When Don and I stopped seeing each other, one day she knocked on my door and asked if I were "finished with him."

I found a fresh towel and quickly dried off, then threw on a shirt and some underpants. I planned to tell Kathie to shut up and mind her own business, but when I opened the door to peek outside, it wasn't Kathie standing there. It was Joel.

His blue eyes bulged from his face and he wore the expression of a wax statue at Madame Tussauds. Kathie stood behind him with her arms crossed. "So, are you going out with *him* now?"

"Fuck off, Kathie," I said while wrapping the towel around my waist.

"Yeah, fuck off, Kathie," slurred Joel.

"Who let you in the building?"

"Lemme in," he said leaning into me.

He reeked of gin. I had smelled it earlier when he kissed me, but now it was wafting from every part of him. I held up my hand and pushed his shoulder. "Joel, man, you are too wasted. Really, you should go."

"I love you, Noelle," he said. "I came here to tell you that. And I want to make love with you. I *dream* of making love with you. I love you, I love. . . ." He pushed past me, staggering into the room, then fell back against a chair and clumsily sat down. He possessively clutched a fifth of Tanqueray, like a junkie clinging to his last fix. "I love you."

"I know," I said. "I *know.* Look . . . why don't you go back to your room and sleep it off?"

"NO!" he said too loudly. It was the word printed on his shirt. "No!" he said again. "I'm going home tomorrow and it's our last chance."

"Our last chance for what?"

He set the bottle on my desk and it looked like it would fall so I lunged for it. As I steadied it, a few drops spilled on my hands and Joel grabbed my arm and pulled me on top of him. He breathed sickening, hot gin into my face and it burned my eyes. "Let go of me," I said. My towel fell to the floor and he tightened his grasp around my waist. I felt his jean shorts and hairy legs chafing against my bare skin. Struggling to break free of his grasp, a hot anger churned inside my stomach. I felt the cut on my foot throbbing with each heartbeat. "Let me go," I shouted.

"I came here to tell you I love you and I'm going to tell you I love you," he said, babbling.

"I GET it!" I yelled in a shrill, unrecognizable voice. I elbowed him in the chest and with a forced exhale, he released his hold. I popped up and grabbed his NO! shirt by the neck and pulled him out of the chair.

He was as heavy as a giant sandbag as I led him toward the door.

Opening it, I found Kathie still standing there. "Take him," I said. "I'm finished with him too." I pushed him out and slammed the door, only to spy a series of small puddles of blood that marked my path across the floor like dropped breadcrumbs.

Joel hit the door once. A hard, angry fist.

I sighed and shook my head then slumped to the floor and fought back tears. As I reached to my nightstand for a tissue to hold against my foot, I wondered if Ruby had a band-aid somewhere. Still holding my foot, I grabbed another tissue and crawled on my hands and knees, wiping up the blood. I made my way to the desk and back again to the door and sat leaning against it, feeling the cold tile on my thighs. I thought I heard Joel breathing on the other side of the door and it made me angry again.

"Drunken fool," I said. "Go away."

I got up and went to the stereo and put the needle down on the record already there, then moved to my bed and listened to the music.

*"There's a lady in the city and she thinks she loves them all,"* sang Joni Mitchell.

As my foot continued bleeding, I couldn't sit still. I had one more final in the morning, Ecology, and I couldn't study for it anymore. I knew the material. It wasn't time for dinner yet. I didn't know what to do with myself. I was trapped in my room. My cell.

Across from me, next to the bed that was once the home base for Cleo King, a line of pink, flowered suitcases stood, fully packed. Ruby was ready to go. She planned to leave for home on the morning train. When I came home from my Ecology final, she would be gone.

She was leaving me behind.

I got up, hobbled toward her suitcases and rifled through her cosmetics case where I found a box of band-aids. As I perched my foot on the sink and covered the gaping wound, the odor of Joel hung in the room.

What the hell was he doing? Ruby had told me he started seeing someone else. The black-eyed girl named "Anita." Did he even realize he was talking to me? We were just friends.

Weren't we?

*"She will love them when she sees them. They will lose her if they follow. . . ."*

I paced around the room without any answers. I wished Ruby were there, but I'd have to go back over to Baker Hall to find her, and I didn't want to risk running into Joel again. For all I knew, he was still camped outside my room. Plus, I still had to get up in the morning. I couldn't get sucked into a party. It would be too easy to let that happen.

I never should have gone over there in the first place.

My hair, still wet, curled around and tickled my face. I reached for a brush. Grabbing the ends, I worked through the tangles and then tossed the brush into the sink. It was no use trying to comb it anymore. It was better just long, free and wild, curling in ringlets—almost dreadlocks.

Louie had dreadlocks. Yes, Louie. He's the guy I was seeing now—or hoping to see now. He worked in the sheet exchange. I didn't know his last name, but had had my eye on him for at least a month, and things were finally getting interesting between us. Earlier in the week he held my hand a little too long while handing me a round, brass sheet token that I carried with me during dinner. Then later when I turned in the token for a fresh pair of sheets, he winked and whispered, "Meet me on the roof Thursday night." I blinked a few times and wondered if I had actually heard him say that or only imagined it.

The roof of his dorm, an off-limits area like the tunnels that wound through the campus underground, sounded to me like a code for "lovers lane." Mostly people went up there to party, but the way he had said it . . . *meet me on the roof* . . . it was bathed in potential intimacy. But that was tomorrow night. What would I do with myself tonight?

# 12.
# Joel. 1981.

As we began our six-hour drive north to Chicago through the infinite cornfields of southern and central Illinois, I stared out the passenger window of Kim's van, still thick with the previous day's drunk. I pressed my forehead against the cool glass, hoping it would soothe me like a compress. We sped by even rows of crops, farmhouses, barns, and silos, and in the distance they looked surreal, like fake scenery in the movies. We passed a pig farm—the smell was unmistakable—and as the rancid odor filled the air with the pointed force of a finger stuck down my throat, I suppressed the urge to hurl.

Kim, in command behind the wheel, spoke in dissertations. He moved from subject to subject but lingered on something called "cogeneration," which I think he said was recycled steam. Each time we passed a quaint, stationary windmill, he launched into the possibilities of wind power. He ranted about how under-utilized our alternative sources of energy were and said he would switch his major to Environmental Engineering when he returned to school in the fall.

I stopped listening and couldn't even muster the energy to grunt in agreement.

When he noticed I'd lost interest, Kim changed the subject. "You just didn't want to leave her door," he said. "Finally, Don dragged you away and wheeled you back to Baker Hall in my chair. I've never seen anyone so pathetic."

"Don't tell me anymore, okay?" I moaned. "It's better if I don't know what happened."

"You're probably right. But you owe me, man. I packed up all your shit after you passed out on my bathroom floor. And it wasn't easy. I had to have fucking drunk Doug carry me up and down the stairs. I swear, if you left anything behind you better not blame me."

"I won't, I won't. Trust me, man. I know I'm the one responsible for putting this ice pick through my temple."

As I fell into the hypnosis of the rumbling road, my eyes finally succumbed to the weight of sleepiness and I plunged into disjointed and bizarre dreams. Swirling in my head like windmills were haphazard visions of corn and grain, vast fields of growing crops, enormous crows cawing and haunting the cloudless sky like black ghosts. I saw Anita with her hands plunged into the dirt, and Noelle—faceless and statuesque—holding a paper with the word "cop-out" circled in red—circled in blood.

I was lost—searching—late for class and unprepared for an exam.

When Kim stopped in front of my parents' house, I awoke in a panic. Opening my eyes, the first thing I saw was my childhood home—a place that resided in the far reaches of my mind and formed the shape of my brain cells. Although it was usually from the inside, this home was the setting of nearly every dream I'd had since I left. I rubbed the sleep from my eyes and focused on this faded eggshell Cape Cod, a dwarf of a home squashed between two brick Georgians. Had it always been so small?

It looked lifeless. My mother usually had the window boxes filled with geraniums and cascading ivy; however, the boxes were barren and in need of a fresh coat of green paint. Brown leaves from last fall were matted into the untrimmed lawn and three yellowing newspapers dotted the walkway.

"Is this it?" asked Kim, looking back and forth between the house and a small piece of paper in his hand. "It's the number you wrote on these directions."

I blinked my eyes and felt embarrassed to admit that yes, it was my home. I tried to moisten my dry lips, but my tongue was desert dry and my teeth wore sweaters. I reached for a can of Coke on the dash, cringing because of a pain in my neck from sleeping against the window. "This is it," I said.

"Good. Then this is where I dump your sorry ass."

"You have no idea."

"Hey, by the way," said Kim, "you snore."

"Anything else you want to tell me?"

"Yeah," he said. "Your breath could wilt a plant."

"Thanks for the ride," I said, managing a smile.

"I'd help you with your bags, but well, I can't walk."

"You make up for it with your mouth."

"You forget I packed those bags. You could at least thank me for that."

"I'll thank you when I see you didn't steal any of my records."

"You're the only one I know who listens to that crap."

"Don't let my old man hear you say that."

"I didn't even know you had an old man," he said.

"I don't. Hey, did you manage to come up with a plan to save the world's energy sources?"

"As a matter of fact. . . ."

"Never mind, dude. I didn't really want to know."

"Have a good summer, Joel. Get a job and forget about that redhead. I'll call you next week."

I climbed out of the idling van, grabbed my first load from the back, and hauled it to the front porch. The screen door and storm doors were closed and I wondered if anyone were home. I returned to Kim's van, which purred quietly after the long drive, and collected first my albums and then my stereo boxes. Nodding my aching head instead of waving, I said goodbye to Kim. "See you soon, buddy."

"Stay out of the playpen," he yelled.

"Fuck you!" I called after the van as it tore down my street.

"Well, isn't that nice?" said Mom, from the front porch.

I spun around, startled. "Mom?" Blinking a few times to bring her into focus, I gasped. I hadn't seen her since Christmas and she looked like she'd aged ten years. She was as gray as a foggy day and her once smooth skin was deeply creased with sharp parentheses surrounding her lips. I stared at her dumbly.

"I don't see my only child for months and I find out what kind of language he's picked up at school?"

"Sorry, Mom. It didn't look like you were home. I would have had you meet Kim."

"Why didn't he come to the door?"

"He's in a wheelchair. It would have been a pain."

"He drives?"

"The van has a special setup. He rigged it himself."

"I'm not sure I like the idea of you riding in a rigged vehicle."

"Mom, I'm home. I'm safe, see?"

"Of course you are. Welcome home, Honey," she said, not all that interested in Kim or his van. She gave me a loose, awkward hug, kissed me on the cheek, and ran a shaky hand through my hair. "You need a haircut, you know. You look like a hippie!"

"Mo-om!"

"I know, I'm sorry," she said. "C'mon, let's get you fed. There's something I have to tell you."

With one eye on the empty flower box beneath the dining room window, I picked up as much as I could carry while my mother grabbed the duffel bag closest to her. She held the door open for me with her foot and I followed her inside the tiny living room. I set down one of my bags on the worn blue carpet and looked around.

It was the same—the regular backdrop to many of my dreams. Same blue sofa, same reading chair. The ceiling was lower, though. Had I grown taller?

The odor of smoke fouled the air and I spied a full ashtray on the coffee table in front of the fireplace. "You're smoking in the house now?" I asked. "What does Dad say about that?"

"That's what I have to talk to you about," she said. "Dad's gone."

"What?" I set down my stereo box. "What do you mean he's gone?"

"Gone—as in left . . . me. Just gone." She reached for a crumbled pack of Kents on the fireplace mantle. Her hair seemed to grow even grayer as she forced the unlit cigarette between her pale lips. Her eyes—*my* eyes—looked sunken and dark with restrained emotion. Half moons swelled beneath them. "Don't look so shocked, Joel. You had to know this was coming."

"Know *what* was coming?"

"He was merely waiting for you to go back to school so he could stick me with the mortgage *and* your tuition. Well, I'll tell you right now that I can't afford both." She struck a match three times before it burst into flame, and then she held it to the end of her cigarette and sucked deeply. The red ember glowed brighter and brighter—like a warning. "I'm just surprised he didn't do it the day you turned eighteen."

"Mom?"

"Look Joel, I know I said you could go back to school if you managed decent grades but Honey, I'm afraid I just can't afford it." She took a step toward me and then stopped. "You'll have to get a job and save some money."

"But Mom. . . ."

"Don't do it, Joel," she snapped. "Don't *but Mom,* me. I can't help it. I'm sorry but I can't help it."

"When exactly did he leave?"

"Three months ago." She reached back to the mantle for the ashtray. Grabbing it, completely disregarding the ashes spilling to the floor, she sat down in her reading chair—the place I always imagined her sitting in the house. "I think he's in California."

"California?"

"Listen, don't worry. I've got a friend at school who has a brother who works at the Chicago Board of Trade. I've set up an interview for you downtown to work at an entry-level thing for his firm. They call it a runner."

"Board of Trade? Runner? Mom, I don't know the first thing about that business. And you want me to work downtown? How am I supposed to get there? My Volkswagen? I don't even know if the thing will still run."

"You can take the train. I'll drop you at the station on my way to work."

My mother nervously tapped her cigarette on the ashtray and then she angrily stubbed it out, sprang up and walked into the kitchen. A cloud hung over her chair and a steady stream of thick, swirling smoke smoldered upward from the ashtray like a genie's snake lifting its head to test the air. I brought my hand to my temple and felt a throbbing pulse. Falling into the sofa, I closed my eyes.

I had heard her say "train" and it felt like one was crashing through me. Was I still dreaming?

I picked up my mom's fraying afghan and tossed it on her chair. Still holding my head I tried to piece together everything that had happened in the last twenty-four hours. I was sure I started out happy. I aced my finals . . . I got drunk . . . and . . . and then what happened?

Oh yeah, I thought. I finally kissed Noelle.

Noelle? Jesus! I kissed Noelle. I raised my head and my heart beat a little faster. Did I say goodbye to her? What *did* I say to her? Did Kim say Don pulled me out of her dorm room? What was I doing there? Oh shit! What did I do? I dropped my pounding head back into my hands and swore out loud. How could everything change so much overnight?

\* \* \* \* \* \* \* \*

For the next three days a silence hung over the house. My mother and I passed each other like strangers, barely uttering "good morning." She sat at the kitchen table or in her chair and smoked pack after pack of cigarettes. And even though her own hurt was tangible, I was determined to hang onto my anger. It gnawed at me like a mosquito bite and I freely scratched it.

I didn't know if I were more angry with her or with Walt. Did he give any thought to the idea that he was leaving me too?

On Monday she dropped me at the Westmont train station, and without saying goodbye, I boarded the Burlington Northern commuter train. I sat in a four-seater with three businessmen, each who wore a dark suit with a white shirt and a pale yellow tie with small red spots. It was the same tie—like they were seventh grade girls and had called one another the night before and planned it. Was it a uniform of some kind? I watched as they buried themselves in *Chicago Tribunes* and *Wall Street Journals* and their bodies swayed with the imperfections of the train tracks. I had an urge to take out the Swiss Army knife from my back pocket, cut off their ties, and then wave them in the air like an oater Indian actor who had just scalped his enemy.

Rudely thrust into a world in which I didn't belong, I decided right then and there that these men were not who I wanted to be. I told myself the whole thing—the train, the job, the time away from school—was temporary.

This was *not* how my life was supposed to turn out.

As I did on the ride home from Carbondale, I pressed my face to the tinted glass of the train window. I stared at the tranquil suburban landscapes where crab apple trees with bright pink flowers nearly reached out and kissed the train. We stopped at the Hinsdale station and then the LaGrange Station, where I craned my neck in vain to see if the Troves of Treasure store was still there. I was desperate for some familiarity.

Zooming past the tiny Brookfield Zoo station without stopping, we then paused for a while at the Riverside stop, where passengers streamed in and every seat filled. From there we stopped once more in Berwyn before it was a straight shot to Union Station.

The closer we got to the city, the tighter and darker the neighborhoods became. Lumbering like a crabby old man, the train didn't stop in these tenements, in these areas where high finance executives never considered living. We, the moneymakers and the potential moneymakers, were on our way to downtown Chicago—to the land of money.

Finally curving into a massive conglomerate of train tracks and railcars, smokestacks and industry, and what looked to me like urban blight—especially compared to the pastoral and forested neighborhood where I had lived the past year at school—I felt sick. I couldn't stop wondering if all of this was happening to someone else.

Sweat formed on my upper lip. My palms felt clammy.

On the verge of panic, I took a deep breath and devised a plan. I planned to meet with my mom's friend's brother, tell him thanks-but-no-thanks, and then maybe walk to the lake and watch the waves for a while. Maybe I'd head to the Art Institute and stare at the Monet paintings until each impressionistic dot devised the meaning of my life. Or maybe I'd just go to Buckingham Fountain, throw in a penny, and wish this wasn't happening to me.

Did Walt know what affect his leaving would have on me? Couldn't he have written and told me he was moving? He had a Master's Degree for crying out loud! Didn't he know how important it was for me to go to school?

I kicked myself for not knowing. I should have known. I should have seen it coming. Really, he was hardly around during my last few years at home. He was always working at the prison—if that's what he was really doing—and I don't remember eating a meal with him the entire time I was in high school.

"Bastard!" I said as the train came to a decisive halt.

Stepping onto the noisy platform, I walked with the crowd. Carried by a suited, workforce undertow, we filed off the train platform and into the station. We climbed the stairs and emerged into the bright city day and dispersed to our hundred different destinations.

My mother had prepared a crib note map for me to follow, but I knew where I was going. I'd taken the train many times before and walked from Union Station to the Northwestern Station, and got off in Ravenswood to visit my Aunt Sue. Or along with Keith and Joe we'd catch an El to Wrigley Field for a Cub's Game.

The city, the Loop, wasn't hard to figure out. I walked several blocks and then turned left on LaSalle, where the Chicago Board of Trade loomed at the end of the street like a thunderstorm in the sunrise. The gray, marble façade was a temple defining the city of broad shoulders. Huge, vertical windows reflected what little sky could penetrate the fortress of surrounding buildings, all of which paled in comparison to the mighty monolith, crowned by a prominent statue—perched like a cross on top of a basilica. As I drew closer to the gilded doors, I craned my neck and focused on the statue. On her.

It was Ceres, the Roman goddess of grain, looking down on LaSalle and Jackson and towering over me.

I studied her, mesmerized like a farm boy in the city for the first time. Taxicabs whizzed by. Horns honked. And there I stood, staring at this faceless, shining goddess—this woman who ruled the world of commodities. Why, I wondered, was there always a woman?

Inside the building everything was regal and art deco-cold—like an Orson Wells movie. And everything was trimmed in gold: The doors, the windows, the newspaper stand, and the elevator that opened on the fourth level, the observation area for the Trading Floor. Stepping off, I looked through the giant windows and gaped at the massive room before me. Filled with desks and phones and television screens, it looked modern and sophisticated, as surreal as the Starship Enterprise.

A bell rang, loudly, like a recess bell or the start of some kind of race, and as I moved to cover my ears, a stampede of people in colorful jackets burst out of the door and flooded onto the floor. The room became awash in purple, orange, yellow, green, red, and every shade of blue. It was an artist's palette of color as jacketed men rushed to their stations. Some moved to the pits where their arms gestured wildly. Others sat on stools and had telephones tethered to their ears. Paper flew through the air like a ticker tape parade while worker bees buzzed back and forth between those on the phones and those in the pits.

"Wow," I said, studying the high-speed maneuvering. How would I ever hope to know what was going on down there?

I remained in the hallway watching with an open mouth until I realized it was time for my appointment. Returning to the elevator, I continued my ascent to the twenty-fifth floor where the commodities trading firm, Rosenbaum and Co., was located.

Except for the enormous silver sign behind the receptionist's desk, the atmosphere was as plain as that of a dentist's office. And like dental assistants and hygienists in their cotton smocks, everyone around me wore purple jackets with more pockets and notes pinned to them than Ray Rayner's jumpsuit.

"I'm here to see a Frank LaRoque?" I said to the receptionist.

"Just a moment," she said, reaching for the phone. "Oh, never mind. He's right here. Frank this is yours."

He was tall and thin. Looked to be about twenty-five. "Follow me," he said without looking at me.

I followed him to a conference room where he tossed a file folder onto a table and gestured for me to sit. "I don't suppose you want a donut."

"Why not?" I said, reaching into a box of Dunkin Donuts. I hadn't seen a box of Dunkin Donuts in years. Walt used to bring them home and always got an extra strawberry glazed one for me, mocking me because I liked the pink ones.

"This is a runner job," said Frank. "Doesn't take much to learn, just a lot of well, running, I guess. You take the orders from the phone clerks and give 'em to the traders in the pits. It's not rocket science and it's pretty much where we all start."

He needed a shave and I had to keep myself from staring at his orange whiskers by focusing on the reflections glinting off his aviator-frame glasses.

"What'd you say your name was again?" he asked.

"Joel," I said. "Joel Rolland."

"Right, Joel," he said. "Look, don't take this the wrong way, but everyone and his brother sends people to the firm for runner jobs. You wouldn't believe the dolts that walk into this office."

"I think I was sent here because of someone's brother. Someone my mom knows," I said. "By the way, if I get this job, it's only for the summer. I'm going back to school in August."

"They all say that too," said Frank. "You can start tomorrow if you like." He stood up and held open the door. "C'mon. I'll show you around."

I followed him to the elevators and we returned to the fourth floor mayhem of what would soon be my portal—my reality—for what turned out to be the next year and a half.

College would have to wait.

# 13.
## Noelle. 1981.

Lisa Leigh was the most popular girl at The Point. From a distance she was always animated and happy, wore her bleached hair like a spiky porcupine, and she had a nose ring. I had never considered the idea of anyone piercing a nostril let alone seen such a thing; however, after five minutes with Lisa, my provincial horror had disappeared.

I attribute our first meeting to mutual insomnia. We met in the hallway sitting area between our rooms, where I sat reading the same sentence in my history book over and over. I didn't hear her walk up but turned when I felt a hand press the aqua Naugahyde of my chair. "I've got chamomile tea," she had said "What to join me? My roommate's out again, no doubt getting laid."

"My roommate snores," I said, "which I don't understand because she sleeps on her stomach. I thought it was the back sleepers who were supposed to snore."

"Hey, you learn something new every day in college. C'mon. I'll warm the water on the base of my popcorn maker."

Lisa's room was a mirror image of the room I shared with Ruby, but the walls were celery green instead of blue. I curled up on her roommate's bed and watched her steep teabags.

"I don't think I could live in this room without my popcorn maker," she said. "And to think I never had one in Springfield."

"Ah, the state capitol. You don't sound like you're from a city."

"Springfield, a city?" she laughed. "Yeah, I guess it is. We call it 'The Patch'. Don't ask me why. I'm from Indiana originally, but

I was adopted and my new folks took me to The Patch. Hey, do you know why they call Indiana the Hoosier state?"

"I don't even know what a Hoosier is," I said.

"Oh that's easy. It means, *hoosier daddy?*" She threw her head back and laughed. "Told ya you learn something new at college every day. To this day I don't know who my daddy was."

"I hardly knew my dad either," I responded, trying to be empathetic. She handed me a cup of tea. It was only lukewarm, but the smell was as soothing as her voice.

"Hey, you wanna look at my high school yearbooks?"

At that moment I knew I'd found a friend.

Lisa was a good student—majored in social work—and was a kind person who, like a queen bee, attracted a swarm of people always willing to please her. She was responsible for arranging most of the afternoon parties we had on the veranda during the spring semester. After class she set up camp, spread her picnic blanket and played guitar and sang like Joni Mitchell. I always arrived late after my student job and by then a crowd had formed and everyone sang with her, harmonizing like a folk band until just before dinner. Then Lisa strapped her guitar to the sissy bar of her motorcycle and returned it to the friend's house in town where she regularly stashed it.

Before the school year ended, Ruby, Lisa, and I made plans to live together in the fall in a "sophomore approved" apartment. And while they both went home after their last final, I didn't know where I was going to go.

Watching them leave was like watching my sister Janette walk down that hallway on the day she dropped me off. My spirits sagged like the sycamore leaves steeped in summer sun and humidity. Battling with my choices, I wondered, should I go home? Should I go to Memphis and stay with Janette? Should I stay in Carbondale, attend summer school and find a job? How I wished there were someone there to tell me what to do.

All my life I thought I hated having my mother and my sister tell me what to do. And now, when I finally had to tell myself what to do, I couldn't make a decision. The only thing of which I was certain was that my childhood was officially over.

Unlike my new friends, whose northern homes were filled with parents and siblings and childhood bedrooms crammed with dried prom flowers, picture collages of kids in Halloween costumes, and shelves filled with trophies and blue ribbons waiting for them to return, I had no reason to return to my mother's home. She made it very clear that all my high school paperwork, stuffed animals, and old clothes had been pitched.

On the day I left home nine months earlier, my mother began the first trimester of living in an empty nest. Emily Moncada had taken down her widow/mother shingle and experienced a metamorphosis. The bank promoted her twice and she started dating, traveling, and dining out instead of cooking. Janette's bedroom turned into a "study," and mine, I was told, had the new moniker of "guest room."

Janette wasn't too interested in having me stay with her, either. She suggested I find a summer residence in my new hometown. "Better to stay put and find a job," she had said. "You'll need the money."

Janette, of course, was right.

I enrolled in summer school, taking a Spanish course to maintain my student worker status, and found a job typing a book about bugs for an entomology professor named Dr. McPhillips. And it was my new friend, Louie Gardner, who offered me a place to live. On the night I met him on the roof of his dorm building, he told me about a house on the far north side of town, which he planned to share with two other guys named Bo and Steve. The rent was only seventy-five bucks a month.

I got what I paid for.

The house was a dump. It smelled of fried food and urine and no one ever cleaned. But knowing it was only for the summer, I spent as little time there as possible. Each day I rode my bike to campus while my lazy roommates slept in, fried food, pissed all over the toilet seat and didn't clean.

Louie lasted three weeks. One day I came home from work and found a note pinned to my door saying his money had run out. Bo said he hitched a ride to Chicago.

What I remember most about those summer days was the heat. The days were hot. Sweltering hot. Armpit hot. The hot roaring flame from a pizza oven hot. Each day I arrived at the Life Sciences building dripping with sweat. After locking my bike and walking into the air-conditioned building, my body temperature plunged before the door closed behind me, and it was like stepping out of the pizza oven and into a meat locker.

The Life Science building was not only cold, but also sterile. It reeked of formaldehyde and I was sure the stink penetrated my skin as I spent the afternoon making typos on an IBM Selectric typewriter while typing a book for Dr. McPhillips.

McPhillips was a flirty stinkbug specialist who called me "Colleen" because of my red hair. He was tall and reedy and had no hair at all. Each day he burst through the office door,

startling me with a loud, musical whistle and a cheerful good
morning. He had a vast collection of Mr. Rogers cardigan sweaters in primary colors and constantly hummed as though singing
"It's a Beautiful Day in the Neighborhood."

*"Top o the mornin' to ye,* Colleen," he sang.

"I'm not Irish," I said, my standard response.

"Well you should be," he had said, putting the latest stack of
manuscript pages on my desk.

I labeled him "Dr. Bug," and we got along in spite of the
lousy job I did typing his book. I could handle the common
names of his precious shield-shaped bugs—green stinkbug, brown
stinkbug, and southern green stinkbug—but their Latin names
didn't flow off my finger tips: *Acrosternum hilare; Euschistus
servus; Nezara viridula* (Linnaeus), and so on. Each time he
delivered new manuscript pages, red pen corrections stained
the margins like blood. I swear I went through as much White
Out as typewriter ribbons.

Summer ended, the trees turned yellow and under the aca-
demic sky, time flew by. Lisa, whose strict parents took one look
at her spiked hair and pierced nose and forbade her from renting
an apartment with Ruby and me, spent sophomore year in the
dorms. Meanwhile, Ruby and I moved into a small apartment
near campus. It was a two-bedroom unit, and a baby step away
from dorm life. Still surrounded by loud music and students,
we learned to cook for ourselves and wash our bed sheets at
a nearby laundromat without an exchange service. I dove into
my studies and fell into a serious rhythm of classes and work,
studying and testing. The year included Spanish Conversation,
Advanced Composition, European History and Economics, Philosophy, Nutrition, Intro to French, Government, and Biology. Except
for a physical education requirement or two, my general studies
classes were nearly complete. And since I no longer had any
math classes, I managed Dean's list grades.

Out of the dorms, our parties became more bohemian. We
gave up the cheap beer, moved on to cheap wine, and engaged
in pseudo-intellectual literary and political debates. We got deep,
sought out odd people—artists, poets, musicians, theater people.
As our political soldiers in a far off place called "Washington
DC" faced conflict with the Middle East, talk of the hostages and
sanctions, then ABSCAM and the Olympic boycott penetrated our
discussions. The air, always charged with possibility and question,
made us yearn for information and truth. We were liberal paupers
with nowhere to go beyond our womblike college classrooms
and ill-furnished living rooms, all the while wanting desperately
to become something.

During our junior year, Lisa was sprung from the dorms like a prisoner out on parole, and she, Ruby, and I lived together in a three-bedroom townhouse. I applied for and received an Illinois State Scholarship and a Basic Educational Opportunity Grant—which were virtually wiped out the following year when Ronald Reagan settled into the White House; however, while Jimmy Carter was still in charge, the government paid my tuition. It was a good thing, because while my mother arranged a student loan at the bank where she worked for me to pay for my second year, she said they incorporated much stricter rules about multiple loans and labeled students too high a risk. I couldn't believe that all her years on the job there didn't serve as some kind of collateral! We Moncada women were nothing if not hard workers.

After one more year working for Dr. Bug and the zoology department professors, I landed a job as a reporter at the campus newspaper, *The Daily Egyptian*. The pay was the same, $3.60 per hour, but the experience for a wannabe journalist was invaluable. Writing, having a byline, was pure validation. It was as though I finally existed.

My first assignments were lackluster and insignificant—merely tests of my potential. I worked on the calendar, interviewed students and teachers who won minor awards, or wrote about changes in operations at the recreation center or the Bursar's office.

The newsroom was a fun and lively place to be, but it was cliquey too. Older, more experienced reporters clustered around each other's desks, showing off their experience like a club membership. Occasionally one would glance in my direction as though daring me to try to become a part of it; but I just went about my business, typed up my stories, and dropped them in the copy editor's basket. On paste-up day I always checked to see if anything I wrote got a byline. If it did, I made sure my name was spelled correctly. "Noelle with two Ls," I'd say.

Then, just before the holidays, my status in the newsroom changed. It was December 1980. John Lennon was killed and it changed everything—especially my fledgling career as a student journalist.

On the day after he was shot, a professor in my reporting class began the session with a moment of silence for the lost Beatle, and then went on with business as usual, telling us that we were all probably "too young to understand what his death meant to the world."

We responded with a collective groan. "How old do you think we are?" someone shouted. "You are as lame as you look," shouted someone else. And, "Do you understand what his death means to the world—not to mention us?"

At once I began scribbling in the margins of my notebook: *"Before my father died, I played* "A Hard Day's Night" *on the record player in his den and danced wildly—did the pony— knowing not a soul could see me. I felt so free—released. And the first time I heard my sister play* "Sgt. Pepper's" *and John Lennon's haunting voice echoed through* "Day in the Life," *I felt forever haunted by his rare talent."*

I used my notes, our class reactions, and our professor's assumption that John Lennon had only touched people "his age," and incorporated everything into a tribute piece. It impressed my editor. He ran it and then shortly thereafter, awarded me the arts and entertainment beat. It was a big step up in status in the newsroom, and soon I was in the clique.

The best part was that I got tickets to all the campus performances—concerts, the circus, lectures, and traveling ballets.


It's now my final year of school. Ruby, Lisa, and I left behind our apartment and moved into a house near the newspaper office. Our house is on a cobblestone street, and like most of the little white dwellings in the neighborhood, a coal miner originally owned it. Carbondale was a coal town and coal town lore held that miners, stuck in the dark caverns all day long, liked to come home to white houses. It has everything we need: Three bedrooms; one bathroom; a small kitchen; large living room; and a backyard to store Lisa's motorcycle and her dog, George, a lean, high-strung yellow lab who babbles like Scooby doo.

We rent it from the local slumlord, Arlen Sabljak, who owns nearly every house in the neighborhood. No one knows how many houses he owns. Arlen is plump, young, and as southern as a cotton baron. He relishes his role as the local real estate mogul. He roams the town like it's his own plantation, and we, his peons, often spot him uptown drinking at the bars. Ruby rarely lets him escape without buying our table a round of drinks. He requires a year's lease—even though most students were there only for the duration of the regular school year (August through May), and all twelve monthly checks must be written up front and post-dated. Lisa took on the responsibility of writing all the checks and Ruby and I pay our shares, $130 each, to her on the first day of each month.

Our three-bedroom house was originally a two-bedroom house; however, the additional bedroom, an enclosed front porch, is an Arlen Sabljak trademark. Arlen was known for having work crews descend upon his houses on a Saturday morning like covert CIA operatives who hammer and saw without a building permit as they attach random extra bedrooms. They were in no danger of getting caught—since inspectors didn't work on the weekends—and by Sunday night, two-bedroom units become three-bedroom units and three-bedroom units blossom into four- and five-bedroom units. Rents go up accordingly.

Lisa chose the front porch bedroom because she liked the window looking out at the street and the prolific flower garden left behind by the previous tenants. Kind-hearted soul that she is, Lisa claimed she wanted Ruby and me to have the two bigger bedrooms. She maintained that generous disposition until last week when along with Halloween came an unexpected cold snap.

"Roger won't sleep here anymore," she said. "Says it's too cold."

"Dump him," laughed Ruby. "You don't need a wimpy boyfriend."

Lisa was the only one who had a steady boyfriend. Ruby didn't have the attention span for anything steady. She changed her major twice per semester. Currently, I think she's a psych major.

I dated a few guys—it was easy to find a date with my free concert tickets—but never got serious with anyone. As soon as they got too close, I pulled away. After a while, and especially when a guy got mean about it, I heard the long-since disappeared Joel Rolland's gin-soaked voice accusing me of dumping Don and thought maybe he was right about me. Ruby said I wouldn't go out with anyone steadily because I had a fear of abandonment. She said it was because my father abandoned me by dying when I was so young, "You're afraid they might leave you," she said. "So *you* leave first."

Really, it was a much kinder diagnosis than Joel's.

I occasionally wondered what had happened to Joel, but my relationship with him had become like last semester's notebooks, stored in the closet of my memory. After professing his so-called "love" in a drunken tirade, he left me, and what I thought was our friendship, behind.

\* \* \* \* \* \* \* \*

Each year for Halloween, Carbondale turned into a giant costume party, a veritable Mardi Gras, where students from other state schools made a pilgrimage to southern Illinois's most notorious downtown area—"the strip," a narrow band of nightlife throbbing like an artery. Nothing in glass containers was sold within a twenty-five mile radius of town for a week prior to Halloween, and on the night of the monster bash, the bars stayed open until four in the morning.

I dressed as Leonardo da Vinci. Lisa was Mae West and Ruby was Lt. Uhura from *Star Trek.* Just after sundown, we locked arms and took to the strip like *Charlie's Angels,* with more energy than a trio of seven year olds on a sugar high.

The hangover hit us like a cavity in a rotting tooth.

On Sunday morning, Lisa and I lay together in Ruby's king-size waterbed. We called it "Ruby's womb," and while the radio played soft tunes in the background, we felt the heated water shake below us as we laughed and recounted the previous night's escapades.

"I am so totally hung over," said Lisa.

"I used to collect candy corn on Halloween," I moaned. "I never imagined I'd be trading in the corn for kamikaze shots. Whose idea was that anyway? Ouch!"

"Can you believe that sow Trina Wilson got it on with Jack-the-Beanstalk Barnes last night?" asked Ruby.

"You're kidding!" I said, sitting up. "Trina Wilson was dressed as a old English hag selling bread on a street corner in a Dickens novel."

"I liked Jack's beanstalk costume. I thought it . . . it suited him," said Lisa.

Jack Barnes was a tall, skinny guy we knew, a neighbor, who we actually thought was gay. "I didn't see those two pair off at all. Damn, that girl is such a skank. She'll sleep with anyone."

"I slept with Jack-the-Beanstalk Barnes my sophomore year," said Lisa.

"No way. You didn't!" we shouted. I couldn't help but laugh.

"He used to be cuter," said Lisa. "Shut up, you two."

The music stopped and we heard the low, melodic tone of the morning DJ on the university station. "Hey, turn up the radio," I said. "It's the contest."

"You and your contests," said Ruby. "Turn it up yourself."

I pulled myself out of the waterbed womb and leaned toward Ruby's stereo and turned up the volume.

*"This is when we play a note or two from a song and the first caller to get it right wins free tickets to . . . what are they winning free tickets to this week?"*

"Must be a good one," said Ruby sarcastically. "Lisa, get the phone. I'm sure I'll know it."

*"Well whatever. We don't have any tickets on hand, but we'll be sure to give you something,"* said the announcer.

"Just watch," said Ruby, punching the numbers into the phone. "This will be the one we get and we win *bupkis.*"

"It doesn't matter." I moved close to the speaker and pressed my ear against it as though I were listening to a long-distance broadcast. "I get tickets to everything anyway."

*"Okay,"* said the DJ. *"Name the artist. Name the tune. First caller wins."*

"Wins *what?"* Ruby wrapped the telephone cord around her wrist like a bracelet.

*"Bleep, Bleep,"* went the music. Two notes.

I had no clue what song it was. Lisa looked equally perplexed.

"Manfred Mann!" shouted Ruby as she punched in the last number and unraveled the coiling phone line from her wrist. "It's called 'Machines.' Quick Lisa, give Noelle the phone. Don't use my name or I'll kill you."

"It's ringing!" I said, suddenly nervous.

"Ringing?" asked Lisa. "That's a good sign, right?"

"Ruby, are you sure about this?" I asked. "God! How do you know this?"

"My parents have the album," she said. "I'm totally sure."

"Hello, WIDB. Can I have your name please?"

"It's Noelle," I said. My voice didn't sound like my own. I immediately wished I'd used a different name.

"Okay, Noelle," said the DJ switching to a fake French accent. *"Comment t'allez vous?"*

Why did people assume I spoke French? I had only taken one class and everything came out of my mouth with a Spanish accent. *"Muy bien,"* I said. *"No hablo francais, amigo. Estudio Español.* Okay?"

"Right," he said. "Well, have you got a Name-That-Tune guess?"

"Manfred Mann. 'Machines.' "

"That is one-hundred percent . . . correct, *Señorita!* Hold on and we'll get your details. Way to go. That one wasn't easy."

"Holy shit, I don't believe it!" I said, covering the phone. "We won! We actually won!" Lisa laughed, whooped, and jumped up and down while Ruby lay in the waterbed as regal as Cleopatra.

"Told ya," she said.

Composing myself, I asked the DJ if my reaction was going to be on the radio. But I was on hold while a commercial for a local car dealership played through the telephone, slightly ahead of the stereo in Ruby's room. As I laughed and held on, the phone clicked.

"Noelle Moncada?" said a familiar voice. "Is that you?"

"Yes?" I said, not remembering whether or not I had given my last name. I shot a questioning look at my roommates. "Who is this?"

"Don't you recognize my voice?"

"Should I?"

"It's me!' he said. "It's Joel."

"Joel?"

"Don't tell me you've forgotten me."

"You mean Joel Rolland?" Ruby perked up like George when one of us called his name. Lisa looked confused. "What are you doing? Are you . . . are you at the radio station?"

"I work here," he said. "I do the weather report."

"You're kidding," I said. "I didn't know you were in town."

"I wasn't until last semester. I had to drop out for a while but now I'm back. I live with Kim Harper. Remember Kim in the wheelchair?"

"Of course. Yes, I remember Kim."

"So, Noelle . . . how the hell are you?"

"I'm fine. I can't believe this. I haven't seen you since. . . ."

"The dorms," he said quickly. "Look, I'm going to put you back on with Jimbo, and he'll get your address and phone number for the prize. I think it's an album or a gift certificate to one of the music stores or something. Say, can I call you?"

"Yes . . . yes. By all means yes." I didn't know what I was saying. It felt like a Halloween ghost had entered my body and taken over my voice. "I'd love to see you, Joel." I shot another wide-eyed look at my roommates. "Call me."

The next thing I knew I was reciting my name and address to someone named Jimbo.

"Are you nuts?" asked Ruby.

"What?" Lisa asked. "What's up?"

"Don't look now," said Ruby, "but I think Noelle is about to regress to freshman year at The Point."

"What's wrong with that?" asked Lisa.

Neither Ruby nor I answered her.

# 14.
# Joel. 1981.

I spent the first six weeks scratching my head about what went on in the world of commodities trading, but I learned my runner job without much trouble. Turns out it was no more complicated than running bases on the ball field.

Each day after taking the train downtown, I put on a purple jacket, waited for the bell, and braced myself for the ensuing clamor that would surround me for the next six hours. I, a mere peon in the trading world hierarchy, awaited orders from snappy phone clerks who were never without phones welded to their ears. I watched as they scrawled buy and sell orders dictated to them from places like New York, Boston, Miami, and Los Angeles and then clipped the tickets on a metal line. This was my cue to snatch the orders from the clips like a short-order cook and run them to other purple-jacket-clad brokers in the pits.

The pits were a feeding frenzy. Traders were like colorful fish swimming in tanks, their red, yellow, orange, purple, and blue jackets swirling as they went after order tickets like sharks after chum.

*"New York: Buy! Boston: Sell! Fifty lots. Buy a hundred. At the orders! SOLD! SOLD!"*

Soybeans were king. Soybean oil and soybean meal; corn, oats, iced broilers—which I later found out were frozen chickens—mortgage futures; treasury bonds; orange juice; cotton; plywood; pork-bellies . . . or as it turned out, bacon.

Within two months I was promoted to phone clerk and then it was I who snapped at the runners. My salary increased from $800/month to $1,000 and I thought I was rich. The hours were excellent. I worked a six-hour day, with trading sessions lasting only four hours. If we had worked any longer than that in one day, we would have probably killed each other.

August came and went and I hardly noticed that I didn't return to school.

Within a year I was again promoted—this time to Broker's Assistant—and helped take orders from the runners. I skillfully organized orders like a Vegas dealer shuffling a deck of cards, and dispersed them to the brokers. By this time I truly knew what I was doing. And I liked it. I also liked the salary increase. Each week I deposited my paycheck and carefully studied my little blue bankbook, watching the numbers increase with satisfaction.

I had more than enough money to go back to school. And yet, what was it that kept me from returning?

Throughout my stint at the CBOT, I thought about her often but never heard from Noelle. I imagined she was still in Carbondale, progressing with her journalism major the way I once expected I would. Kim Harper called occasionally and we got together during his breaks when he came home to Chicago. Each time I saw him, his hair was longer. Soon he had a ponytail hanging down to the middle of his back.

He was at the top of his engineering class, and I envied his focus and drive. I mean, there were days when I felt passionate about what I was doing, but I only pushed paper—spent other people's money—and pretended I was immersed in the commodities produced by our country's farmers.

I thought of my former roommate, Sam the pig farmer. He went to college to major in Agricultural Economics in order to better run his family's business. He had the background of farm living to set him on that path, while I facilitated the trade of pork products each day, never having seen a live pig. I also thought of Anita Dambra and her vision of owning a nursery and growing things—her love of the soil.

The history of the Board of Trade revolved around the rich soil of the Midwestern prairies and grew out of the productive grain markets of the mid-nineteenth century. And yet, in the course of my daily job, I never once got my hands dirty.

It wasn't long after I thought of Anita that I heard from her. It was during her winter break and shortly after New Year's. She was in the Chicago area, staying with her roommate's family. I remember the conversation perfectly:

"Hey stranger," she had said on the phone. "Remember me? The girl who liked to play in the mud?"

"Anita? Is that you?"

"Sure as I'm standing here in Evanston," she said. "I looked you up in the phone book. Still living at home?"

"Yeah," I said. "And working downtown."

"Well, can we get together? I'd love to see you, Joel."

"Sure. How long will you be in Evanston?"

"I don't know," she said. "Another three days or so—at least through the weekend. But that's it. It's too cold up here and I want to get back to Nana."

The next day Anita rode the El train from Evanston to the Board of Trade. I saw her from the floor looking at the chaos through the large observation windows, and she wore the same dazed expression—an open mouth, a furrowed brow—that most people exhibit the first time they try to take in that scene. I waved at her, but she didn't see me.

When the closing bell rang, I went right up to her and she threw her arms around my neck. "Joel Rolland," she said, "you're more gorgeous than I remember."

"So are you," I said, meaning it. She had cut her bangs and they glanced gracefully across her forehead. It softened her look. I remembered she had deep, mysterious eyes, but those two dark-obsidian orbs looking back at me made me shiver.

I spent the next three days with Anita in my arms.

She collected her things from her roommate's massive house in North Evanston, which she said was as large as a hotel, and we took the train to my mother's house. Anita compared it to her roommate's coach house. "There's a big difference between the suburbs to the west of the city limits and those to the north," she had said.

"No kidding."

"My neighborhood in New Jersey is somewhere in-between the two."

"Have you called your parents to tell them where you're staying?"

"Not on your life," she said. "They'd kill me if they knew I was staying with a guy—even if your mother is in the next room. Don't you feel the least bit weird about that?"

"No. She doesn't care," I said, laughing. "Besides, she likes you."

The entire time Anita and I were together we never stopped talking about our lives—about our hopes and dreams, our plans and our disappointments. We made love in my boyhood bed and I thought about all the hours I'd spent in that very bed fantasizing about girls—especially Maria, who moved to Boulder, Colorado, and became a ski instructor. Actually having this beautiful, sexy woman in my bed was overwhelming.

Was this what falling in love felt like?

"Why don't you come back to school?" she asked as day three drew to an end. "Let's call the Bursar's office and see if you can get back in."

"Don't think I haven't thought of it. But where would I live?"

"You can stay with me until you find a place. My housemates won't mind. They've always got their boyfriends coming and going."

I had enough money and I knew it was possible. And I felt that if I didn't go back—if I didn't make the decision to return to school at that moment—I might not ever go back.

And so it happened. Two weeks later I left my mother and her small home with the peeling window boxes and was once again in Carbondale.

I stayed at Anita's place for less than a week before hooking up with Kim, who hadn't yet been able to secure a roommate for that semester. We shared a small, white house close to campus.

In May Anita headed north to take an internship at the Chicago Botanic Gardens, and Kim and I both stayed through the summer so I could catch up. Finally enrolled in reporting and editing classes, at last I felt like I was learning something. I also took a job at the student radio station, researching news stories and giving the weather report. I had learned to use my voice in the trading pit and it made for a pretty good radio voice—at least that's what they told me.

The world of commodities trading was far away, and I was again, back on track.

# 15.
# Noelle. 1982.

After a chaotic fall semester Ruby and Lisa went home for the holidays, leaving George and me to share our drafty, wooden house. Although it was eerily quiet, for a week I reveled in my aloneness. I slept until noon, ate cereal for dinner, and read the novels stacked next to my bed. It was like a literary leaning tower of Pisa. *The Magus, The World According to Garp,* Richard Bach's *Illusions.* Sinful as ice cream, they represented a Christmas present to myself—an escape from required reading. As I read, curled in a blanket with George at my feet, the winter wind whistled through the windows and crept under the front door like an uninvited guest. Rafters ached and cracked, letting out sighs of relief, while the walls whispered about years of temporary inhabitants, all passing through on the way to their lives.

My mother came on Christmas Eve. Already dark outside, the twinkling lights strung around my front door danced on her beautiful, smiling face. "Hello my darling," she had said. "Merry Christmas." Her hair was cropped short and teeming with golden highlights—a new look. While in the past she wore only lipstick, leaving behind blotted pink kisses on tissues in the bathroom trashcan, she had thin lines of eyeliner surrounding her feline, green eyes, an echo of my own.

I suppressed the urge to burst into tears at the sight of her. "Come in, come in," I said reaching out.

She stepped inside and crinkled her nose as the crisp industrial smell of disinfectant greeted her. I'd been maniacally scrubbing the kitchen floor, sterilizing the bathroom, and throwing out mounds of papers preparing for her, hoping for her approval. Her thin eyebrows arched as she surveyed my home. It was her first visit to any of my college abodes.

"Whom do we have here?" she asked as George slowly approached her like a shy child.

"Oh, it's George. He's my boyfriend."

"Hello, George," she said, awkwardly patting his head. "I don't recall you mentioning you lived with a dog. He doesn't belong to you, does he?"

"No. He's Lisa's dog," I said. "I made up Ruby's room for you. Let me take your suitcase."

"That's okay, Dear. I've got it." She set down her black suitcase at the threshold to Ruby's bedroom. "Now, take a step back. Let me look at you."

I instinctively straightened, stiff as a soldier ready for inspection, and hooked my thumbs into the front pocket of my jeans. How I hoped my outfit of a loose-fitting red sweater and a sterling butterfly pin that Ruby and Lisa had given to me for Christmas would live up to her scrutiny! To me it seemed dressed up.

"You look pretty," she said. "Tired, but pretty. You might want to rethink those bangs. Is that the style now?"

Brushing the wispy bangs from my forehead, I tried to brush aside her comment as well. Somehow I was never quite good enough. "You look beautiful, Mother. I don't think I've ever seen you invest so much time in yourself."

"That's because you've stopped investing time in your looks, Dear. A little make-up wouldn't hurt."

"Maybe you can give me some for graduation, Mom." I walked toward the kitchen hoping to mask my annoyance. "Make-up doesn't really play in this world."

"You should see your sister these days," she said following me. Her high heels clacked on the hardwood floors. "She's moved in with her boss. He's head of the Audiology and Speech Pathology Department down there in Memphis."

"I've heard. He's like, what, twenty years older than Janette?"

"Yes, well," she said, opening the refrigerator, "I can't say I approve. But it has sure made her clean up her act. You wouldn't recognize her. Janette wears more gold jewelry than Cleopatra and talks about fancy restaurants and trips to Bermuda."

"Are you looking for something in particular?"

"Wine in a box?"

"College delicacy," I said. "Want some?"

"You bet."

We polished off the box while baking sugar cookies and then ate the entire batch in front of Ruby's tiny, black and white television watching *It's A Wonderful Life*. By the time Bedford Falls returned to normal and Jimmy Stewart ran screaming through the snowy streets shouting Merry Christmas to all, my head rested heavily on my mother's lap. She combed her long fingers through my unruly strands.

Each stroke conjured faint reminders of my childhood. They were feelings only my mother could stir, like memories of Christmases past when I still believed in Santa Claus. Like when I believed the full moon followed me as I glared at it through the dark windows in the backseat of a Pontiac. Like when I still had a father.

"Do you have to leave in the morning?" I asked through a yawn.

"I can stay until afternoon," she had said. "I think it's less than four hours to Memphis. But I do want to get there while it's still Christmas. I don't suppose you want to come with me. Janette's rich boyfriend is bound to have more than one spare bedroom."

"No thanks," I said. "Janette wouldn't want me hanging around. Besides, my friend Joel is coming back in a day or so and, well, I've got to take care of George."

"Who's Joel? Is he a boyfriend?"

"No," I laughed. "Not a boyfriend. Just a friend. I've known him for a while—actually, since high school. He used to go out with Lara Romano. We have the same major so we've been studying together lately."

"Just a friend, huh?" murmured my mother suspiciously.

"Yes, mother. Just a friend."

The first words out of my mother's mouth on Christmas morning were, "you look tired."

"Thank you. And merry Christmas, Mom," I said kissing her. "What time are you planning to take off for Memphis?"

"Earlier than I thought. The weather report is calling for snow. And since I'm only going to spend tonight and maybe one more night with Janette, I had better get a move on. I didn't even bring a pair of boots."

"Snow? We rarely have snow here. And you're traveling south."

"Farther south than you know. I'm going down to Long Boat Key."

"Is that a Florida Key?"

"Sort of. It's an island on the gulf coast. Near Sarasota. Mr. Hutchinson, the bank president, told me about a condo for sale in his building and I'm actually thinking about it for my retirement. Sure you don't want to come with me?"

"Thanks, Mom. But no. Let me know what happens."

She slipped me fifty bucks before she left. "Buy yourself something decent," she said. I tucked the bills in my pocket, watched her drive down our cobblestone street, and the feeling of loneliness took over.

It was the kind of loneliness one can only feel on a holiday like Christmas.

My mother had been right about the weather forecast. That night snow fell like salt pouring into my lonely wounds. I tried to like the feeling of being solitary—tried to wrap it up in a pretty bow of sophistication. From my bedroom window I watched fat flakes float through the air and allowed a certain melancholy to take over my spirit. Snow was romantic on Christmas Eve. On Christmas night and beyond, it only became something to shovel.

I fell asleep and dreamed of how I might spend the fifty bucks my mom had given me, and when I awoke, I knew I never again wanted to spend Christmas alone.

The snow fell for two days. It covered the streets and shrouded everything in a thick blanket of white. When it finally stopped and the sun attempted to shine through holes in the thick, gray clouds, I cleared the walkways surrounding our house and walked with George through the drifts of the neighboring sidewalks. George lunged at squirrels and rabbits and I reined him in while humming the "Twelve Days of Christmas," rearranging the words by counting the days until Ruby and Lisa were scheduled to return. Visions of them singing and dancing in our living room, pouring wine, and laughing filled my head.

I also thought of Joel and heard my mother's voice: *"Just a friend, huh?"*

At the end of our street, I turned right and walked toward his house. Joel and his roommate, Kim Harper, lived in another Arlen Sabljak house only two blocks away from me and two blocks nearer to campus. The close proximity to campus made it easier for Kim to get to and from classes in the Technology building. I didn't know how he'd be able to get around in a wheelchair with all this snow. Was there such a thing as a sled chair? From what little I knew about Kim, I thought he'd probably be the one to invent something like that. According to Joel, Kim maintained a 4.0 grade point average, and Joel gave credit to his roommate for helping to make him a better student.

Joel had completed his general studies requirements in record time and then landed a coveted student job at the radio station, which made him consider changing his major from Journalism to Radio and Television. He did, after all, have a deep, liquid voice, perfect for radio.

In the weeks following our accidental phone encounter when I called the radio station to play "Name That Tune," Joel and I rekindled our friendship. We became study partners—spent many evenings going over our assignments and quizzing each other for exams. Our meeting place was always at his house where it was as quiet as a library.

I turned onto his street, another cobblestone lane lined with white, wooden houses, and stopped in front of his empty house. Snowdrifts leaned against the front porch and icicles hung from the eaves like long, jagged dinosaur teeth.

Our relationship had frozen into place. Would it be the same when he returned?

* * * * * * * *

The phone rang and startled me. It was the first time I'd heard it ring in over a week. I ran from my bedroom, my socks slipping on the hardwood floors, and lunged for the receiver. "Hello?"

"I'm back," said Joel. "Why don't you come over?"

My boots were on my feet so fast I didn't care that my socks were mismatched. As my heart raced with anticipation, I grabbed my backpack and threw in a few books. I couldn't go to his house without study materials.

George wagged his tail, expecting to go for a walk. "Not this time, buddy," I said unplugging the Christmas lights surrounding our front door. I patted his head and stepped into the cold.

Joel's face parted the curtains of his front window. He was waiting for me the same way George waited each time I left him behind. I climbed the wheelchair ramp leading to the porch of his house, stepping in footsteps that looked like they'd been made by the Abominable Snowman. When I reached the top, the door opened. We both breathed visible white clouds.

"Hi, you," I said, panting slightly and stamping the snow off my boots. I stepped inside and he kissed me lightly on the cheek.

"You're cold."

"No kidding. It's like Russia out there," I said, taking off my coat. I looked past him and saw Kim stationed in the living room like a piece of furniture. "Oh hi, Kim. I didn't know you were back too. How did you get up those stairs?"

"I carried him," said Joel. "And I promise I'll have the area cleared before morning."

"We drove down together," Kim said. "I drove. I can do some things for myself."

"Just a few things," said Joel.

"I'll leave you two alone," said Kim as he grabbed hold of his wheels, spun them forward and disappeared toward the back of the house.

"That was a little abrupt. Don't you think?" I asked in a hushed tone.

"What do you mean?"

"You don't think that was strange?"

"I don't know."

"Please, Joel. He was unquestionably cold."

"It's probably because he's a big fan of Anita. We had some words about it on the drive down."

"What words? Who's Anita?"

"Anita Dambra. You remember her from The Point. She and I, uh, she and I have been sort of together—I mean, dating—you know—for the last year or so."

I stiffened. Did he say he was dating Anita Dambra? Why hadn't he mentioned this before now? "I remember her," I said. "Black eyes? Bangor Hall?"

Joel nodded.

"You're *seeing* her? God! I can only imagine what she must think of me coming over here so often. She knows we're just friends, right? She's okay with that?"

"Why wouldn't she be?"

"Please," I sighed. "Back in the dorms she sneered every time she saw me talking to you."

"She didn't sneer," said Joel.

"Yeah, whatever." I tossed my coat on a chair. I looked around for a Kleenex. "I've seen that look on plenty of women's faces. I know when I'm not liked."

"What look?"

I shook my head, not wanting to explain. "It's not important. I didn't realize you were seeing someone, that's all. Don't you have any tissue?"

"This is a house of men, Noelle. We use toilet paper. Wait here, I'll get you some."

He disappeared momentarily behind the bathroom door and emerged with a wad of toilet tissue. "We leave the seat up too."

"Thanks for the warning," I said, wiping my nose. "So you and Anita Dambra, huh? I guess that answers any questions I might have had about what we've been doing together lately."

"What do you think we're doing together?"

"We're friends, right?"

"Of course. I've always had girls as friends. You've heard me talk of Maria."

"Yes, your neighbor, Maria. I remember you talking about her. Fine," I said, stuffing the used tissue into my front pocket. "So, am I like a Maria or an Anita? I mean, did you tell Anita we've been studying together?"

"Is that what we're doing together? Studying?" He stepped toward me and turned his head, drawing me into his watery gaze. His blue eyes were hypnotic and I felt utterly pinned in place, like a butterfly studying her captor. He looked tanned, and his hair was wispy and blond with natural sun-streaks, like a beach boy. I liked how the fine strands fell freely into his face, his soft, pure and kind face. And those lips! My God, they were so full and pale pink and . . . and . . . oh no. Was I about to be kissed?

*Noelle! Get a grip!*

"Wait a minute," I said, stepping back. "You should have told me you had a girlfriend."

Joel smiled widely, exposing the smile of a toothpaste commercial, and all at once he blinked—a tight squeeze—his eyes shutting and opening like a camera lens. He looked childlike and playful, like he was cooking up an idea. If we had been outside, I'd expect a snowball to hit me in the face.

I felt awkward. Not knowing what else to do, I turned away and paced around the room without direction. "Hey, do you know anything about marketing?" I asked. "I'm taking this stupid marketing class next semester and the course outline says I have to plug statistics into the mainframe computer at Faner Hall. I never thought I'd be one of those students walking around with a fat deck of orange computer cards, but I will be!"

"Noelle," whispered Joel. He walked toward me, grabbed both my hands in mid gesture and squeezed. "Stop talking about school."

"What do you mean stop talking about school? That's what we do. We talk about school."

"Not tonight we don't. Not now." He pulled me toward the large fraying sofa taking up most of the space in the living room and gestured for me to sit. "Listen," he said, "I've been wanting to do this for a long time. School doesn't start for another week. Why don't we do something else? How about . . . how about . . . I take you out to dinner."

"Uh," I stammered. "You mean, like a date?"

"Yes. A real date where I pay and everything."

*"Everything?* Well, I don't know about everything. What about Anita?"

He lifted our hands together and brushed wayward strands of hair away from his forehead. "She's in New Jersey," he said.

No one had offered to take me out on a real date since I entered college. My friends and I traveled in packs. We went to parties and passed the hat to buy a keg of beer; or we took in movies at the Student Center where we flashed our purple student ID cards—the same ones we once altered to make us appear old enough to buy liquor—and paid a buck for the show. The only restaurants in my realm were on the strip: Booby's for a sub sandwich; Burts, for a cucumber, sprouts, and cream cheese sandwich on pumpernickel; or Ahmed's Falafel and Gyros joint. If we wanted to splurge on dessert, there was the Dairy Queen where we could pick up a chocolate-chip, banana Blizzard, which we called a "C-squared/B-squared." Other than that we lived on Quatros pizza, nineteen-cent boxes of macaroni and cheese, and tins of tuna.

Joel's invitation had me thinking of white tablecloths, wine glasses, salad forks, and candles. It sounded sophisticated—like Janette's world.

"I'm free tomorrow night," I said, smiling.

\* \* \* \* \* \* \* \*

Joel rang my doorbell at six and George, who anticipated my excitement, barked and ran in circles around the living room. I felt my heart race as I opened the door where I found Joel standing on the porch wearing an army green parka. His nose was pink from the cold and he sniffed before he said hello. "Would you like to come in or should we just get going?" I asked.

"Let's go," he said. "I'm starved."

We rode in his burly Chevy Impala to the far west side of town and entered a Chinese restaurant, where Joel ordered nearly everything on the menu. We had pot-stickers, hot and sour soup, bean curd with Chinese mushrooms, lemon chicken over rice, Mongolian beef, Moo Shu pork, and two other bowls full of spicy things that I couldn't figure out—or pronounce. We fumbled with our chopsticks and didn't stop eating, talking, and laughing.

He was as easy to be with as Ruby or Lisa.

Halfway through the meal, however, the conversation shifted. Joel grew serious and stared at his plate for what seemed like a long time. With his chopsticks, he forced bits of chicken and grains of rice from one side of the plate to the other. Where I hadn't before, I noticed the plucking Chinese music trickling from the speakers like drops of water, and looked around the room at the stark décor.

"Noelle," he said, recapturing my attention, "why don't you ever talk about your father?"

"My father?"

"Yes, your father."

"I hardly knew him," I said lightly. "He died when I was very young. So young that I'm not sure he really existed."

"I wish my father never existed. The bastard."

I set down my chopsticks. "Well, except for that, you don't talk about your father either."

"That's because he took off during my first year of school. It's why I didn't come back. I had to go to work to afford my tuition. Didn't you notice I wasn't in town?"

I nodded. Of course I had noticed. The last time I had seen him before he disappeared, he professed his love for me. No one—no man—had ever before said those words to me. Drunk or sober.

"Joel, I'm not sure what to say. I think. . . ." The waitress cut through my words as she reached between us and removed an empty dumpling plate. We watched as she robotically moved away, in step with the music, which now seemed louder.

"It's just one more thing we have in common," said Joel. "We're both fatherless children." He shoveled clump after clump of the spicy, no-name dish into his mouth and sweat formed on his brow.

"Yeah, well, if that's the way you want to look at it."

Abruptly, he changed the subject. "I can't believe what I thought was a summer job on the trading floor could so easily turn into a career."

"But did you like it? I mean, wasn't it good making money and getting promotions?"

"Sure, but I knew I wanted to go back to school. I was thinking I might somehow incorporate a reporting job with the commodities market."

Ideas flashed like blinking Christmas lights over his head, and I continually asked questions, drawing him out, interviewing him like a reporter. I felt his passion and his sense of direction. His excitement was infectious.

"C'mon," he said after paying the bill. "Let's go uptown and shoot pool."

"I'm a terrible pool player," I said.

"Perfect," he said. "So am I."

As the snow fell from the darkness above us, we drove to town and parked across the street from Gatsby's pool hall, an underground watering hole. The stubborn Impala jumped and snorted and didn't want to turn off. Joel pumped the gas pedal, and as the engine hiccoughed, I stamped my cold feet on the floor, trying to feel my toes. The car continued its tantrum— gasping, moaning, and clinking—and Joel was patient, obviously accustomed to its quirks. I watched the wipers hesitate along with the engine as clumps of snowflakes hit the windshield. When the engine finally gave in, the wipers stopped on their way up and were instantly buried with snow.

"Get out this way," said Joel. "There's a snow bank on your side." He stepped out of the car and reached for my hand. Taking it, he pulled me out and into the puffy arms of his parka. "C'mon," he laughed. "Let's get inside."

The normally busy street was empty of traffic and pedestrians as we crossed. And before we reached the snow bank on the other side, Joel stopped. He took off his gray, rag-wool gloves and jammed them into his pockets.

"What are you doing?" I asked, looking over his shoulder for oncoming cars.

He put his hands on my cold cheeks and I felt snowflakes land on my nose. Then he smiled and pulled my face to his.

Very softly and very briefly, he kissed me.

"There," he said. "I wanted to get that out of the way. I knew I was going to kiss you at some point this evening and I guess I just couldn't wait any longer. Now c'mon," he said. "I'm freezing."

"Not so fast," I said. "It's my turn." I lunged into his pillow soft jacket and pressed my freezing cheeks next to his smooth face. For another second, we stood in the middle of that snow-covered street, face-to-face, eye-to-eye. I closed my eyes and kissed him. It was long and deep—a kiss like I'd never before given. And even before it was over, I somehow knew I'd never live a moment like that again.

# 16.
# Joel. 1982.

Noelle gave me a book for Christmas, *One Hundred Years of Solitude*. She said it was on her top ten list, and I believed if I read it, I would learn more about her. On the morning after our date, I opened it, slumped into a chair next to the front window and was at once met with a complicated family tree. Hmmm. Would I like reading a book that required a road map of the characters? It felt a little like studying.

I read about a young man seeing ice for the first time and my mind wandered. I pulled back the curtain and stared at the long icicles hanging in front of the glass like a protective cage. It was a gray day and more snow was expected. I conjured up childhood memories of winter break—days filled with sledding at a place we called the "British Hill" and ice skating on Salt Creek. We always fought with the neighborhood girls who wanted to use the space for figure skating while we suited up in our Chicago Black Hawks hockey gear found under the Christmas tree.

I shivered as frigid air seeped through the panes of my bedroom windows. The room was formerly a front porch, but Arlen Sabljak, the landlord, had a crew turn it into a bedroom and there was no insulation. I could hang meat in this room. Pressing my face to the glass and exhaling a cloud onto the window, I drew a tic-tac-toe grid and saw a car pull up and stop abruptly. A figure emerged from the driver's side and made its way around the front of the car. Using my palm I cleared the glass and at once drew back, reacting to what felt like an electrical shock.

It was Anita. She wasn't supposed to be back for another week.

*One Hundred Years of Solitude* fell to the floor. Glancing down, it looked as sinful as contraband. Anita would see it. She'd read the inscription. She'd know. Without another thought, I kicked it under the bed and rushed to the front door.

"Anita," I started breathlessly. "What are you. . . ." I stopped. Her face was pale. Her eyebrows in a tight, angry knit. I opened the screen door and reached for her. "What's the matter?"

"I'm pregnant," she said. "I'm not coming in right now, I just came here to tell you." Without waiting for me to respond, she turned and headed down the ramp with the same speed in which she had ascended it.

"Anita!" I said, stepping into the cold and trying in vain to grab the sleeve of her jacket. The cold air hit me full on and I lost my breath. "Wait a minute," I managed.

She continued toward her car.

"Stop! What the hell are you doing?"

"I found out on Christmas morning," she said. Her voice was thin and her eyes glazed over, two dark orbs. "How do you like that? It was a great big merry fucking Christmas surprise and I spent the entire break puking up my figgy pudding. My parents thought it was the flu."

"What?" I asked in disbelief. Again, I reached for her arm and she abruptly pulled it away. I dropped my head, not knowing what to say.

This couldn't be happening.

My toes curled under, fighting to stay warm inside a thin pair of socks. I stood as still as a snowman with an unmovable mouth, hugging my frozen torso.

Anita continued moving toward her car and I once again tried to grab hold of her arm. "Anita, you've got to talk to me about this. Why didn't you call me when you first found out?"

"I needed time for it to sink in. Time before I said it out loud."

"Wow. Well, I think I know the feeling."

"Don't tell me you know the feeling. You *don't* know the feeling."

"Anita," I said shaking my head, "This baby *is* mine, right?"

She squinted her eyes and the white breath that shot from her nose in a quick burst made her look like a bull ready to charge. "That was the *exact* wrong thing to say," she spit through tight, narrow lips. She yanked her arm from my grasp and trudged through the snow to her car. Slamming the door, snow fell from the car roof in a large clump and she sped off without looking at me. As her taillights disappeared around the corner, I looked down at her footprints in the snow. They were elongated and strangely non-human.

"Hey, man," called Kim from behind me. "Was that Anita?"

In my stupor, I turned and saw his wheelchair filling the front door. I really needed to get the ramp and the walkway shoveled for him. "No," I said. "I mean, yes. Yes, it was Anita."

"What's going on?" he asked. "Did she find out about you and Noelle?"

"Son of a. . . ." I said, stomping up the ramp toward the door—toward him. I leaned over and put my hands on his arm rails. My face felt like it was going to melt. "No wonder she was so pissed off. Did you tell her I was seeing Noelle?"

"Back off, man," said Kim. "What's the matter with you?" He wheeled himself backward into the room, and my hands fell to my knees. I kept them there. Stooped over, I looked at him from the doorway. His long hair rested on his shoulders and he hadn't shaved in so long it looked like he was growing a beard. "Shut the door," he said. "It's freezing."

I stood up, kicked the door closed, and buried my face in my numb hands. "Fuck ME!" I yelled through my fingers. "I'm such an idiot!"

"You had to know you were getting yourself in trouble," said Kim, poised in the center of the room. "I didn't say anything to her. But there are plenty of ways she could have found out."

"Oh just shut up for a second," I said. "It's not Noelle. It has nothing to do with Noelle." I walked into the kitchen and tore a paper towel off the rack and blew my nose. Kim followed me. "She's pregnant. Anita's pregnant," I said.

"Oh shit," said Kim. "Bummer. Guess I didn't call that one." He leaned his head back so that his Adam's apple pointed upward like a directional signal, and then he let out a small laugh.

"You think this is funny?"

"Kind of," he said. "It's the thing that's *not* supposed to happen."

"No shit," I said.

"Haven't you two heard about birth control?"

"I figured she was on the pill. If I hadn't gotten her pregnant in a year, how could it happen now?"

"That's using your head," he said sarcastically. "You're sure it's yours?"

"That's why she left here even more angry than when she came," I said. I wiped my nose again with the rough paper towel. "I asked her if it was mine."

"Oops," said Kim, turning his wheels. "Well, you had to ask." He laughed again and then shook his head. "Man, it's hard to picture you as a daddy."

I bit the inside of my cheek. It was a nervous habit I'd had since I can remember, and I'd done it so much in the last few years that I'd actually developed calluses on each side of my mouth. "There's no way I'm ready to raise a baby right now. NO WAY!"

I didn't even think of a baby—a real live human being—until that moment. Anita said the word "pregnant" and I only thought of myself. My stupid, horrified, humiliated, and embarrassed self. This was the last thing I wanted to deal with on the verge of my twenty-first birthday. I wasn't ready to be a father. Shit!

"You should be thinking about Anita right now," said Kim. "She's the one in trouble. You just helped get her that way."

"Anita!" I gasped, and ran toward the front door, knowing I had to follow her.

I grabbed my coat from the closet, stepped into a pair of rubber boots, and ran for the door. Once outside I reached into the pockets for my gloves, and an image came to mind of Anita's New Jersey father standing behind me with a sawed-off shotgun shoved up my ass while I said "I DO!" to a white-clad bride the size of a house.

My car engine thankfully fired up on the first try. Pulling the gearshift into drive, the word "abortion" rang inside my head like a warped church bell. I pressed the accelerator and headed toward Anita's house.

I had money. I'd offer to pay for it. It couldn't cost more than two hundred? Three hundred? Who would know the going rate for an abortion? Is that kind of stuff published somewhere? Would she do such a thing? Shit, would I?

When I get there, I thought, suddenly aware of the icy streets on which I drove, I'll be supportive. I gripped the wheel tighter. I'll tell her it's her decision and I will support whatever she decides. Yes, supportive. Kind. Not like my father. I'm not a bastard. I'm not like him.

She'll have to choose abortion, I told myself. "She has to!" I said, banging my hands against the steering wheel. Anita had only one semester left before graduation and had a job lined up at the Botanic Gardens up north. She wouldn't want to spoil all that with a kid!

I slammed the gearshift into park and walked toward Anita's front door with my head down. I told myself again that I was there to be supportive.

And when I looked up, I saw her standing on the front porch with her arms open. She was waiting for me.

# 17.
# Noelle. 1982.

Each time a new semester begins there's a shuffling of schedules and a period of adjustment. It means pristine notebooks and textbooks—that is if you can afford to buy new instead of used—and all kinds of reasons to panic before settling into a new routine. I spent the first few weeks having nightmares where I couldn't find my classroom, or I had forgotten about a big project due that day.

Ruby, Lisa, and I posted our schedules on the refrigerator. We were less concerned about the classes listed than we were about whether or not we'd all be able to meet for lunch and watch our soap, *All My Children.* Together we made up a three-person Liza Colby fan club, and each day we loved to hate this snobby character as she interfered in the love affairs of Pine Valley.

I had only two important classes left before graduation: Journalism History and the Advertising and Marketing class I regretted taking from the minute I enrolled. My counselor said learning the basics of marketing would be helpful in any occupation I chose. I supposed she was right, however, I hated selling anything. It made me feel pushy.

My schedule included an introduction to Stage Acting, which was filled primarily with freshmen theater majors. It made me the *grande dame* of the classroom. I also took Horseback Riding, which fulfilled my last required Physical Education credit. And finally, the best blow-off credits of my college career came from the equivalent of underwater basket weaving—a crafts class.

Crafts class was held in the basement of the oldest building on campus, home to the funky and talented art students.

Campus standouts, my instructors were like original works of art themselves. There was Julia, the fabric witch, who constantly brewed up some potion for dying bed sheets vivid colors. She hung them outside the building where they flapped in the wind like exultant, Christo banners. And there was Jake. He called himself "Mr. Multi-Media," and incorporated a little bit of, well, everything into his work: photography, paint, fibers, metals, etc. Eccentric and probably seriously disturbed, he always exposed a toothy grin and offered to show the women in his class his latest etchings.

Our first crafts project was papermaking. It was a useful method of recycling a lot of past term papers, class syllabi, and old notebooks. Since my mother didn't allow me to store my college papers at her home, I had accumulated boxes and boxes of my education and enjoyed the paper shredding process.

By the second week of class, square sheets of handmade paper covered my bedroom walls like patchwork wallpaper.

"Haven't you made enough paper?" asked Lisa. "There's no place left to hang it."

"I'm just starting on my second semester sophomore year notebook. Want me to do your room next?"

"Don't go near my room with that stuff. The potion looks like vomit," she said.

I stood atop a stack of blue plastic milk crates that I used as bookshelves and stretched to the highest part of the wall. Turning around, I saw both my roommates standing just inside my room. Their arms were crossed and they looked at me like I'd gone crazy. "Where are you two going so early on a Saturday?"

"To the National. Need any milk or anything?"

"Could you get me some more liquid starch? I use it in the paper recipe."

"Sure," said Ruby. "I like your paper. You should bundle it and make stationery."

"Don't fall off those milk crates while we're out," called Lisa. "And I still say it smells like vomit."

I heard the door close and stepped down off my makeshift ladder. George wandered into my room, sauntered up to me, and licked my palm. "Hi, buddy," I said. "It's nice outside today. Maybe we can go for a walk later." Checking my desk calendar to see if I had anything planned, I realized it was the last Saturday in January. How did we get to the end of the month so quickly?

Sitting, I went through the squares, the days of January, and counted back three weeks. It had been three weeks since I last spoke to Joel.

I'd be lying if I said I hadn't noticed he didn't call after our date. Surely he'd had as good a time as I.

My stomach tingled as I thought about our brief, romantic icebreaker in the middle of the street. I smiled, remembering the ten games of pool that followed the kiss. Neither of us wanted the night to end. And he had lied about not being a good pool player—an old pool shark line, he finally admitted. He showed me how to hold the pool cue and we drank glass after glass of beer until the room grew fuzzy. I remember laughing. A lot. Just before we left to again brave the cold and snow, we stole a full glass of beer and smuggled it out the door inside his rag-wool glove. We drank from it together, calling it our "well insulated goblet."

"I loved tonight," was the last thing he had said.

I had loved it too. And I was sure I loved him. A lot had happened since he first told me he loved me that day in my dorm room. But did he mean it then? And did he love me now? He didn't say. Instead he had said, "I loved *tonight.*"

It must be because of Anita.

"He has a girlfriend," I said to George.

But do guys with girlfriends take other girls out to dinner? Do they kiss them in the middle of a snow-covered street?

I pulled a piece of handmade paper hanging on my wall and set it on my desk. Flipping through a notebook, I searched for a poem I had started writing the day after our date. With a blue felt-tip marker I tried my best hand at calligraphy by copying the lines on the bumpy paper. The words, in blue, trickled down the page like snowflakes, and I was happy with the end result.

I attached it to a multi-layered piece of navy blue felt, which acted as a frame.

"C'mon, George," I said. "We're going for a walk."

George immediately sprang into action. He found his leash, stored in the corner next to the front door, and panted expectantly as it dangled from his mouth. When I opened the door, he burst outside and ran to the corner and back three times before I reached it. Together we turned toward Joel's house.

I knocked on the door and waited. Nothing. I knocked again and peeked through the glass looking for movement. Clearly, no one was home. I decided to leave the bag with the poem tucked inside against his front door.

George, who sat on the sidewalk below the wheelchair ramp, waited patiently for me. "Good boy," I called, and he sprang up the ramp and planted his damp paws on my stomach. I hooked the leash to his collar for the walk home. Looking back once, I had the urge to take back the poem. But I didn't. It was like dropping a letter in the mailbox. Once you leave it, you live with it.

I took a deep breath and slowly walked back toward my house with the carefree knowledge of no schedule lying ahead for the rest of the day.

The snow had almost completely disappeared. There were still small patches clinging to street corner curbs where giant piles created by the town's snowplow stood only weeks before. But a dramatic warming occurred in the past few days and rivers of melting snow flooded the streets, filling the air with the sound of a tinkling waterfall and the smell of earth. Everything was mushy and as damp as a terrarium. Around the bases of mature sycamore and oak trees, daffodils and tulips poked through the ground weeks ahead of schedule.

I wore my winter coat but noticed others walking around in sweatshirt jackets and even short-sleeved shirts. This was how people got sick, I thought. It happened every year. Everyone wanted spring to come so much they willed it into existence by breaking out their happier and lighter wardrobes.

George pulled me toward a tree and lifted his leg. I wondered if those daffodils and tulips stood a chance. Would it be another early spring like the spring we had freshman year at The Point?

Feeling the need to keep walking, I passed the street leading to my house, and once again thought about Joel and the night of our date. As George pulled me off the sidewalk to yet another tree, it dawned on me that his statement—I loved *tonight*—had sounded so final, like it was the fulfillment of a last wish before a death sentence. Or like he made me Cinderella for an evening and then scurried away before the stroke of midnight defined his true fate. Maybe I should have left behind a glass slipper.

It had been too long since I heard from him. I yanked on George's leash and walked a little faster, wondering what—if anything—was happening between us. Did we have a future together?

Just then a couple rounded the corner, catching my attention. They walked toward me, arm-in-arm, and when I recognized them, I stopped.

The girl's jacket was open and her shirt screamed the word, "NO!"

# 18.
# Joel. 1982.

"It was that Noelle, wasn't it?" said Anita. "She ran!"

"What are you talking about?"

"Please, Joel. You didn't see her take off and run with a big yellow dog?"

"Anita, I don't know who that was," I lied.

"It was Noelle. That redhead from the dorms. I know it."

She was right, of course, and I wanted to run after her. But I couldn't. Instead I squeezed Anita's hand a little tighter. I couldn't leave her—not after what we'd gone through together.

Anita had decided to have an abortion the moment she found out she was pregnant. She confessed she sprang it on me the way she did just to see my reaction. It was a test that I had failed, which made me adamant about trying to make it up to her. I didn't want her or anyone to think I wasn't willing to take responsibility for my actions.

I drove her to a clinic in the town of Marion that, of all people, her Nana had told us about. And it was horrible. As we sat in the purgatorial waiting room, it felt like I was waiting outside the principal's office. I prepared myself for a reprimand.

The door opened and a nurse who was shaped like an outhouse stepped into the room. "Ms. Dambra?" she had called without taking her eyes away from the clipboard in her pudgy hands.

"Yes," said Anita in a small voice. "I'm here."

I instinctively rose with Anita, and the nurse looked up. Her dark eyebrows pointed into an evil V and her narrow gaze burrowed into me.

"You sit tight," she barked.

I quickly looked away from her and into Anita's pale face—her ruined expression.

"I'm scared," she said, whispering.

"I know. I'm sorry," I said.

"Today, please!" snapped the nurse. She kicked open the door with her foot and they both disappeared behind it.

All I could do was wait. And so I did. I sat in a room where hundreds of sorry-ass guys like myself had sat before, doing time like a prison sentence.

I looked around. Everything was upholstered in a harsh shade of orange. Framed posters on the walls showed couples holding hands and had headlines reading things like "Plan Your Family."

Unable to relax, I got up and shuffled through the magazines fanned out on a glass coffee table. *Newsweek, Time, Sports Illustrated* . . . I guessed they knew their audience. I flipped through an old edition of *Newsweek* without reading any of the articles. All I could think about was whether or not I should burst through that door and stop the procedure. I'd marry Anita and we'd move up to Chicago and have that baby. I'd go back to work at the Board of Trade and Anita could still work at the Botanic Gardens. My mom would help us work out the babysitting. We could make it work.

I stared at the door. And stared, and stared. I was frozen.

"It's my decision," Anita had said. "You know this is the best thing to do."

Did I?

Anita and I approached the corner. Walking atop Noelle's recent footsteps, I felt her presence. I hadn't seen her since that night—that wonderful, winter night when we finally connected. Stepping off the curb and onto the cobblestone, I craned my neck and looked down the street toward her house. Nothing. All was quiet and there was no sign of her.

I couldn't help myself. I sighed.

"What?" asked Anita, stopping at the corner.

"Hmm?"

"What's the matter? You look far away."

"I'm not," I said. "I'm here. Let's go to my house and open a bottle of Carlo Rossi."

"Can't," she said. "I've got to get to the greenhouse. I'm helping the new T.A. with his hybrids for lab on Monday."

"I thought we were spending the day together."

"I'll call you after," she said. "Thanks for lunch." Then she kissed my cheek and turned toward campus.

I watched her walk on the cracked and slanted sidewalk. The spring was back in her step. Her stride was long and her arms dangled at her side, carefree.

She disappeared around the next corner, and I turned and looked again toward Noelle's house. Still no sign of her. I replayed the memory of her turning from us and bolting like a deer shocked by headlights on a back-road highway. Her red hair flew through the air, a blowtorch of color.

I stood on that corner for too many minutes, indecisively wondering which way to go. I didn't call her after Anita told me the news. But Noelle hadn't called me either. I didn't know what was going on between us.

A voice inside my head told me to go home.

I arrived at my house and ascended the ramp instead of the stairs. About to open the door, I looked down and saw a yellow 710 Bookstore bag leaning against it. "What's this?" I said out loud. I picked it up and peeked inside. It looked like a small, wool rag. Reaching inside, I pulled it out, and stared at the colorful, confusing creation in my hands. It was a slab of thick, blue wool and a piece of paper with the consistency of oatmeal placed on top of it. Written in a delicate hand, there was a poem. It was called, "A Winter Encounter."

The words traveled down the page like soft, blue water drops. I scanned them from top to bottom, knowing it was from Noelle. She must have just dropped it off. She must have walked over, leaned it against the door, and walked home. And then she saw Anita and me together.

I sat down on a paint-chipped Adirondack chair and read the words aloud:

*"A Winter Encounter . . .*

> *Two beings ignoring the cold*
> *And sipping from a well-insulated goblet.*
> *Sharing complexities while*
> *Building on instincts.*
> *Traveling to an unknown place.*
> *A long clear vision of*
> *Warmness is exchanged*
> *Between out-stretched arms*
> *And enterprising minds.*

*Dispositions are easily*
*Understood with*
　　*Expressions so*
　　　*Limitlessly expressed.*
*Technicalities become trivial*
*As the two come together.*
*Vacancy does not exist.*
　　　*The outside is inside*
　　*Yet remains insulated*

　*While the two cling to*
　*The comfort of warmth."*


My eyes filled with tears. "Noelle," I whispered. A tear fell from my eye and landed on the letter "D" of the word, "Dispositions," turning it into a puddle of blue ink.

# 19.
# Noelle. 1982.

I scampered down the middle of the street as fast as a jack-rabbit, feeling my feet pound against the irregular cobblestones and jarring my insides with each stride. I didn't stop until I reached my front door. Pressing my body against the rusty screen as though hiding, I fumbled for the keys attached to my belt loop. I didn't dare look back down the street. I didn't want to see them together again—to see Anita's smile and the word "NO!" across her chest.

I couldn't believe Joel had given her that shirt. It might as well have been an engagement ring for the way it made me feel. It was like being slapped without the benefit of seeing the hand coming toward my face. Or like a car accident when I didn't realize another vehicle was about to crash into me until it had already happened.

Betrayal. Humiliation. Stupidity. It was an icy, bitter cocktail. George, panting at my side, barked as I tried to turn my key in the lock. Finally the door opened—that front door lock always gave me trouble—and George rushed past me, going directly to his water bowl. I dropped his leash in the corner and then threw myself on my unmade bed. My chest rose and fell as I tried to catch my breath. I stared at the stained ceiling tiles and saw the word NO! I felt the word NO! I rolled to my side and looked at my desk, the place where I had spent the morning creating the gift for Joel.

"Oh, no!" I said, sitting up. "That stupid poem!" How could my humiliation get any worse? I got up, paced around the room and then heard the front door open again. Ruby and Lisa were home and I heard the rustling of brown paper grocery bags.

"Noelle?" called Ruby. "You here?"

"In here."

Both their faces dropped when they saw me. "What happened to you?" asked Ruby.

"You look like you saw a ghost," said Lisa.

"It was a ghost all right," I said. "A banshee! And it screamed the word "NO" at me!"

"Are you okay?" they asked together.

The floodgates opened and I raged like a river providing hydroelectric power on a hot day. Enough electricity pumped from my pores to power a small town. I told them about my date with Joel and how wonderful it had been and how I hadn't heard from him since, even though I thought we really connected. I told them about the poem—GOD! That ridiculous poem—and how I saw them together. And the tee-shirt . . . and the sense of betrayal . . . and how silly I felt for thinking he was ending it with her . . . and that we were going to be together . . . and . . . I couldn't stop babbling.

"You want to take this one?" said Lisa to Ruby.

"Sure. Go open a bottle of something." Ruby transferred her bag to Lisa, grabbed my hand and led me out of my room and into the living room. "Sit," she said.

I did what I was told and slumped into our thin-cushioned and lopsided sofa. The threadbare Indian tapestry used as a slipcover pulled from the corners and one corner fell over my shoulder. George perked up his ears, trotted over and sat in front of me. His large, dopey face snuggled between my knees and he let out low moans as if to say, "Pet me."

"You're in love with him, aren't you?" asked Ruby.

"No!" I said, too quickly. "I mean, I don't know. I thought I might be but there's no way now—now that I know he was just using me while Anita was back in New Jersey. I just assumed he was going to end it with her, and I guess I didn't even care until today that it's been three lousy weeks since I've heard from him. I feel so stupid. Especially because I thought we were friends."

"Men suck," said Lisa, who carried three glasses of white wine. "You can't be friends with them. Don't you know that?"

"You have guy friends, Lisa," I said.

"Yeah, but none of them are as cute as Joel. C'mon. Forget him. Let's get drunk."

"You didn't sleep with him, did you?" asked Ruby.

"No, thank God." I picked up the glass and took a big sip—too big and some wine spilled down my chin and onto my shirt.

"Look at me. I can't even drink wine." I shook my head.

"What?" asked Lisa.

"I just liked him," I said. "I liked him a lot. He was so easy to talk with—and we talked about everything."

"Not *quite* everything," commented Ruby. "Sounds like you didn't discuss that sow Anita Dambra too much. I remember her from the dorms. She always gave me the once over and was so jealous whenever I talked with Joel."

"Lisa's right. Let's just forget it," I said. "Let's forget Joel, forget Anita, and forget all of it. This is my last semester and I'm headed for pomp and circumstance and an official B.S. degree."

"For BULL-SHIT!" sang Ruby and Lisa together.

"Let's put on some tunes."

"Okay," I said. "I'm going to put him out of my mind. The same way I did after his drunken Marlon Brando afternoon at the dorms."

"They're not worth it," said Ruby.

"Men leave," said Lisa.

"Men die," I said.

Ruby walked to the stereo and picked up a tape. "Think of it this way," she said. "Men are like cassette tapes. When you get sick of them, you can just rewind and tape over it with better music." At once the room filled with dance music from Little Feat, and we set down our glasses and turned our living room into a dance floor.

Ruby and Lisa and I lived for music. Our evenings out were filled with performances by our favorite bar bands: Terrapin Station, who played Grateful Dead covers and Lisa once sang with; and Swing Set, whom we particularly loved for the Commander Cody tune they always dedicated to us; and a punk band called Cal and the Current Events, which Ruby turned us onto because she was sweet on the lead guitarist. We always sang and blasted our stereo and attended every concert that came to campus with my free tickets.

The next two months leading to graduation went by quickly and I never saw Joel. With only one class in the communications building and my afternoons spent at the newspaper, our schedules failed to coincide. I thought I saw him once in the distance, but I quickly moved in another direction. Since he didn't call, I knew he had no intention of being my friend—let alone my boyfriend. He had Anita, I had my studies, and before I knew it, May arrived and I collected a royal blue cap and gown, brought it home, and paraded it around the living room. Since Lisa didn't plan to graduate until August and Ruby still had another year—as long as she didn't switch majors again—they fawned over me on my graduation day, dressing me like I was the bride and they were my attendants.

My mother and Janette showed up for my graduation—an affair with little pomp and circumstance. I was one of many seated in a metal folding chair on the floor of the arena, who stood and hollered when our particular school—the School of Journalism—was named. Mortarboards and champagne corks sailed through the air, and my newspaper pals and I snapped pictures of each other before wandering off to lunch dates with our parents and siblings.

Janette was no fun. She should have stayed home. She was currently between homes and out of sorts because she had just broken up with her boss. (What a relief!) She intended to swear off men and I toasted her on that thought.

My mother, however, was in good spirits. She didn't even comment on my hair or my makeup-free face. Together, she and Janette gave me a three-quarter carat diamond pendant as a graduation gift and a check for five hundred dollars.

"I still can't believe you want to move all the way to California," Mom had said. "But you'll need this when you get there."

"Wow," I said. "Thanks. But Lara's not expecting me until August, when she moves into her new place in Berkeley."

"Why do you want to live with Lara Romano in Berkeley?" asked Janette. "I hear it's a slum."

"It's not a slum," I protested. "Honestly Janette, your standards have gotten way out of control." Her nose was turned up in distaste from the moment she entered our house. Apparently the new lifestyle had altered her idea of good taste. She may have left the man and sworn off men, but she had tasted riches, and it was a hard place to leave.

"What are you going to do for money in the meantime?" she asked.

"I got a job working on production for the alumni magazine this summer and it pays top dollar."

"What's top dollar?" asked my mother.

"Four-ten an hour. I know it sounds like nothing," I added quickly. "But it's the highest student wage right now."

I was excited about moving to California and living with Lara. I hadn't seen her in over two years, but we kept in touch through letters and occasional long, expensive phone calls. She finished her liberal arts degree at Mills College and planned to attend the University of California, "Cal," as she always called it like it were an old friend, in a Master's program in business administration. Unable to swallow the corporate sound of the letters M-B-A, she assured me it wasn't an MBA program, just a master's degree that happened to be in the business department. Lara, even more liberal since she moved to the Bay Area, wanted to work in a non-profit sector and thought about pursuing the issue of public health. There were lots of jobs in San Francisco, she said, and I would have no trouble finding one.

While all the engineering and computer science students went off to high paying jobs in the Golden Triangle cities—Chicago, Houston and Denver—Ruby and Lisa said they'd like to move to California too. Eventually.

I didn't want to imagine life without them, but I wanted to leave Carbondale. Once I had my degree in hand, I felt I no longer belonged there. Class was OVER and I was tired of being hungry and broke. I had lost so much weight during my last two years of school that I was once again shaped like a needle. My hipbones protruded from my frame like a skeleton and were often bruised as I constantly bumped into doorframes, always in a hurry to get somewhere. But I still had one last hot Midwestern summer, and I decided to stay with Ruby and Lisa in our Arlen Sabljak house on the cobblestone street.

I enrolled in a creative writing class. It was a small group, consisting of students of all ages—undergraduates, graduates, adults. The instructor was a salt-and-pepper-haired poet who asked us to call him "Creth." No one knew if it was his first name or last. No one cared. Our biggest concern was with the length of our fellow classmates' stories. Anything over ten pages was guaranteed to raise a groan.

After class I rode my bike to the newspaper office where we put together the alumni publication. I worked in the same room as my now former coworkers at the *Daily Egyptian,* a pared-down group that stuck around for the summer to continue pumping out thin, daily papers. At night Ruby, Lisa, and I either sat on our porch swing and watched the events unfold in our neighborhood, or sat on someone else's porch swing and watched their neighbors. Someone was always walking home from town with a brown bag full of beer and passed them to us like we were kids looking for trick-or-treat handouts.

It was August—the dog days—and just when I thought it couldn't get any hotter, it did. Ruby and Lisa were off somewhere one evening while I sat on the porch swing praying for a breeze. I had spent the afternoon tie-dying a sheet and hung this bright purple creation on the vacant plant hooks along the eave of the porch to dry, but the air was so damp that water droplets continued to amass below it, forming miniature, purple lakes.

"That's a great sheet," called a bearded man as he strode by.

"Thanks," I said, surprised to see him walking toward me. He reached out his hand and stroked the sheet, his eyes on a wide-eyed acid trip. "I made it today."

"I like knowing this is in the neighborhood," he said. And then he skipped away.

Another Carbondale character, I thought, shaking my head. I had to get out of town.

I heard the faint ringing of the phone and went inside to answer it.

"Hello?"

"It's me, Cleo."

Of course it was. No one else had a voice like that. "As I live and breathe," I said. "What's happening, Cleo?"

"I'm graduating in a couple days. Getting that degree in forestry and dig this! I'm *magna cum laude*. Ever since I left that hell dorm I've pulled nothing but A's. Can you stand it?"

"That's great. Good for you."

"Listen," she said. "I'm leaving for Colorado on the day after graduation to take a job with the forest service. I haven't seen you in too long. Since I started this whole adventure with you, I want you to come to my graduation. But in the meantime, c'mon over and we'll go out and celebrate."

Cleo still lived on the east side of town. It was a long walk, but I had nothing better to do than watch my fabric dry, so I leashed George and made my way to her apartment.

George looked regal in his purple collar and he trotted proudly in front of me as I held the matching purple leash loosely in my hand. The night air was sultry and my clothes were damp. I wore a jean skirt made from a pair of worn out Levi's, a white tank top and a pair of Birkenstocks, which Lara had sent as a graduation present. (They were all the rage in Berkeley, she said.) I braided my hair and tied the two ropes together in back of my head in a square knot. I couldn't stand the feeling of thick hair on my sweaty neck when it was so hot.

George led me across the train tracks dividing the east and west sides of town and I stopped at a busy street and waited for the traffic light to change. A car horn honked and some drunken guys yelled at me like I was a streetwalker. I was grateful to have an eighty-pound dog on a leash to protect me—just in case—since the side of town I was about to cross into was a bit removed from the womb. It was certainly closer to the real world than it was to campus.

The light changed. I crossed the street and walked into the bright lights of a gas station on the opposite corner, when an old blue car parked and facing the street, caught my eye. It looked like a cop car because it had a spot light dangling where the rearview mirror was supposed to be.

As I neared it, I saw the smiles of two men. Pulling George's leash, I stopped and narrowed my eyes, focusing on the growing smiles. "Do you see those guys?" I asked George. "Are you ready?"

One was behind the wheel and the other was behind a beard. I narrowed my eyes and momentarily thought I recognized them. "It can't be them," I said.

But it was. It was Joel Rolland and his former roommate, my old boyfriend, Don Juan Carver. "You've got to be kidding me," I said, laughing.

Don was the first to emerge from the car. "Noelle!" he called. "I *thought* that was you. See Joel? I told you."

"Donny the Moax," I said. "What are you doing here?"

"Living with Joel. I'm starting school again."

Joel stepped out of the car, smiled, and I zeroed in on his familiar white teeth. He didn't speak. He just looked at me. His blue eyes penetrated the night sky and looked right into my soul.

"Hello Joel," I said with a quickening heartbeat.

"I knew it was you all along," he said. "Get in this car."

Without thinking, I did. George and I sat in the backseat as the car roared to a start. The dog's panting was as loud as the engine and beads of saliva dripped out of his mouth and off his nose. He moaned and grumbled as if to say, "Where are we going?"

"I've got a new place on this side of town," offered Joel as he pulled out of the parking lot. "Kim graduated in May and took an engineering job in Houston. And then I heard from Don who said he was thinking about coming back, so I found us a two-bedroom. We'll show it to you."

"I wondered what happened to you, Don." I said. "What made you want to come back to school?"

"My mother kicked me out!"

"Told him he was a moax," said Joel.

"She really did," Don said, laughing.

I thought about how happy the use of the word "moax" would make Ruby. "Whose car is this?"

"Mine," said Joel. "The Impala died a month ago. Finally. She gave it her best shot, but the old girl just wore out. I sold it for fifty-bucks to some airplane mechanic who wanted it for parts."

"Airplane parts?" I asked.

"Who knows?" said Joel. "I took the fifty bucks and put it toward this beauty. What do you think?"

George licked my face and just then, Joel turned sharply into an alley, and all eighty pounds of George landed on top of me. He put the car in park, stepped out and opened the back door. George instantly jumped out, found a tree and lifted his leg.

"That's my boy," I said, brushing stray hairs from my skirt.

Joel reached into the backseat—offering his hand the same way he had done months earlier when the temperature was sixty-degrees colder—and he pulled me out of the car. "Noelle," he said, "it's high time we continued our conversation."

"Joel, I. . . ."

"Noelle," he said as if to scold me, "I'm not going to let you get away this time. Not tonight. Our relationship has been like a never-ending sentence. Don't you think?"

"Right," I said. "We're a run on and I'm a run off. That's the last time I saw you, you know. That day with. . . ." He put his hand over my mouth and told me to come inside.

I don't remember seeing Don any more that evening and I never made it to Cleo's apartment. I only remember Joel's eyes. And then I remember his kisses, and his tongue, exploring and thrusting and covering my body.

It was a "conversation" that was long overdue.

"What about Anita?" I asked.

"It's over," he said. "It has been for some time. She graduated in May and moved to Chicago to work at the Botanic Gardens. I know I should have called you. I thought about it. Really, I did. I guess I didn't have the nerve."

He said Anita had returned from New Jersey right after our dinner together—our date—and then said something about a potential shotgun wedding. When I asked him what that meant, he said, "I don't want to talk about Anita when I'm with you."

Although I couldn't get the phrase "shotgun wedding" out of my mind, I didn't want to talk about her either. It was all suddenly very unimportant. I knew I was leaving for California in less than a week. I was leaving behind college, Carbondale, my youth, my insecurities, and my confusion. Graduation had taken on a new meaning. And I was about to complete a well-defined curriculum.

I had followed a program preparing me to face a world

where anything could happen. I was no longer just a girl—or a woman. The degree on my wall said that I was a *journalist*. Having immersed myself in four years of grammar, sentence structure, and a myriad of diacritical marks, I realized this so-called "sentence"—this rambling, run-on sentence between Joel and me—was in need of some punctuation.

I intended to end it with an exclamation mark.

And I did.

# 20.
# Joel. 1983.

The cancer began in her breast. As was her way, she didn't tell me about it until almost a year after her diagnosis—until I came home for Christmas. I knew something was wrong—or at least different—the minute I walked in the door. Since the day she told me my father left, I almost expected to be greeted with bad news each time I came home.

It's not that my mother looked sick. She looked great. It had been three years since my father left and she had successfully moved ahead with her life. She quit smoking, started fixing her hair again (always talking about "Joseph her hairdresser"), and formed a steady relationship with Ralph Howrey from the business department at the community college. She'd known him since high school. Everything seemed to be back to normal and my mother was happy again.

But she told me the day I came home for the long December break that a lump developed in her left breast. She had been diagnosed with Stage Three breast cancer last January.

"Last *January?*" I had asked. "January?" I shook my head in disbelief. "That's practically a year ago! You didn't think to tell me?" I thought back and equated the timing of her diagnosis with my learning about Anita's pregnancy. *And I thought Anita waited too long to tell me that!* What was with these women in my life? "Mom, why didn't you tell me?"

"I was trying to protect you," she said. "I knew how hard you worked to get back to school. I hoped I could defeat this thing and not have to bother you with it."

"Bother me? BOTHER ME?" I walked to the sink, picked up a sponge and squeezed it. My knuckles turned white as soapy water ran through my fingers.

"I honestly believed I was ahead of it, Joel," she said. "I had very few side-effects from the chemo. Yes, I was tired and sometimes I felt nauseous—but no more than when I was pregnant with you. I thought that not losing my hair was a sign." She ran her hand through her short, dishwater tendrils. "Well, not all of it anyway. Thank Christ for Joseph. And I kept working. I took the treatments at night."

The doctors told her that the lump was two inches wide, and by the time they detected it through a mammogram, cancer cells had spread to the lymph nodes near her breastbone. She had had a radical mastectomy, followed by four months of chemotherapy, a resting period and then radiation.

"Honey, there's more," she said, "I looked in my old *Webster's* and saw your checkmark next to the word *metastasize,* and, well it breaks my heart to tell you this. . . ."

"It's spread. Hasn't it?"

"I just found out," she said. "It's what they call Stage Four and I have to do another round of chemotherapy and maybe more radiation. This time I'll probably lose my hair."

"Where did it spread?" I asked, not sure if I really wanted to hear the answer.

"My lungs, Honey." She reached for me with both hands and put them on my shoulders. "I have lung cancer, Joel. And the prognosis isn't good. What I'm trying to say is there is no Stage Five."

I didn't return to school. I called Don and told him to find a new roommate, and I called my old boss at Rosenbaum to see about getting another job on the trading floor. My mother needed me, and I needed to prove to her *and* myself that I wasn't like my father. I wanted to show her that I wouldn't leave.

Rick Rosenbaum said there was always a job waiting for me. He suggested a position with what he called a sister company—A.G. Beckman—one of the largest operations on a different trading floor, the Chicago Board Options Exchange.

Options were a new ball game. Simply put, instead of commodities we traded options on stock. The building was the same, yet options traded on the floors above the commodity pits. Options were the clouds hanging over commodities and like the dark cloud hanging over my head.

Just like my initial impression of the commodities world, I

didn't think I'd ever get the concept. But everyone told me to give it "two weeks." They actually said that: *"It takes two weeks to get the gist of options."*

And they were right. After two weeks, I got it.

Simply put, options are speculations on the future price of an underlying stock. It's like a Las Vegas twist on the world of commodities. And while soybeans ruled commodities, IBM— Beamer—was the king of stock options. Chicago traded all the big ones: Boeing, Honeywell, GE, Coke, and DuPont. We put clients' money on the line based on whether or not they or we believed the price of a stock would fall or rise. *Fall and Rise—Put and Call—Port and Starboard—Yin and Yang—Mutt and Jeff.* It's all bullshit—just money for the sake of money.

Because of my experience I was placed in an assistant broker's position and groomed to become a floor broker. The hierarchy was the same as commodities, but the product was different. And my rise through the world of options was quick and steady. It was as quick and steady as my mother's demise.

Watching my mother in the last months of her life was like watching Don Carver and his rock-climbing friends rappel down the cliffs at Giant City State Park. With tubes attached to her like climbing ropes, she progressively rappelled down a harsh and irregular wall of pain. Each day I watched her suffocate a little bit more. Her cough was guttural and fierce, and some days she didn't want me to come in her room, which more and more resembled and smelled like a hospital ward. She lost her hair. I thought she'd be upset, but she never mentioned it. She wore an aqua-colored turban on her head, showing off the remaining blue in her eyes, and she never let me see her hairless head.

Mom was worried about me. I saw it in her eyes. As her skin turned as sallow as a worn out chamois, her eyes remained uniquely blue—like two turquoise stones. Sometimes I just sat with her in her room and we didn't speak. We watched Cubs' games on television together and once in a while she swore at Ryne Sandberg for striking out or commented on Mark Grace's "nice ass."

"That guy is the epitome of a baseball player," she had said. "That's what you looked like on first base."

"You're not going to tell me I've got a nice ass, are you?"

"I never should have let you give up baseball. And now you've relinquished school too."

"School will always be there, Mom," I said. "All I need is sixteen more hours. Besides, I like the stock market. I'm getting pretty good at it."

"Just promise me you'll finish school."

I squeezed her hand and nodded.

Ralph hired a hospice nurse—a Jamaican woman named Blossom—who guarded my mother like a treasure. "Don't come now, *chyle*," she often said to me. "Mama sleep now."

Mom managed to stay at home through July, and then she died in the hospital in September.

My old friend Maria came to the funeral and stood by my side like a sister. She had recently moved back to Illinois after tiring of the Colorado tundra, and she worked at the local YMCA as an aerobics instructor. Having known her since we were children, she was distraught over my mother's death.

Keith had long since moved away—to Texas like the rest of the college graduates carrying engineering degrees—but my old buddy Joe showed up, unbelievably with his girlfriend Carol Wright—the very same girl we once called "Carol Wrong," whom he had to marry in Consumer Education. I hardly recognized her as her skin condition had cleared and she was nothing short of a fox.

As we all suspected, Joe became the most sought after auto mechanic in town. His old man gave him a loan so he could open his own shop and Carol worked with him, taking care of the books. By her stained fingernails, I guessed she was pitching in with a few oil changes as well.

We had a small service for my mother, attended mostly by fellow teachers from the junior college and several former students, many of whom I recognized from high school. I remembered St. Matthews—the Episcopal Church from my childhood—a place to which I followed my mother each Sunday morning until I got to high school—when she let me off the church hook. There she kissed me on the cheek and left me in a classroom where we put stars on an attendance chart and fished name tags from a plastic bowl. Then we colored pictures of Jesus and his disciples and ate snacks before joining our parents for communion. And even though we were allowed to take the host in our hands, my mother never let me because my hands were colored with crayon and marker from Sunday school class. She insisted I stick with the old-fashioned way of receiving, which was to say "amen" and stick out my tongue.

The priest was different—in fact she was a woman—but St. Matthews hadn't changed. Except for a photograph of my mother stationed on an easel beside the lectern, it had the same naked and lonely cross hung above the altar and the same hard pews, the same tattered prayer books, and the same hymnals full of bland songs you wouldn't even think of dancing to. That's what Mom always said about church songs. She held up her fingers and rated them like *American Bandstand* kids snapping their gum.

My father, of course, never went to church. He was an atheist. (I had to look up that word the first time I heard it.) Therefore it seemed fitting that he wasn't in attendance. At least that's how I felt at first—until my mother's name, Patricia—Patty—came up again and again during the service, and it became clearer to me why I was back in this sanctuary.

A small voice in my head kept reminding me that it was my mother's funeral. And as much as I didn't want to believe this nagging voice, the previous nine months of my mother's spiral into the throes of cancer were fresh memories. How could I have ever thought that her ultimate death might bring relief? I felt anything but relief.

Aunt Sue got up and spoke first and talked about what a great older sister my mom had been. She cried softly as she spoke and twice stopped to blow her nose. As she paused, sniffling sounds filled the quiet, hollow church. I sat stoically and listened, trying to picture my mother as a young girl holding up the water-skis attached to Sue's skinny legs, and getting hit in her own legs with cut up steak when Sue decided to become a vegetarian and threw her meat under the table.

Then my mother's boyfriend, Ralph, took the podium and talked of her vitality and her amazing vocabulary. Her students laughed and nodded their heads. He pointed to me and told those same students that it was I who was responsible for her requirement to mark each word they looked up in the dictionary and to provide a term paper using the words as a final exam in her English Composition course.

"She said that kid—Joel—hunted words like a pig hunted truffles," said Ralph.

There was polite laughter—the kind you only hear in a church—and it hit me in my sinuses like a sudden head cold. The back of my throat ached and my eyes filled with tears.

Maria squeezed my hand. "It's okay to cry," she whispered. "We're all here for you."

I swallowed a hard lump. *All?* Whom did she mean by all? I looked around and saw mostly strange faces—a blurring of pitiful eyes, noses, lips, ears, jewelry inappropriately glittering in the light, hairstyles . . . *Who were these people?* The organ blared and the scent of burning wax crawled into my head and made me dizzy with grief. Sweat beads formed on my brow and words I wanted desperately to shout were caught in the back of my throat. Someone needed to yell to the congregation that my no-good excuse for a father was nowhere in sight. Didn't anyone notice? Didn't anyone care?

I shifted my weight in the hard pew. My pants felt tight. I'm not sure anyone heard, but I started growling and wasn't certain how long I could contain my need to scream. I visualized myself getting up and yelling, *"My mother is dead! She believed in God and came to church when my father the atheist sat at home and read the newspaper. Now's she's dead and he lives on somewhere in California. Was he right? Is God dead?"* I loosened my tie and pulled at my collar and thought I might suffocate if I didn't get out of that church. I dropped my face into my hands and became Nietzsche's madman. "God is dead," I said. "How could He take her and leave my father somewhere on earth and completely indifferent?"

Maria was concerned. She stroked my arm. "It's going to be okay," she said. "It's almost over."

"That's just the problem," I said to her. "It will *never* be over. My mother will always be dead."

She walked with me, holding my arm like an escort as we made our way to the back of the church. All eyes were on us like we were a black-clad bride and groom. But no one smiled. They offered somber nods, pitiful expressions, and reached out, touching my shoulder with an endless series of pats expressing disappointment and encouragement. It was like returning to the dugout and taking your place at the end of the bench after striking out.

I just wanted to get outside. I stopped looking from side to side and focused straight ahead.

And that's when I saw her.

She stood alone in the vestibule of the church—a silhouette in the streaking sunrays blasting through the glass doors. As still as a statue, she waited for me with her arms open, the same way she had waited for me on her front porch a year earlier when she told me another life would end.

"Anita," I said. "How did you . . . how did you know?"

"Your mother's boyfriend called me," she said softly. "He said she wanted me to know so I could be here for you." She wrapped her bare arms around me and I buried my face into her shoulder. "I'm so sorry," she whispered. "I'm sorry for all of it."

We stood together and tears fell from my eyes and trickled down her arm. She stroked my hair and continued to whisper and soothe, the way a mother talks to her child.

"So, this is Anita," Maria finally said. "I've heard a lot about you."

I pulled away and wiped my nose on the back of my hand. "Yes, this is Anita. Anita, meet Maria."

"I was his first true love," said Maria.

"I'm not sure what number I was," said Anita, reaching inside her purse for a tissue. "But I'm definitely on the list." She motioned toward me, like she intended to wipe my nose. I took the tissue from her hand.

"Joel didn't tell me how much we looked alike," said Maria. "He always did have an exclusive interest in Italian women. Unless, of course, you count Noelle."

Anita's eyes hardened as she handed me a second tissue. *"You* know Noelle?"

"Maria," I said quickly, "let's go outside, okay? If I don't get some fresh air I'm going to pass out." I grabbed both their elbows and walked toward the door. They were like tall, matching bookends on either side of me.

"If you ask me," Maria continued unmercifully, *"she's* the true love of his life."

I turned to her, mouthed the words "shut up," and pushed the door open with my foot.

"What?" Maria asked. "Joel, what's the big deal about Noelle? She's in California and you and Anita broke up ages ago. What's the matter?"

"What's the matter is his mother just died," said Anita. "I think we should just deal with that right now." Sentient where Maria was not, Anita took charge and offered to drive us to a banquet hall at the college, which Ralph had reserved for the reception.

I don't remember much after that besides a series of people telling me what a great teacher my mother was or how much they admired her. I spent the entire reception—perhaps it was three hours—on my feet in a state of suspension.

Losing my mother, I knew, was an enormous event in my life and yet I didn't feel a part of this ephemeral gathering. I was young, too young I think, and impatience got the best of me as I overheard tidbits of laughter and reunion. I was waiting for something—ANYTHING—to happen to change me—or to tell me that my own life wasn't over too.

Wine and triangle sandwiches with the crusts cut off passed before me. Business cards were exchanged. People of all ages in dark clothing, out of place on such a colorful and warm Indian summer afternoon, swirled around me like ravens—hungrily circling—attracted to death for the morsels of humanity it provided. I was at the center of it all and yet completely removed.

Anita and Maria took turns checking in with me. I knew where each of them were throughout the gathering—from when

the room was thick with people to when it thinned down to
Ralph and his son, Mike, my Aunt Sue, her husband Jack, and
their young kids, Billy and Amie.

And finally, Anita and Maria were the last ones. They were
like surreal and identical twins with one dark gaze boring into
me and reading my thoughts. Was it possible for them to know
I was thinking of Noelle and wishing it had been she standing
in the lobby of St. Matthew's and extending her arms to me?

Noelle and I had exchanged a few letters since she moved in
with Lara. I first wrote about school and joked about Don never
going to class. She wrote of her job hunt and her inability to
find anything other than work as a typist. She wrote that her
boss was a real character and dragged her all over the Bay Area
to social events like yachting voyages and wine tastings. She
said it was a great way to get to know San Francisco, but she
still wanted to work somewhere else—maybe as a reporter—or
anything where she could keep learning. I wrote about my
new job in options and then my promotion to Floor Broker. I
wrote about Blossom, and how she sacrificed a chicken in our
kitchen to try and help heal my mother. Noelle wrote of poetry
readings on campus and at local bookstores and how she and
Lara attended Grateful Dead shows. At night she took writing
classes at Cal's continuing education program, and she combed
the newspaper daily looking for another job.

Then finally, I wrote of my mother's death.

As I composed my letter to Noelle in California, I thought
of my father in the same state and wondered, was he anywhere
near the Bay Area? It dawned on me that I didn't even know
if he was alive or dead. Did he know my mother had died?

I held the one page letter to Noelle in my hand, stared at
the words and the handwriting blurred. California seemed so
far away—a place where they nearly ran out of numbers for
zip codes and had to begin them with nine. The way Noelle
wrote about the Golden State and all her tourism escapades, it
sounded like heaven. But to me, California had always been the
hell my father went to after he left us.

The words, "my mother is dead," came into focus on the page
and grew more and more bold. I quickly folded the letter in
two and sealed the envelope. With the sickening taste of glue
on my tongue as I wrote Noelle's zip code, 94709, I succumbed
to reality. My mother was really gone. I had to let go.

As for my father, I had spent the last three years trying to
forget him—to bury my memories of him. But in the pain of
losing my mother, the memories resurrected like a weed with

severely long and fibrous roots. I visualized his face—his gray-blue eyes, his crumb-infested beard—and his body suffering from the worst kind of cancer that rotted him from the inside out. And this vision became my scourge. For a time I imagined it was *his* death instead of my mother's. It was he who died alone. Without a wife. Without a son.

Why did he leave me? Would I ever know?

I could only think of myself as an orphan. Now I had lost them both.

# 21.
# Noelle. 1984.

The Berkeley apartment I shared with Lara Romano was small and dark. And when the *El Niño* winter kicked in with its endless torrential rains, it was small, dark, and damp. There were no windows in the galley kitchen or bathroom, and each featured a fan that roared like a freight train. My bedroom window, as well as the one window in the living room, looked out at walls of brick. I was convinced that someone pushed apart two large apartment buildings just far enough to drop in our building, and then lined up it and the neighbors like plastic houses on an expensive Monopoly board property.

In a land of color, dramatic beauty, and lush growth, where the plants I once had in small, terra cotta pots in the Midwest now grew as hedges in front of picture windows, our apartment seemed like a crime against art. When I fantasized about life in California, I dreamed of living in a watercolor on the cover of a Joni Mitchell album. Alas, I didn't know until I arrived that I couldn't afford to be a lady of the canyon. Instead I had to settle as a broke chick of the flatlands.

We rented the middle two-bedroom apartment of a three-unit complex and, thankfully, the neighbors were kind and quiet. It was a lovely, tree-filled neighborhood, close to the University of California campus—important to Lara—and more importantly to me, close to a BART station. Bay Area Rapid Transit. We spoke of Bart as if 'he' were a neighbor or a boyfriend. The high-speed trains connected us to all inlets of the landmasses surrounded by the salty waters of San Francisco Bay, known to locals as the

East Bay, the South Bay, the Peninsula, and The City.

College and California had transformed Lara. Her long hair was gone, but it was blonder because of the intense California sun. She wore it cropped short and spiked like a sweet gum pod. She was thin, wore long, gauze skirts and an ankle bracelet made of small bells that tinkled as she walked. She no longer wore contact lenses but instead wore gold granny glasses that she found at the Ashby Flea Market—a weekly gathering of junk vendors, outside another BART station that smelled like a combination of clove cigarettes and fires burning in fields of third world countries.

As she was in high school, Lara was an excellent student and seemed to know not just a little bit about every subject that arose in conversation, but a lot. Intellectually, we were opposites. While Lara always knew what she wanted and how she felt, I saw both sides of nearly every issue.

I thought I was objective. Lara said I was wishy-washy.

We went to a lot of movies, which in Berkeley was always a political experience. Audience members couldn't contain themselves from shouting opinions. After we saw *The Year of Living Dangerously* Lara expressed her outrage at the concept of "horror as beauty" and discussed—at length—President Sukarno's Indonesian hell as portrayed in the film. While all I wanted to talk about was Mel Gibson's blue eyes and Sigourney Weaver's fake English accent, Lara talked about the aborted communist coup in 1965 that slaughtered 400,000 Indonesians, and then went on further to discuss Viet Nam and all of Southeast Asia.

Any subject I brought up seemed to pale in importance. Perhaps that's why I didn't immediately tell her about my relationship with her old high school boyfriend, Joel Rolland. Part of me still felt a tinge of disloyalty for having slept with her past boyfriend, and when I finally brought it up, it felt like a confession.

"You mean you slept with the guy I lost my virginity to?" she had asked. "What a loser."

"Me or him?" I asked.

Lara set down her textbook and looked at me over the top of her granny glasses. Her rolling eyes made me dizzy. "He never finished college, did he?"

"Is that what it boils down to for you?"

"Honestly," she said rising and walking toward the kitchen, "how much does it really take to graduate from a simple state school? And he couldn't manage that?"

"Lara, his father left. And then his mother got sick."

She shrugged her shoulders, walked back into the living room with a glass and poured sun tea from the pickle jar perpetually steeping in our sole window. "Want some?" she asked.

I didn't. I tried to like sun tea, but it was an acquired taste that eluded me.

"I just think you should set your sights a little higher," she said. "That's all."

It took nine weeks and every last dollar of my meager savings, but I finally found a job working for a small San Francisco publishing company, a producer of tourist publications. The publisher, Joellen Newhouse—Jo—told me she hired me as a "publisher's assistant," because she liked my looks and thought it would help sell advertising. I snapped up her offer to work for an annual salary of $14,000 with health insurance, a few paid holidays and, what Jo called a lot of "perks." I told her I wouldn't be good at selling advertising, though, or selling anything for that matter. Surely I'd take every rejection personally.

As a working girl, each morning I walked to the North Berkeley BART station and filed aboard the swift, tooting trains with the other East Bay commuters. The younger workers wore long skirts and backpacks—where we stored the shoes we'd change into out of our tennis shoes once we arrived at our offices—and the older workers had more sophisticated business suits and briefcases. It was a hierarchy of age and social status. Most everyone carried Styrofoam coffee cups and buried their heads in the green newspaper pages of the *San Francisco Chronicle*.

It was a newspaper world and I longed to be a part of it.

Instead, however, at the office of Joellen Newhouse, I typed and answered phones with a system that may as well have been Dixie cups and shoestrings for how frustrating it was.

"Newhouse Communications," I sang in my most professional phone voice. "Hold please." Then I depressed the receiver button twice and prepared to push a two-digit extension for the art, editorial, or sales department; however, instead of getting a hold tone, I'd more often get a dial tone. I lost countless calls and gained tongue-lashings from the advertising sales staff.

Whenever I came home and complained of my menial job, Lara scolded me further and said things like I was "giving women a bad name" by staying there. She gave me some credit for scratching the surface of my chosen field and for working at a small, woman-owned business, but working for Joellen Newhouse was the biggest problem with the job. She was always late with the paychecks and redlined nearly every item on her employees' expense reports. She hated to hire outside services and often sent her sales staff on deliveries across town, just to save money. "And while you're at it, try to sell them an ad," she always said.

Out of the office, however, Jo put on a more glamorous show. I followed her around from event to event like a lady-in-waiting, collecting my so-called perks, and learning the meaning of the term "schmooze." There were gallery openings and fashion shows at Union Square, Cable Car Bell Ringing Contests, Nob Hill lunches, Fleet Week parades, and photo opportunities at Fisherman's Wharf where I often felt like a fashion failure—a snapshot of a *"Glamour* Don't." My ensuing fashion shame led me to Macy's department store where I ended up spending most of my paychecks during lunchtime shopping trips.

As my wardrobe improved, so did my technique. I grew more comfortable at my job of passing out business cards and establishing a presence for our publication. The faces at the events became familiar. So did the meals. Salmon for lunch. Rubber chicken for dinner. Too much white wine. Too many self-important people babbling on about themselves and telling me why they should be profiled in Newhouse publications.

"I am the highest ranking female concierge in the City," said one.

"I've single-handedly brought more conventions to San Francisco than any of the other top hotel executives in the business," said another.

"The City is yesterday's news," said yet another. "Contra Costa County is where the growth is."

As the months passed, the City got smaller and smaller. With all the same people at all the events, it seemed cliquey and gossipy and I grew bored.

"It seems to me that someone needs a trip to Napa," said Jo.

"Would that be a perk or do I have to work?" I asked.

"Both," she said. Jo pulled up a chair, sat down, and placed both her elbows on the desk just as the phone rang. "Joellen Newhouse," she chirped into the phone. "What? No. Oh no. I don't need any toner cartridges. Please take me off your call list." She slammed down the phone. "God, I abhor salespeople."

I glanced over her shoulder at three members of her own sales staff, all housed in open-air cubicles. One gave her the finger. Another rolled her eyes. The third shook his head and picked up the phone, loudly declaring himself an advertising SALESMAN from the Newhouse Publishing Company.

"Ungrateful babies," Jo hissed. "Never mind them. Come with me this weekend to Napa. I'll let you write the recap for next month's issue."

How could I refuse? I loved Napa Valley. It was beautiful at all times of the year. In the summer it was warmer than perpetually fog-covered San Francisco, and the heavy shade trees made it feel like the Midwest. In Fall those same giant trees lining the narrow highway that tunneled tourists and tasters through the valley from Napa north to Yountville, St. Helena, and finally Calistoga, changed color, and by winter the vineyards burst into blinding fields of yellow mustard plants. Come spring, the panoramic views of endless vineyards nestled between mountain ranges in the east and west exploded with the color of California poppies. At every time of year, the heady aroma of fermenting wine filled the air.

Jo and I left the office after lunch on a Friday afternoon. We journeyed north to a weekend extravaganza put on by the Napa Valley Chamber of Commerce to attract the meetings and conventions industry.

"You have to drive," Jo said as we approached her blue Jeep Cherokee in the parking lot. "My driver's license is expired and I don't want to get a ticket."

"But I guess it doesn't bother you to drive to and from Marin County to the City each day, does it?"

"The cops are rabid north of Novato," she said, pulling down the sun visor in front of the passenger seat. She checked her face. "You'll have to watch your speed once we get out of the City."

Traffic was light in the City but bottled up near the Presidio, a red-roofed military base near the water. Soon we were northbound on the Golden Gate Bridge. As we drove over the expansive bridge between elegant towers of lollypop orange and toward the rainbow-painted tunnels leading to Marin County, Jo rambled about her staff and her ambitions and I hardly listened.

I had just received a letter from Joel, telling me of his mother's death. He had waited until after the funeral to let me know—so that I wouldn't feel obligated to come. He didn't want me there. It felt like I wasn't important enough to share his grief.

Didn't he realize I knew what it felt like to lose a parent?

Our relationship had faded into memories. Only thin cobwebs—brief letters and occasional phone calls—connected us. It could hardly be considered a long-distance romance. It was just plain long-distance.

Jo and I shared a room, however, we didn't attend any of the same parties until the Saturday night grand finale. It was a wine tasting banquet at the beautiful Austintini winery. I sat with Jo and four men in suits at one of a dozen exquisite tables. Draped with white linen cloths, each was set with fine bone china and as many sterling forks, knives, and spoons as various-sized crystal wine glasses. The centerpieces were Waterford vases filled with delicate and graceful white tulips, just cracking open. Single spotlights, stationed above the tables, shown on the cut crystal of the vases and made them sparkle like diamonds in the sun.

The suited men spent every breath droning on about themselves. They were worker bees trying to impress the queen.

The queen, of course, was my raven-haired and blood-red-lipped boss, Jo. She never stopped trying to sell advertising in a coquettish way. "You should tell ten-thousand readers what you just told me in a half-page horizontal!" she said, batting her eyelashes.

I looked away from the table, surveying the room for anyone I might have met at an earlier party. Most people were heavily engaged in conversation. I stared at the closed double doors. There was no out.

Sipping my wine, I saw the doors open. A man entered the room. He was tall and lean and had long—yet styled—dark hair and blue eyes, glinting like aquamarine gemstones. He sashayed toward a central podium, and as he moved, the room hushed as though someone had turned a dimmer switch. He pulled the microphone forward and a sharp tone burst through the room.

"Sorry about that," he said, and cleared his throat. "Don't want to disturb." Again he adjusted the microphone. I turned in my chair and fully faced him.

"For those of you who don't know me—and I imagine there are a few of you—my name is Nick Austin and I'm your host this evening," he said. "Ladies and gentlemen, our mission begins now." There was polite applause. The overhead spotlights highlighting our tulips extinguished and the wall behind our host became a screen. An image of the same white tulips gracing our tables projected upon it.

"Our mission is simple, my dear friends," he said. "It is to harvest great beauty, art—if you will—in the form of the world's finest wines. You've no doubt already tasted the elegance in the first two prize-winning selections, the Sauvignon Blanc and the Pinot Noir."

His liquid voice was in itself beautiful and quenching. I picked up my goblet of Sauvignon Blanc and drank like a dehydrated nomad in the desert. Salads were served. The next course followed. With each, Nick Austin returned to the podium and introduced a new wine, explaining how each complemented the sorbet, entrée, and dessert and cheese courses.

"What a control freak," scoffed Jo. "If you please ladies and gentlemen," she mimicked, "do not taste the wine poured by our fine stewards until it breathes the appropriate length of time. I will indicate that moment."

I ignored her. Jo whispered derisive commentary about everyone. Finally, we ate crème brûlée and drank sweet wine, and the
lights came up. Sipping the last of my dessert wine, I noticed
Nick Austin approaching our table. I nudged Jo. She was digging
through her oversized purse for her compact and lipstick. "Here
comes your control freak," I said.

Quickly, she ducked her head and refreshed her lipstick. With
her index finger, she rubbed her front teeth. "Am I clean?" she
asked, grinning.

Before I could answer, she turned up her one-hundred-watt
smile and reached her outstretched hand toward Nick Austin.
"Hello to the handsome Mr. Austin. I'm Joellen Newhouse." He
clutched her hand and I watched Jo's smile fade into two
freshly painted, pursed lips. It was a "wet fish handshake," her
pet peeve. "Uh, yes. I'd like you to meet my protégé, Noelle
Moncada," she said. "Stand up Noelle and let our host get a
good look at you."

Embarrassed, I stood like a trained Irish setter and extended
my hand. Nick Austin grabbed both my hands and held them
in a firm grasp. I felt my face grow hot and looked away. He
squeezed my hands and I faced him again.

I recognized his expression.

"Ms. Newhouse," he said keeping his focus on me, "you have
exquisite taste in protégés."

My cheeks must have turned the same color as the dessert
wine. It wasn't only because of his intense gaze, but it also an-
gered me to be called a protégé. As if Joellen Newhouse were
training me for anything useful! "I think I've had too much
wine," I said dumbly.

"Nonsense," he said. "A fine wine will always make a true
beauty blush after dinner." He winked one of his perfect blue
eyes and released my hands. I watched, dumbstruck, as he pro-
gressed to the adjacent table.

Jo again dug through her purse like a dog trying to relocate
a bone. "Let me find a business card," she whispered. "You need
to get him to buy an ad."

"I'm not selling advertising for you, Jo."

"Fine. That's just fine. Then I'll give him the card. But you're
missing a great opportunity." She found a card, flattened it on
the table and then pushed past me and caught up to Nick.
He greeted her again as if for the first time and she slipped
her card into his pocket, talking rapidly through her high-beam
smile. I couldn't hear what she said, however, Nick looked at
me and nodded.

I sat down, sipped my wine, and rolled my eyes, a little

disgusted with myself for thinking someone like that might be interested in me. Three half-empty glasses of wine were displayed before me like a color wheel, from almost pure white to amber to dark red. I finished all three.

The following Monday when Nick Austin called the office of Newhouse Communications and invited me to dinner, Jo was happier than I. She was like a publishing madam and expected me to sell adverting like a prostitute sells sex. But his call wasn't about business. It was personal. And I didn't want to talk about publishing or advertising when I was with Nick Austin. I just wanted to hear about his fascinating world.

Nick's grandparents raised him on a Napa Valley ranch. It was home to the exclusive Austintini Vineyards. Everything about grape growing and wine tasting permeated his conversations. He was so passionate and sure of himself. I had never met anyone like him.

Our first dates were dinners at the Bay Area's finest restaurants. Each meal with Nick was an experience in etiquette and wine tasting. He prided himself on selecting the correct vintage and went through a series of dramatic motions each time wine was involved. Studying the label, feeling—not sniffing—the cork, swirling the glass like a centrifuge and examining the wine's "legs," and then taking a full nose inhale, he sucked the wine into his mouth and swished and swirled. Half the time he'd proclaim the vintage, "excellent," or "superb," and direct the wine steward to "pour." The not-so excellent or superb offerings were met with no comment and a raised eyebrow. Depending on his mood, the bottle was either sent back or we drank it.

In his presence I felt like a student, and I was terrified that one night he'd expect me to read the wine list and make the proper choice. But it never happened. I was merely an audience for him.

I fell for him. Hard. Slept with him on the third date.

I don't remember him asking if I'd marry him. I simply remember my shock at seeing the ring on my left hand and hearing his schedule for presenting me to the family and meeting with his priest.

When I called Janette in Memphis and told her I was getting married, she cried. Then I called my mother in Florida and she didn't say anything, until I told her I had already called Janette and that I had asked Lara to be my bridesmaid.

"You didn't tell me first?" she had asked. "You told your sister and your friend before you told your own mother?"

"I didn't know I was supposed to."

"You're also supposed to ask your only sister to be your bridesmaid," she said.

"I didn't know that either," I said dumbly. "Maybe I should go out and buy a copy of *Bride's* magazine and read all the *DOs* and *DON'Ts* before I get it all wrong."

*"Don't* be smart," said my mother.

"You don't sound as though you're very happy for me."

"How can I be?" she said. "I don't know this person. And you've known him for how long? Three months?"

She was right. I hardly knew Nick Austin. And Lara hated him. She couldn't believe I was planning to marry a Republican. And a Catholic Republican on top of it "Do you realize how much the Catholic Church oppresses women?" she asked incredulously.

My introduction to the Catholic Church followed shortly after he placed the ring on my finger. It became a subject I had to study. Like philosophy. Or history. Nick, on the other hand, was a devout attendee of Sunday mass and insisted we be married in a Catholic service. His grandparents suggested that I convert, but I found a loophole to conversion. I signed a proclamation indicating I'd have each of my children baptized Catholic and raise them in the church.

I continued down a mysterious path, walking without a sense of direction. I kept doing what I thought was expected of me. Each week we attended prenuptial classes in a room as small as a jail cell, which was painted blood red and had a gold crucifix on the wall where Jesus Christ hung watching over us. I had a hard time keeping my eyes from the nails protruding from the statue's hands. No wonder there was such a thing as Catholic guilt. I couldn't imagine having to look at that in every room of the house.

Nick and I sat in desk chairs across from the young, pasty-white priest assigned to us. His name was Father Steve. It was hard calling a man who looked to be about my age, "father." It wasn't a word I had used often in my life. He was new to the church, fresh out of the seminary, and like everyone else, took a backseat to Nick's flamboyance. When the soft-spoken rector managed to get a word in, he asked us to confess our previous relationships. He said it just like that. "Confess."

I didn't know previous relationships were considered sins.

"I've had two," said Nick. "But they both ended and each is married to someone else. I have nothing lingering." He folded his arms and leaned back in his chair. His blue eyes bore into me suggesting it was now my turn to speak.

"I've never had a serious relationship," I started, "Except for

one. But I don't know how to categorize it. I'm still friends
with this person."

"What person?" asked Nick. "Noelle, you never told me you
had a boyfriend."

"You never asked," I said. His dark eyebrows shot up. He took
it like a slap in the face. "Really, Nick," I said with a small laugh,
"did you honestly believe you were the first man in my life?"

He didn't answer. Instead he stood up and walked toward
the door. Father Steve sat silently at the opposite end of the
table taking notes, afraid to look up from his pad. I hoped he'd
intervene but realized that since Catholics worshipped a virgin,
I was in unfriendly territory. Did they expect all their brides to
be virgins as well?

"Joel was never my boyfriend," I said. "We're friends. Do you
expect me to give up my friends because we're getting married?"

"Did you sleep with him?"

Father Steve looked up from his pad. He wanted to know
too.

"We're friends," I said. "That's it."

Nick didn't buy it. "You have to cleanse your palate of this
guy," he said. He was big on cleansing palates. "Cut him off
immediately."

"Is this person a threat to your pending marriage?" asked
Father Steve.

"Hell no," I said.

"Noelle," scolded Nick as though he never swore. "If you're
still friends then why haven't I met him?"

"He lives in Chicago and I haven't had any contact with
him since his mother died, which is right before I met you. I
don't know why you say I need to cleanse my palate. Do you
think I can just chew on some saltine crackers or something
and wipe away my past?"

I didn't want to wipe away my past. I wanted to keep my
memories of Joel in a special place—a mental scrapbook. Even
though I had stopped writing to him when Nick came into
my life, he was like one of those trick birthday candles with a
small flame that keeps lighting itself again and again. I couldn't
douse the flame. I didn't want to. He was my friend!

But I knew I had to tell Joel about Nick. Somehow, I had
to tell him I was getting married.

It took all afternoon on a busy day at Newhouse Communications to compose and type a letter to Joel about my engagement. As I wrote I imagined the warm breath of Nick on my

shoulder, dictating my words. I was sure he'd ask to see what I had written, as if it were a school assignment and he was responsible for determining my final grade.

Ultimately, I wrote the letter not for Joel's sake, but for Nick's.

*Dear Joel,*

*I hope you don't mind an impersonal, typed letter, but killing time at work looks better when I appear as though I'm working on something. I've been meaning to write you or get in touch with you for a while. I feel a sense of obligation to you—for reasons explainable only through wordiness and lengthy detail. And even though I'm sure you wouldn't mind too much putting up with my gibberish, I'm going to avoid it.*

*I'm writing to tell you I'm getting married. His name is Nick Austin and he's from Napa. His grandparents own a winery and he's Catholic. We're taking prenuptial classes.*

*Last Wednesday we spent a marathon session discussing . . . are you ready? Discussing you. I almost hate to tell you this because I can't image your reaction. But Joel, you've played a large role in my life the past few years. And in committing to Nick, I had to ask myself why and how I could suddenly or even gradually put you out of my mind as a lover rather than as a friend. The passage of time—not seeing you and subconsciously avoiding your phone calls—did I do that?—I'm sure made it a whole lot easier for me. It's just that when Nick came into my life, my longing for him and the pleasure I received just by hearing his voice or being at his side was something I knew I didn't want to be without. I've never met anyone like him. He's older than I, certainly smarter, and he's shown me a world I didn't know existed.*

*I keep getting interrupted in this hectic office and I can't decide if there's a whole lot more I need to say to you or if I should just end this letter. I'm afraid that once I finally sign "sincerely yours," I will be signing off our fleeting conversation for good. And Joel, that's too hard to give up.*

*If you do want to write me back you don't have to address the letter to "Mrs. Austin." Although that will be my new title, I have decided to keep my name. His family disapproves, but I can't imagine not being called "Moncada." I still live with Lara and we haven't yet set a date, but once we do, my wish is that you'll either address a letter to both Nick and me, or write with the understanding that I don't want to keep anything from him. Not knowing what in the world your reaction is to all this typing, you of course are free to do whatever you want.*

*Joel, please know that I still care about you very much and I always will. You will always have a special place in my heart—you will always be my* Soulful Joel. *And being the understanding person that you are, I'm hoping that you still care about me enough to be happy for me and realize that this is the best thing for me. And for Nick.*

*Sincerely yours,*

*Noelle*

# 22.
# Joel. 1984.

Her letter cut through my heart. Left field. Line drive. Over-throw. Error. It was cold and rambling and, felt very impersonal. I couldn't believe it. Any of it. A Catholic named Nick from Napa? It was like hearing about a cartoon character. How could she do this? The girl who ran away from all her relationships was suddenly deciding to settle down for the rest of her life? At twenty-three? She couldn't be thinking clearly. Must be drunk on all that Napa Valley wine.

I searched for my address book on the desk in my mother's room and finally found it under a stack of bills addressed to either Mr. and Mrs. Walter Rolland, Ms. Patricia Rolland, and the newer variety, like cable TV and American Express, to Mr. Joel Rolland. It was the largest bedroom in the house and had the best windows, but I never moved in. I kept my room on the second floor, and it looked much the same as it did in high school. A place to store bills and papers, Mom's room was more like a home office.

Finally locating my tattered address book, I turned to the 'P' section and looked up Ruby Pappas's phone number. She and Noelle had been such good friends. I was sure she'd have more information about what was going on in California, even though she was still in Carbondale.

"Yel-low," she answered after the first ring.

"Ruby, is it you?"

"Jo-el Rolland," she said at once. "Even though I haven't heard it in far too long, I'd know that voice anywhere. What's shakin'?"

"Noelle wrote and said she's getting married."

"I know," said Ruby. "Hard to believe. But if you ask Lisa and me, we don't think it'll ever happen. What's the guy's name? Nick?" She exaggerated the 'N' and the 'K,' so that the 'K' cut through the phone line like static.

"Nick from Napa."

"Sounds like a Svengali to me," she said. "She'll never go through with it."

"I don't know what to make of this letter. I mean, I thought we really had something together and suddenly after months of no contact she writes and says she's marrying some guy?"

"Face it, Joel," said Ruby. "She was never your type. I know about your mom and gosh, I'm really sorry. Was it awful?"

"Yes." What did she mean, 'she was never your type?'

"I'm sure it was," she said. "It probably sounds cliché, Joel, but you need someone more like your mother. Don't you think?"

"Christ, Ruby," I swore, "Do you think I've got an Oedipal complex or something?"

"You said it. Not me."

I hated psychology majors.

We chatted a while longer and I found a reason to hang up. I grabbed Noelle's letter and headed next door to Maria's house. I knew I could count on her for an unbiased opinion.

It was a warm June day and as I walked up the driveway, I saw her in the backyard helping her mother hang laundry on the clothesline. Men's white tee-shirts dangled next to dripping bras with enormous cups. Mrs. Tinnerello was not shy about displaying the family's underwear.

"Hello Joel," said her mother in a thick, Italian accent. "How's my boy?"

"Fine, thanks Mrs. Tinnerello," I said. "I just need to talk to Maria about something."

"Okay, okay," she said dropping a handful of clothespins into her apron pocket. "I know when I'm not wanted. Come inside and have some soup when you're finished talking. It's wedding soup—with the little meatballs." She lifted a basket of dry clothing and walked inside the door leading to the kitchen.

"What's up?" asked Maria.

"Read this letter," I said, handing her Noelle's folded letter.

"What's this?"

"Just read it and let me know what you think."

Maria opened the letter and scanned the typing from the top to the bottom of the page. "Noelle?" She sat down in a metal lawn chair and read.

I watched the underpants flap in the breeze in a graceful rhythm. The yard was small but impeccable. Mrs. Tinnerello's budding rose bushes were on one side and the opposite side, lining the next-door neighbor's garage like a fence, enormous bushes were heavy with white, lacy flowers—bridal wreath. A purple lilac bush filled out the corner next to a horseshoe pit, where Maria's dad spent his summer evenings after work.

Maria frowned as she read and when she got to the end, she shook her head. "A cry for help," she said. "Clearly this girl wants you to come and stop her from marrying the guy."

"You think so?"

"What else?" she said. "You will always be my *Soulful Joel?* Give me a break!"

I snatched the letter from her hands and asked her to tell her mother thanks for the offer for the soup, but I had to go. Maria got up and walked behind me as I made my way back down her driveway.

"Joel," she called. "Do you love this girl?"

I stopped, turned around and looked at my friend, standing in her driveway wearing shorts and a plain, black tank top. Her unruly hair blew in the breeze and she didn't keep it from blowing in her face. She had on hot pink thongs and her toenails were painted bright red. "When did you start painting your toenails?" I asked.

"I've always painted my toenails, Joel," she said. "You just never noticed."

I drove my mother's car around the town without a sense of direction. I didn't want to go home and I had nowhere else to go. I drove past Joe's service station and saw him and Carol talking with a customer. They didn't see me drive by. I went past the old gas station where he once worked and sold dime bags out of the back room. The station had a new name and the car wash was no longer there. Fast food restaurants had sprung up where paint stores once were, and banks had sprung up in place of fast food restaurants.

I had the terrible feeling that I was going to grow old in this town and nothing would become of me.

I made my way along the railroad tracks, the route I took each day to work, into the next town and then the next town. I saw that my favorite store, Troves of Treasures, had metamorphosed into a record store called "It's a Beautiful Day." I parked on the busy street, put a quarter in the meter, and went inside.

The walls pumped with the sounds of the radio's latest most overplayed tune, Prince and the Revolution's "When Doves Cry."

Silent browsers dressed like bikers or Cindy Lauper flipped through stacks of records, bobbing their heads to the music. Tina Turner and Boy George posters decorated the walls. As I looked at albums in the rock and roll section, the music changed to Phil Collins's ballad, "Against All Odds." I listened and thought of Noelle.

*"How can I just walk away from you. . . ."* sang Phil Collins. This was a song I didn't need to hear. I looked at the oblivious kid behind the counter and internally accused him of putting on that song just for me.

I had to get out. *"But your coming back to me is against the odds,"* I heard as the door closed behind me. I practically ran to my car and drove home where the kitchen sink was full of dirty dishes and the foul odor of garbage permeated the air.

I'd clean up later.

I reached for my phone book, still sitting next to the phone, then looked up her number and made the call.

# 23.
# Anita. 1984.

I worked for the Chicago Botanic Gardens in the plant evaluation unit, which was established the year I graduated. My work was what I had dreamed of doing during long afternoons in my Nana's greenhouse, and I felt like the luckiest person on earth.

My parents bought a small house for me in Deerfield, and I live with three cats, two fish, and a bird. I enjoy living without other people in the house—especially after my college years when roommates had guests coming and going at all hours.

Deerfield is classic suburbia—curbed streets, sidewalks, neat family homes, square patches of lawn, and trim flower gardens—not unlike the New Jersey town where I was born and raised. I missed Southern Illinois and the small town where I spent my summers with Nana. But there were no jobs to be had down south, and after my internship at the Gardens, this was the only place to come.

The fledgling plant evaluation program was staffed with experts who took me under their wings, and I must say I learned even more on the job than I did in school. The Gardens cover three hundred eighty-five acres and had twenty-six varietal gardens. During my internship I spent time in each of the gardens, weeding and maintaining, but my favorite places were the greenhouses. I loved moist mornings in the tropical rainforest, immersed in colors and sweet smells, and then in the afternoon I moved to the desert to be among prickly cacti and spiked succulents. The contrasts from rich, aromatic peat to grainy, dry sand and everything in-between was like a soil smorgasbord.

In the evaluation and test gardens where I now spend my days, I focus on perennials, as well as vines, shrubs, and small trees. Through experimentation with soil and sunlight, our purpose is to determine what plants are best suited for Midwestern landscapes. The studies are long term, so I spend most days making notes and treating my plants like they were my children.

I don't have much time for a social life. In the evenings I come home, feed my animals and myself, and then tend my organic garden in the greenhouse out back. I grow all my own vegetables.

Nana calls every weekend and I always speak with her from the greenhouse. It's our way of being together—our familiar territory. I last saw her when I went to Murphysboro to celebrate her eightieth birthday, which was shortly after Joel's mother had died.

Nana looked wonderful. As usual her long silver hair was pulled into a loose bun at the back of her head. She wore her faded denim apron, so filled with years of colorful embroidery of flowers and bees, ladybugs and birds, that the blue fabric background—once a vast sky behind her embroidered garden—was barely visible. Nana grabbed my hand and walked dutifully to the greenhouse the moment I arrived. She was eager to unveil her latest geranium hybrid.

Her almond-shaped eyes sparkled as she presented it, and she whispered in my ear that she had named it "Anita." It was because of the black around the flower buds, which she had said were the same color as my eyes.

I spent three days with her, recovering from the funeral and from seeing Joel again. I had loved Joel's mother, Patty. She was only fifty-six years old—barely middle-aged—and she died in such a miserable way. The cancer strangled her like a vine growing inside her chest, wrapping itself around her airways and stealing all the nutrients from her healthy organs. I had only visited her once in the hospital and it was difficult. She took my hand and looked at me with Joel's eyes. As she was unable to speak, it was up to me to do all the talking and interpreting. Did she want to know what had gone wrong between Joel and me and whether or not there was any chance of fixing it? I didn't know what to tell her.

I suspected the abortion was what went wrong between us. Things weren't the same after that. I wasn't the same. I, who spent my life growing and nurturing plants, wouldn't allow myself to think of the thing inside me as a living being. I was so selfish! All I could think about was my path toward graduation and fulfilling my dream of quiet days in the greenhouse.

I hated that Joel asked if the baby were his. I found that impossible to forgive, even though I tried. He said he would have married me, but I knew he didn't want to. I knew I was his second choice. I was second to that Noelle Moncada—that freakish, Amazon woman always hovering over our relationship.

Well, I wasn't stupid. I knew he dreamed of her. He actually said her name once in his sleep. The night he did it, I got up and left and after that, avoided his calls. As much as I loved him, I wouldn't be anyone's second choice. I deserved more than that.

In the greenhouse on a Saturday afternoon, the phone rang and it startled me. I looked at my watch and thought it was too early for Nana's call. The phone rang a second time and it became more like an alarm. My heart beat a little faster as I thought maybe something was wrong. I took off my left glove and reached for the phone.

"Nana?" I answered. "Everything okay?"

"No Anita, it's not Nana. It's me. It's Joel."

"Joel?" I asked with a mixture of surprise and relief. "What's wrong?"

"Nothing's wrong. I was just thinking of you. I miss you."

Sparkling liquid droplets on a ripe tomato across the room caught my eye. They looked like tears. I took off my other glove and sat in the greenhouse's only chair, where I usually sat to write notes on my home experiments. "Are you still there?" he asked.

"I'm here," I said. "I've always been here, Joel."

"Can I drive up and see you?"

"Now? I don't know, I. . . ."

"I love you, Anita," he said. "I love you and I need to see you."

# 24.
# Joel. 1985.

Six months passed before I heard from Noelle again. I didn't write to her or call her after she notified me of her engagement, and I never received word that she'd gotten married. I didn't expect to receive a wedding invitation but thought maybe an announcement would come my way. I thought she'd let me know.

But nothing like that ever showed up. Instead, I received a Christmas card. It was a cartoon of Santa and his reindeer flying over the Golden Gate Bridge and she simply signed her name, "Noelle." No Moncada. No Austin. And there was no name on the return address, just the street number, which was new. The zip code remained the same.

Was she purposefully being mysterious?

I placed the card on my mother's desk and closed the door to her room. I was supposed to be at Anita's house in an hour and with the holiday traffic and icy roads, it would take an hour to get up there. Normally I'd be spending the night, but her parents were in from New Jersey, and well, I promised her I wouldn't sleep over as long as they were in town. While my parents—at least in my mind—were both dead and buried, Anita still became a child when her mom and dad were around. And since they technically owned the house in which she lived, she followed their rules.

It had been a fresh start for us. And we were happy. A part of me had never stopped loving Anita, and I was grateful to her for welcoming me back into her life.

When I made the decision not to respond to Noelle's letter announcing her engagement, I removed her from my heart. She had never been mine. I knew that. There was no use fantasizing about her or dreaming of what might have been. She left me to move to California and she was ready to marry someone else. She seemed to always find a reason not to choose me, and I was a fool for thinking there might have been a chance for us.

I wondered if, perhaps, at some point we could just be friends.

After Anita's parents finally left, I spent so much time at her house that I had my own drawer and space in her closet. It made more sense for us to stay at her place instead of mine, since it was close to her job and made for an equidistant commute for me. I'm not sure who brought up the subject of marriage first, but the topic came up in conversation more and more, and I grew comfortable with the idea.

Anita was everything I wanted in a wife. She was beautiful, smart, and I knew she loved me. She always said it was "love at first sight" for her. I knew I couldn't claim the same thing, but once I got to know Anita, there was a strong attraction that couldn't be denied. And I'll never forget the winter days just before I went back to school when we fell in love. In that time with her, I understood what my feelings and questions of love were about.

It was about a connection—to her and to the world.

I watched how Anita tended her plants and how she snuggled and nurtured her cats. I knew she'd be a good mother. I would need that in a wife—someone who would care for our children like my mother cared for me . . . just in case, dare I say it? Just in case I turned out like my father twenty years down the road.

Were traits of abandonment hereditary? And wasn't my gut instinct to abandon the first child we conceived together?

Sometimes at night—in that period just before sleep—as Anita snoozed peacefully next to me, I felt a profound loss for the child we almost made together. If we got married, if we tried to do it right, would it be a second chance? Could we atone our past actions?

Anita wouldn't allow us to look back on those dark days. She, instead, looked at it as a success story. We faced the lowest low, made an adult decision and survived, she said. "At least we know we work. We know we can make a baby."

By spring we had all but picked out the rings. I think we both knew we were headed down the aisle and we made plans to sell my mother's house. And it was while we priced items for a garage sale that Anita finally brought up the issues that she said I needed to clear up before we were officially engaged.

"I want you to go to California," she had said. "You need to find your father."

"My father?" I asked. While forming the 'F' in father, my teeth bit so hard into my lower lip that I nearly spit out the word. "I told you how I felt about that, Anita. As far as I'm concerned, he's dead."

"We both know that's not true," she said.

"How do you suggest I find him?"

"Have you ever even tried?"

I placed a fifty-cents sticker on a green, glass vase—the kind the florist delivers—and set it on a picnic table. I had never told Anita—or anyone else—but I *had* tried to contact him. My Aunt Sue, and of course my mother, knew all along where he was. But my aunt didn't tell me this until after Mom had died, when she asked if I wanted to write him.

"I'm not going to tell him she died," she had said. "I'll leave that up to you." She handed me a small piece of paper with his address. It was a P.O. Box in Santa Rosa, California. "There's something else you should know," she said. "He's remarried. And he has a son."

"Remarried?" I asked. "A son?"

"That's right," she said. "You have a brother and they're the reason he left. She was a teacher at the junior college—someone in Patty's department. The baby, his name is William, was a year old when your mom found out. He confessed after he had already made plans to take his new family to California to make a fresh start."

I couldn't speak. His galling duplicity cut me in half.

For weeks after Sue told me, I fought the idea of writing to him. I composed a hundred letters in my head as I lay in bed, not paying attention to the television or the words in the book I was trying to read. But I couldn't bring myself to write a letter. Writing anything seemed like a betrayal to my mother. With the pain of her passing so close, I couldn't bear it.

But the questions—the ACCUSATIONS—swirled in my head with hurricane force. Why was this new woman—this new SON—so much more important than I?

How could I not mean anything to him?

Once I picked up the phone and dialed his area code and directory assistance. I nearly choked when I said his name, Walter Rolland, to the directory operator. I felt guilty, like she knew I was his estranged and ill-wishing son, and that I had no real intention of phoning him. I don't even know why I wanted the number. To fill a blank space in my address book? To torment myself? To believe that an address and a phone number somehow made him more real? More ALIVE?

A part of me didn't want to let him know that Mom had died. I held it close—the experience of her illness, the knowledge of her death. It was like a weapon I held in a vast arsenal meant to defeat him. It was my Hiroshima, my Nagasaki. My emotional nuclear bomb. And if I dropped it, I didn't want his response to be based on guilt.

Now that Mom was gone, I wanted to know that if he acknowledged me at all that he was doing it because of the simple fact that he was my father, which was a fact he couldn't change. I wanted him to acknowledge that he created me along with my mother, who he had married and stayed with for twenty years.

Finally, just after I received Noelle's letter, the letter she wrote to tell me she was getting married, I wrote to him. I asked about his new son and indicated that I'd like to be a part of his life. I wrote that I had news about Mom, but didn't mention the cancer. I didn't mention her death. Her death belonged to me.

I didn't hear back from him. He didn't write, he didn't call.

As the weeks passed and the phone didn't ring, as the mailbox held only bills and circulars, I stopped expecting to hear from him. Weeks became months and still, nothing came. And once again, I found it easier to believe that he was dead.

"My father's dead, Anita. In my mind, he's dead."

"Is Noelle dead too?" she asked.

Hearing her name—Noelle—*was* like a call from the grave. Had I secretly pretended that she, too, was dead? "What do you mean?" I asked.

"I want you to see Noelle too."

I turned toward her sharply, thinking she couldn't possibly have said what she just said. "Noelle Moncada? You mean *that* Noelle?"

"If that's still her name," she said. "I don't care if she's married or not. I just want you to face her once and for all to see if there's anything left. I told you that I couldn't be with you if I wasn't first in your heart. I won't marry you if she's still in your system. That's a promise."

"You make her sound like a drug."

"She *is* a drug," said Anita. "And as far as I'm concerned, she's toxic to our relationship."

We had moderate success with the garage sale and packed the remaining items in Anita's pick-up truck and hauled them to the Good Will. Since Anita brought up her name, I couldn't stop thinking about Noelle. And Anita knew it. "I don't think we should spend the night together," she said. "Let's drop off this stuff at the Good Will center and I'll take you home."

"You're probably right," I said.

I kissed her briefly and as soon as I closed the door of her truck, she tore off down the street. *That* Noelle was one sore subject.

Grabbing a bottle of Budweiser from the refrigerator, I went upstairs to my mother's room, opened a window—the same window out of which she used to blow her contraband cigarette smoke—and sat at her desk. A warm breeze made the curtains swirl and filled the room with some much-needed fresh air. I took a long, slow sip of beer and thought of the spring days in college where drinking beer outside was the sweetest pleasure. Along with those thoughts of college came more thoughts of Noelle. I couldn't erase her from my mind no matter how hard I tried. No matter how good it was with Anita—and it was good—I continually asked myself, wasn't it Noelle who showed up in my dreams as the prize I could never seem to win?

The dreams came less often, but still they came. And there, in a hazy, slow motion world known only to me, she showed up in the oddest places and among people she would never have been with—like Joe and Carol; my Aunt Sue; my boss, Rick Rosenbaum; and some of the other floor brokers. In one dream we were kids in the neighborhood, playing softball, and she was Maria, but then the bell down the street rang and it was Noelle who had to leave. Then we were college students taking classes in outdoor adventure activities—and she was in the class ahead of me, leaving just as I was coming.

In my dreams Noelle was always interested in me—always gave me some indication that it was I whom she wanted, and yet somehow, circumstances never allowed us that knowing kiss—that bond that says, "Yes, it's you and I. It's right." Whenever I woke up from those dreams I was left with a sense of longing—and failure.

But they were just dreams. More and more Noelle faded into fantasy. It was Anita who was my reality. Sure of this, I picked up the phone and called the last home phone number I had for Noelle.

Lara Romano, my old girlfriend, answered.

"I wondered how long it was going to be before I—I mean we—heard from you," she said. "Still in Chicago?"

"Yes, I am. How are you, Lara?"

"I'm well. Very well. I hear you're working for the corporate pigs. Making lots of money are you?"

"Lara, I'm glad to know you haven't changed," I said.   "Is Noelle, is she...?"

"Is she married?" asked Lara.

"I was going to ask if she was still living with you."

"More and more all the time," said Lara. "Especially now that we have a bigger—not to mention brighter—place. She and Nick are on their last legs, thank God. What a creep!"

"So she's not married."

"Christ, no," said Lara laughing. "She's already met someone else, if you can believe it. But hey, you didn't hear that from me."

"That's Noelle all right," I said. "She doesn't like to stay in one place too long."

"I'm not sure what's going on with this new guy. I think he's a law student and someone at her work introduced them. Hopefully he's the nail in the coffin of what's left between her and Nick-the-prick. He was so mean to her!"

"What do you mean? Did he hurt her?"

"I don't know about physically," said Lara. "I think it was primarily emotional abuse. He kept helping her confirm the worst opinions of herself. Exactly what she didn't need."

"What did she see in him?"

"A father," said Lara.

"Now you sound like her old roommate, Ruby."

"Oh, she's got a new job too," said Lara. "She finally got away from the other bad influence in her life and now she's working for my officemate's uncle who owns a small book publishing company in Albany. He says in his books that it's based in Berkeley, but it's really Albany. Close enough I guess."

"How do I get in touch with her?" I asked. "Can I call her there?"

"Sure," she said. "I don't know where she is now, but she'll be at work on Monday. She never misses work. Let me get the number."

I copied Noelle's work number on the back of a telephone bill and wrote the numbers over again and again as Lara talked about her program, the course she was teaching and some of her students. She hadn't yet decided if she'd go for her Ph.D. or try to find work, but admitted she was tired of living below the poverty line. She insisted she'd only work in a not-for-profit sector.

"What about Noelle?" I asked. "Is she a journalist yet?"

"I wouldn't call it that," said Lara. "She might be writing some short stories, but she doesn't ask me to read anything.

I wouldn't have time to read anything anyway. Anything not course related that is."

"What's her job?"

"Editorial Assistant," she said. "I think she primarily proof-reads—and types, of course. Noelle wouldn't be Noelle if her fingers weren't attached to a keyboard. It's not much better than her last job, but you know how she always underestimates herself."

"Is that what she does?"

"She underestimated *you,*" said Lara. "But then again, so did I."

"I'm thinking about coming to see her," I said. "And maybe I'll even look up my father. He's in Santa Rosa."

"Your father? I don't remember meeting your father."

"He wasn't around much back in those days. I don't know if I'll do it. It's been a long time since I've seen him. I'm not even sure he knows my mother died." I pulled another swig from my beer. I didn't know what I was saying. I wanted to get off the phone. "Thanks for the number, Lara. You sound like you're doing well, and I'm glad. Listen, in case I don't get ahold of Noelle, don't tell her I called. I'll call again when I'm more sure of my plans."

I hung up and folded the piece of paper with Noelle's work number into a small square and put it in my back pocket. Finishing my beer, I climbed the steps to my bedroom and pulled a cardboard box from the closet. The box contained notebooks from school, ripped folders with pen doodles and yellowing pages with thin strips of typed copy—my first attempts at the inverted pyramid. I pulled out a yellow plastic bag, the 710 Bookstore bag containing Noelle's poem, "A Winter Encounter," as new and as perfect as the day I first saw it.

I read her words and conjured a cold, thin memory of a night when I was very young and had nothing but possibilities ahead of me. While I thought I had the power to make every-thing right, it didn't occur to me that some of those possibili-ties would be devastating. After the night I slept with Noelle, I thought my future would be with her. But I was wrong.

I dropped the poem back into the bag and set it on top of my notebooks. Racing down the stairs, I went back to the tele-phone and made plans to leave for California. Ralph's son, Mike, lived in Oakland. If he said it was okay, I'd stay with him.

I would do this for Anita. In my soul, I knew she was the one for me.

\* \* \* \* \* \* \* \*

A week later in Oakland, California, a warm and colorful place filled with a lush, patchwork beauty, I phoned Noelle at work from Mike's apartment. She spoke with soft "a's," a new, laid-back accent. She was happy to hear from me.

"I'll take off the afternoon and meet you at the BART station near my work," she said. "We'll get a latté."

I didn't have the slightest clue what a latté was.

Waiting for her to arrive at the train station, I leaned against the wall and read the paper. When I looked up, I saw her riding toward me on her bicycle with red hair flying in the breeze. She was unmistakable. We saw each other at the same moment and her luminous face lit up as if it were internally wired. And there was that huge, familiar smile.

She was more beautiful than I remembered.

We walked together to a coffee shop where I found out what a latté was, and I liked this milky coffee drink so much I had two. Then, as we walked up a steep hill to a park known as the "Rose Garden," I felt shaky.

"I come here all the time," she said, laying her bicycle in the grass. "The beauty and smell of the roses and the breeze off the Bay are romantic, don't you think?"

She rambled on about roses and redwoods and eucalyptus trees. I wasn't listening. I wanted to change the subject—to gain control. "What's going on with you and Nick?"

"He hates me," she said, burying her chin in her chest. Her voice grew small—like the early days when she presented her poems to the Oral Interpretation class. "I don't know how much longer I can stay with him, because I started seeing someone else. I was desperate, I guess. I don't know. Desperate to be *loved*. I haven't told Nick."

"So, are you sleeping with this new man?" It came out like an accusation and by the deep furrow that appeared between her nearly invisible eyebrows, Noelle thought so too.

She didn't answer. Her faced reddened, matching the sweater tied around her waist, and she stared out at the waters of San Francisco Bay. Her hair hung in messy ringlets and blew behind her. She combed it with her fingers. "There's something I have to tell you," she finally said.

"You *are* sleeping with him, aren't you? Man, that disappoints me."

"No, Joel. No. That's not what I was going to say. And what the. . . ? That's not a very nice thing to say to me."

"I'm sorry," I said. "Really. Sorry. I don't know what I'm talking about. What were you going to say?"

"Never mind."

"Noelle. C'mon. I flew all the way out here to see you. Just tell me."

"Whatever," she said. She grabbed her hair and twisted it into a knot. "This is really stupid. But the other night, Lara and I were talking and for whatever reason she asked me about my best—or most meaningful—sexual experience. I didn't answer her but the truth is. . . ." She hesitated, then turned and looked at me. "The truth is, it was you."

Her green eyes filled with tears and she looked away. I was compelled to grab her, to pull her to me and not let go. But I didn't. Instead I reached for her chin and turned her face to mine. A perfect tear fell from her left eye. She didn't wipe it away. "You're very tempting," I said.

"Promise me we'll always be friends," she said. "Okay?" She looked confused and sad as she blinked away more tears. Her nose ran and she used the back of her hand to wipe it.

At that moment, my longing for her transformed into a form of love that I had never known and can barely describe.

It was not a need.

It was not a passion.

It was *not* what I felt for Anita.

Instead, it was a caring and a friendship. And in a way, it was a goodbye.

"Will you promise to stay in touch with me forever?" she asked again.

"Yes, Noelle," I said. "I promise."

# 25.
# Noelle. 1986.

Three weeks after I stopped working for Newhouse Communications—a break I made at Nick's insistence—I had failed to make a single advance in the wedding plans. Instead of fanciful and exciting wedding decisions—a bulleted list in front of me became a mountain of chores and obligations:

- China and silver patterns
- Invitations
- Bridesmaid dresses
- Honeymoon

It was like a pile of unfolded laundry or a stack of dirty dishes—the last things I wanted to tackle. Why did all these decisions fall upon the bride?

Finally, one afternoon at an East Bay bridal boutique, I experienced a white lace revelation: I was *not* who I wanted to be.

The boutique was sparsely populated with mannequins and taffeta. I walked inside and instantly felt out of place. The lone saleswoman, who looked like one of the mannequins, scanned me from head to toe—from my long, unstyled hair, my jean jacket, to my green cotton skirt and Birkenstocks. Sufficiently judged—in her eyes just another young, *Berkeleyesque* woman—I nodded a wordless hello and stood in the middle of the room like I was lost.

"Bride to be?" she asked.

I nodded again and she rose slowly from her desk and strutted toward me, not unlike the way a bridesmaid walks up the aisle. "You've come to the right place," she said. "With your figure, you'll have the pick of the stock. Do you have a theme?"

"A theme?"

"Oh my, you're young. Where's your mother?"

"Florida last time I checked. She may be getting married herself."

"A double ceremony?"

"No, nothing like that," I said.

The woman stroked her chin. "Let's see." She had a prominent moustache above her lip—dyed yellow to match her hair. "Do you know the season? Indoors or outdoors?"

"I . . . I mean we haven't set a date. But I think it'll be outdoors at his grandparent's vineyard."

"Ooh a vineyard!" she said. "How lovely." She grew animated with the thought and danced from rack to rack, pushing dresses from one end of the metal bar to another. As she shuffled dresses the way a Las Vegas dealer shuffled cards, I sat down and watched her work. "Don't you want to look around a bit?"

"Just show me the latest styles," I said. "You're the expert."

"Wonderful. I know just the thing to enhance your ethereal look. My daughter has red hair like you. Only the natural redheads have such translucent skin. I hope you wear sunscreen. You don't want to end up looking like one big freckle, you know."

"Oh no, I wouldn't want that," I said rolling my eyes. I felt a growing contempt for this woman—this representation of the marriage institution—and wished someone were with me, like Ruby. I knew Lara would never step foot into a place like this.

Wait a minute. Lara and Janette were supposed to be my bridesmaids. Weren't they supposed to be helping me? While looking around a sea of white lace poof, I realized I was sorely lacking in the area of bride training. Were these things—decisions regarding wedding etiquette—taught in high school home ec classes? Was this what I had missed by taking Western Civilization and Vocational Typing instead?

The woman suggested I "prepare myself" by waiting in a dressing room at the back of the store. I followed her instructions and immediately regretted it. It was like stepping into a vagina. Everything was pink and red and soft and cushy. Mirrors and sparkles and soothing New Age music engulfed me and I grew dizzy. It was a case of vaginal vertigo. I opened another red velvet drape and then sat down on an equally red velvet bench, half expecting to look around and find a heart shaped bed. Next to the bench was a magazine rack stocked with the current issues of five different bride's magazines. They were filled with skinny, sullen models dressed in five-thousand-dollar gowns. Flipping through one magazine, which weighed about as much as I, I wondered if any carried an article about how to gracefully call off the entire thing.

After five minutes the saleswoman finally entered holding only one dress. "I think I've found the perfect creation," she said. It was an ankle length gown made of Victorian Lace, with a high collar, a tight bodice, and long sleeves.

"I can help you with that," she said, immediately fussing.

I undressed and slipped on the gown, while she stood behind me like a servant, zipping and tying, and finally, stepped back to scrutinize the fit.

"It's a size too large, I think, but it's lovely on you with that neck," she said as I looked at my reflection in the mirror. She smiled until her eyes scanned halfway down the length of my body. Then she frowned. "It should be a little longer. It shouldn't hang to your calf, but rather almost to the floor."

"Story of my life," I said. "Always too tall."

"Don't say that. You could be a model."

I could be a lot of things, I thought.

"That's a problem," she said. "We can shorten, but we can't lengthen. Not this particular dress anyway. Let me see what else I can find for you—now that I know I'm dealing with some extreme height."

She didn't notice that when I walked in? I pulled at the sleeves and placed my hands on the scratchy lace. It was a beautiful dress, but I thought I looked ridiculous in it. Looking at my three-fold reflection in the mirrors before me—a young girl in ill-fitting dress-up clothes—I saw only the triviality of my existence. I turned from side to side and searched hard to find myself inside the kaleidoscope of lace. Instead I grew smaller and smaller, sucked into a narrow tunnel full of restrictions and disappointments.

It was the tunnel that was my future.

Suddenly it was clear to me how shallow my attachment was to this imagined future. I knew I was in a world where I didn't belong. I didn't want to be a bride or a wife. I didn't love Nick. I knew this. I also knew that I wanted to go back to work. I wanted to work as a journalist—a writer—an editor—anything in the field in which I had studied. What was holding me back? Why had I felt so trapped? For months I had followed him around and endured his criticisms. At first I thought he was teaching me—making me a better person. But I didn't see a better person looking back at me through multiple sets of eyes.

"So, what do you think?" asked the woman, returning with two more gowns. "Something else along these lines or something more modern? I have both."

"I think I've seen enough."

"But you've only tried on one dress," she said. "Exactly when is the big day?" Suspicion colored her face as she double-checked my left hand to see whether or not I was a legitimate bride-to-be. When discovering Nick's showy ring, she arched her painted eyebrows. I put my hand behind my back.

"I'm not sure there's going to be a wedding," I said.

"Oh. Well, that's quite an engagement ring you're sporting on your finger. Are you sure you want to give up that *and* a vineyard?"

"It's all pretty superficial, don't you think? I mean, where does love fit into the equation?"

"Ah, yes. Love. You are indeed very young," she said. "So tell me, are you just killing time? Wasting *my* time?"

I reached for the zipper at the back of my neck, practically ripped it open and let the dress drop to the floor. Turning to face her in my underwear, she immediately looked away. "Actually, Ma'am, you should consider your time well spent. You may have helped to convince me that getting married right now is the exact wrong thing for me to do." I bent over and picked up the pile of ivory lace and handed it to her. "And it's not like you've got a dozen customers out there lined up to try on these overpriced dresses, is it?"

"Well," she sighed. "I never. . . ." She opened the curtain, and like a case of *coitus interruptus,* forced herself out of the vagina.

I put on my clothes and then grabbed my purse from the red bench and looked inside for a business card that Lara had given me for a man who owned a small book publishing company, Northside Press. His name was Charlie Hoganson and I had spoken to him on the phone several weeks earlier regarding a position as an editorial assistant. He said I should drop in and see the operation if I were interested in the job.

He had made no promises, but since the bridal boutique was in the neighborhood, I had nothing to lose by going to see him.

"I'm sorry I wasted your time," I said to the saleswoman. "I didn't mean to be rude."

"Just don't throw away a good thing if you've got one," she said. "Fiancés with vineyards don't come around every day."

Thank heaven for that.

The Northside office was only two blocks up the street, off the beaten path on a side street. Charlie, bald with a corrugated forehead and heavy-set like a Teddy bear, hardly remembered our conversation. He gave me the once over—in the same manner as the saleswoman at the bridal shop—and asked me to type some copy. It meant facing another IBM Selectric. I sat down, greeted it like an old friend, fed in a sheet of paper, and typed.

My typing sounded like a rapid-fire machine gun. I finished
Charlie's assignment in about three minutes, and he looked it
over while stroking his mustache.

"Ten bucks an hour," he said. "I pay on Fridays."

Visualizing the smug look on my typing teacher's face, I
silently thanked her for putting up with me as I took typing
test after typing test, refusing to slow down, until I managed
to turn in ten tests at a hundred words-per-minute with fewer
than five errors. In a world just moving into word processors
and personal computers on every desk, typing was getting easier
and more valuable every day.

That night I told Nick about the new job and he was furious.
He set down his wine glass so forcefully that cabernet splattered
on the tablecloth and looked like blood. "We're going to live in
the Napa Valley," he said over dinner. "Do you honestly intend
to commute each day to another menial job?"

"It's not menial," I argued. "I'm an editorial assistant. I'll be
training to be a book editor. This is what I went to school to
become."

"Exactly whom are you trying to kid, Noelle? You'll never be
a book editor. You'll be lucky to work on the newsletter at my
grandparents' winery."

He said things like this to me all the time. But this time I
truly heard him. I digested this insult—this latest attack—and spit
it right back at him. "Is that what you think of me, Nick?"

"Face it, Noelle," he said. "I've read your work. It stinks. You
can't even spell."

I swallowed hard and ate the rest of my dinner in silence. I
left the restaurant without saying goodnight, and headed east to
Berkeley. Maneuvering over the Richmond Bridge through sparse
traffic, sensing the briny air of the Bay and the freedom of the
water beneath me, I realized that Nick and I were destined to
go in different directions. Nick would drive north and I would
drive east. We would both end up where we belonged.

At home I found Lara working at the dining room table and
eating cold cucumber soup. "You'll be glad to know I got a new
job today," I said while dropping my keys on the table.

"You're kidding me," she said.

"It's with your friend's uncle. The publisher. That ought to
make you proud of me."

"Noelle, I *am* impressed. Now all you have to do is dump
that Republican and you'll have my full respect."

"I'm pretty sure I broke up with him tonight," I said.

Lara dropped her spoon.

When I saw Joel Rolland it felt like I broke up with him

too. He touched my face and told me I was "tempting." Then he promised to remain my lifelong friend. After I said goodbye to him at the BART station and rode my bike home, there were three messages in Lara's handwriting sitting next to the phone. All were from Nick. "He sounded pissed," she wrote on the third.

The phone rang and I answered it, knowing it would be he. He didn't wait for me to say hello.

"Where were you this afternoon?" Nick asked. "I called your office and then left a dozen messages at your house."

"I took the afternoon off. I went . . . shopping."

"At work they said you went to meet an old friend who was in from out of town. What friend? You didn't tell me you had a friend coming in."

I looked at myself in the hallway mirror. Did I recognize the girl looking back at me? "You know something Nick? It doesn't matter what I did this afternoon. It's none of your business."

"Just who is it you're sleeping with now, Noelle?" he asked. "Is it that old boyfriend or are you seeing someone new? You think I don't know what's going on with you?"

"Nick, I. . . ."

"Don't bother, Noelle. It's very clear that you've got deep-seated personality problems and someday you'll realize you have to change. I may or may not stick around."

More criticisms. More threats.

In the past my response was to hang my head, cower like a child and then try desperately to regain his approval—to dress just right, to prepare a meal for his grandparents and serve the correct wine—to quit my job and concentrate on wedding plans. The more dinners we attended where he worked the room and showed off his wine expertise, the more alone I felt. He regularly abandoned me at tables full of strangers, where I sat dressed in expensive jewelry and smiled politely while those around me talked about themselves as they poked at their food.

I thought about my sister Janette and her spell with the rich snob she almost married, and I cringed. "Goodbye, Nick," I said, and hung up.

The next day I wrapped up the engagement ring and sent it to him by registered mail.

I wish I could say I never heard from him again. I wish I could say I cut him out of my life with the simplicity of a returned ring. But he made it difficult. Leaving Nick was messy.

I had grown accustomed to clean breaks; however, with him—with a famous family, a priest—the escape route was littered with unfinished plans, diamonds and sapphires, grandparents, and all the expectations and guilt attached to the Catholic Church. Not to mention my mother, who raised me to stick with *it*—whether *it* meant cheerleading or even Nick, whom she hadn't yet met.

After spending the afternoon with Joel, after seeing his kind face and recognizing a certain brand of love and warmth that was possible in a relationship—a friendship—I knew I had to end it with Nick. While Joel and I were destined to be friends rather than lovers, Nick and I were lovers but not friends. It had been clear for months that he didn't love me. He may have loved the idea of me—the nubile redhead—but his constant criticisms proved that a marriage between us would never work.

I was failing Nick, and worse, I was failing myself. Nick didn't like failure and that's all I was to him. He would rather have married me and lived a miserable existence than let me leave and accept the idea of choosing the wrong vintage of a woman. But I was no Eliza Dolittle! I grew strong in my resolve. I knew I could be loved for the person I was—not someone's idea of what I was. For weeks Nick showed up at my office and came to my house. He scolded me like I was a child trying to quit the cheerleading squad before the end of basketball season.

I knew better. My mother was thousands of miles away and I knew that this time, it was okay to change my mind.

Finally, at Lara's suggestion, I threatened him with a restraining order. *"Nick Austin must not come within fifty feet of Noelle Moncada or face misdemeanor charges of harassment."* That did the trick.

* * * * * * * *

I loved my job at Northside Press. It, I decided, was where I wanted to be. I met interesting authors, read their raw material, and delighted in knowing that they, too, misspelled words and made silly grammatical errors. "Everyone needs an editor," said Charlie.

The office was small and we worked in what used to be someone's house—a 1940s stucco bungalow. Charlie's office was the living room. His title was "Publisher," and he did everything from payroll and bookkeeping to writing book jacket blurbs and arranging publicity schedules. The two main editors—the acquisition editor and the copy editor—and I worked in what had been bedrooms. Our conference room was the former dining room, and the kitchen was the break room. The art director worked in an annex off the kitchen and the shipping department was the garage.

I worked five and sometimes six days a week. I arrived early and stayed late and often I took work home. I sought and gained comfort in the unemotional routine of the projects—the books that provided stories, information, and poetry without talking—without judging. My coworkers were kind and appreciative as I helped make their jobs easier, their workloads lighter. I felt truly valued, especially when my salary went up from ten to fourteen dollars an hour.

In this time, Lara and I developed a closer friendship. We attended poetry and literary readings and saw every new movie we could. Some weekends we ventured to the Sierra Mountains with thirty-pound packs on our backs. I trailed Lara as she expertly traversed the rugged terrain, following guide maps she'd picked up at the library or the REI store. Lara sweat so hard there was a constant stream pouring off her body. She wore a dark blue bandana and stopped every fifteen minutes, took it off her forehead, and wrung it out like a sponge.

On one trip, I sat down on a boulder alongside the trail and looked at the azure sky, watching birds of prey soar by at impossibly high altitudes. I told her about a movie I'd seen called *Continental Divide* with John Belushi, who played a big-city muckraker—like Mike Royko. He fell in love with a naturalist, Blair Brown, who lived in the Rocky Mountains. I recounted the story of how they fell in love and how he gave up his job in the busy city to live with her in her remote mountain home. Before I finished telling her the plot, Lara's big marble eyes filled with tears.

"What's wrong?" I asked.

"That's what I want in my life," she said, wiping her face with her damp bandana.

"To live in the mountains?"

"To have a man love me enough to want to follow me to the mountains."

I had never seen Lara cry before. She was always so strong and, I thought, too smart to cry. The thin air and the picture-postcard setting of the wilderness brought out my new strength and I put my arms around Lara and comforted her. Showing me her vulnerability had been a gift she didn't expect to give, but finally, after so many years, she gave me the chance to be the strong one—to assure her that everything would be okay.

Sitting next to a crystal clear mountain tarn with one of my oldest friends next to me—I felt young, alive, and ready to conquer the world. I felt like I had something to offer simply by being there with her. Simply by listening and being a friend, I felt fulfilled. I didn't need a man in my life, and I wasn't looking for anyone's approval.

For the first time, I didn't want to be anyone else. Everything before me was good enough. *I* was good enough.

I realized that afternoon in the mountains with Lara that I was only just beginning to love myself. Everything prior to this day had been preparation for this new consciousness—simply *oral interpretation* of what I thought it meant to live and to love.

Then Joel called. My heart jumped when my boss told me "there's a Joel Rolland on the phone for you," and I couldn't resist blurting out that I had broken up with Nick.

"Then this phone call is bittersweet," he had said.

"Bittersweet? Why would you say that?"

"Because I'm marrying Anita."

# 26.
# Joel. 1995.

Anita and I were married in May of 1985. Our first child, Michael, was born a year later, and it was the happiest time of my life. The day after he was born, I passed out cigars on the trading floor and felt at the top of the crowd. His birth signified my own rebirth—from boy to man to father.

When I became a father, I redefined the term. I could be everything my father was not.

In the evenings I curled up against Anita and the baby and made plans, devising lists of all the things I would teach my son: How to find the North Star, skip a rock, make a proper paper airplane, and throw a ball. When the time came, I would definitely teach him how to drive a stick shift. During slower periods on the trading floor, I found myself thinking a lot about God and creation—about the miracle of birth and the precious gift of life. When I was with my son, I couldn't move my eyes away from his scrunched-up face, his pouting lips, his balled hands. There's so much promise inside the closed fist of a newborn baby. And each time I pried open his warm, curling fingers, it unleashed a Pandora's Box of both past ills and hopes for the future.

Michael's birth resurrected my father. I didn't want to think about him—wanted to keep him buried. But hope got the best of me and I sent him a birth announcement. I hoped he would relate to the birth of a grandchild—be happy for me and finally make contact—maybe even apologize.

He didn't write back.

Anita had given up her job at the Botanic Gardens seven months into her pregnancy, and loved being a mother. She grew more beautiful to me with each passing day. Then, the following year she had a miscarriage. She was fourteen weeks along in her pregnancy and it happened as she pushed Michael in a stroller on her way to the grocery store. The sudden wetness between her legs triggered an alarm and she knew at once that she had lost the baby.

She was inconsolable.

"Miscarriage is nature's way of dealing with defective embryos," the doctor had said. Anita didn't see it that way. She thought the miscarriage was God's way of punishing her for the abortion. She believed the new baby attached itself to scar tissue or remains of her first pregnancy, and it didn't stand a chance. How she had ever managed to hang onto Michael and give birth to a healthy son was beyond her comprehension.

She cried for days. And days turned into weeks. Anita refused to set down Michael and slept in the nursing chair next to his crib each night. She was afraid she would lose him, too, and there was no reasoning with her. It got so bad that I called her parents and they came from New Jersey and stayed for a month—long enough for me to go out of my mind.

Each morning my mother-in-law awoke before me. Wearing a hot pink robe and her white hair piled high atop her head, she served coffee and toast, and asked me what I wanted for dinner. With her, life's priorities were twofold: planning meals and getting to the morning newspaper first. She completed the crossword puzzle, the Jumble, and the Crytoquip well before sunup. I tried to read the stock reports while drinking her weak coffee, while she asked questions about whether or not I believed in global warming or my opinions on cosmetic surgery and if I thought she should have it. My father-in-law, on the other hand, hibernated in the bathroom with the sports page. When he emerged he talked not of sports but of the Navy. He couldn't get beyond 1945 and his last trip to Japan. For him, the world stopped after Truman dropped the last bomb and his World War II mentality melted his mind closed. "Don't ever let me catch you driving a Japanese car," he said. "There are very few things I hate in this world, but one of those things is definitely the *Japs.*"

There was no point arguing with him.

The weeks crawled by. I tuned out my in-laws and focused on Michael. Watching him grow and change was my greatest joy. He had my blond hair and Anita's black eyes. His skin was rosy, his cheeks pudgy. He ran circles around us, threw his food, and babbled constantly. Anita rarely took her eyes off him.

Before I left for work, I tiptoed into his room where they were still asleep and kissed them both goodbye. Sometimes his eyes popped open and his face glowed with love. Anita, on the other hand, was stiff and remote. Her actions were mechanical, dutiful.

Her parents kept telling me to "give it time."

I felt like a visitor in my in-laws' home, and I hated not sleeping with my wife. While we once tried to conceal our sexual relationship when they visited before we were married, now it was far worse. This time it was Anita's choice, and I grew more resentful and angry with each passing day. I had become an insignificant detail in her life.

Meanwhile, I needed someone to help *me* through the loss of our child, but no one seemed to understand anything beyond how it affected Anita. I ached for her—longed for her touch, her love. All I could do was continue to get up in the morning and go to work and hope things would look brighter when I came home.

At work I wasn't insignificant. I flourished. Rosenbaum backed me with $75,000 as a market maker in the IBM pit. It was a good investment as he stood to make fifty-percent of everything I made, with half of my take earmarked to pay off his investment in me.

I didn't disappoint him. Once that $75,000 was repaid, I was on my own. As a market maker I had an obligation to facilitate public orders. Among other trading strategies, my edge was the difference between what I had paid for an option and for what I would sell it. Essentially I had to be on the buy side *and* the sell side of every transaction. And God bless the world of options, making money was easy. My cohorts and I joked that it was like pushing in a wheelbarrow in the morning, filling it with cash, and pushing it home in the evening.

After putting up with them for far too long, I presented my in-laws with two first-class airline tickets back to New Jersey and thanked them for all their support. It was time to get my life back. I bought a new car and had a larger family room added to the house. For Anita's birthday I had a solarium constructed off the new family room. She seemed happy about it, even grateful, but it took a while for her to step inside and claim it as her own—to take over and fill it with plants from the greenhouse. Eventually, as I had hoped, it proved to be therapeutic. Each day she spent a little more time growing and propagating and teaching Michael the finer points of plunging his tiny hands into buckets of mud.

Slowly, like a germinating plant, Anita emerged from her

depression. And as she recovered, a firework of recognition lit Michael's round and small-featured face any time I walked in the room. It was as though their moods and dispositions were directly related—through chemistry or electricity. "Dada!" he shrieked. Like many babies, it was his first word. But for me it was the only word in the world worth hearing from his tiny, pink lips.

When Anita first came back to our bed, it was hours after I had closed my book and turned off my light. I woke up in the wee morning hours sullied and sweating from haunting, recurring dreams, to find her asleep next to me snoozing soundly and innocently, while I struggled with dreams of my father and, God help me, Noelle Moncada.

My dreams portrayed a hundred different lives I might have chosen for myself. Both Noelle and my father soared through the wistful, breathless night air that is sleep. Somehow they were both always just out of reach. In my dreams each had eyes as green as traffic lights. Often, they knew my son. They had impossible, connected relationships. *What does the green light mean, Michael? Green means you GO!* And away they always went, my father, Noelle, Michael, leaving me disappointed, rapacious, panicked. Standing on a street corner, lost or late.

Anita had asked me to do it. I said I'd done it, but I didn't. I couldn't shake her.

And I didn't want to.

We had what Noelle liked to call 'a pact.' We had phone conversations. They weren't frequent and at first seemed unplanned; however, a pattern emerged where we called on each other's birthdays and we sent Christmas cards.

"Is this how it's going to be?" I asked her on my twenty-eighth birthday. "Are we going to call each other on birthdays for the rest of our lives?"

"Why not?" she had asked.

Yes, why not. She saw nothing wrong with it. Why should I? I told her our relationship remained an ongoing sentence, connected by a never-completed past tense. With no future together, we only had insignificant small talk. We were friends. It was what we were meant to be.

Then on her twenty-ninth birthday, she said she had finally found the love of her life. His name was Marc Armstrong and he was an attorney. She had actually met him before she broke it off with Nick from Napa, but it took a while before they became involved. Constantly saying she was "scared to death" of being engaged again, they dated and even lived together for two years before she married him. And from what I could tell through the long distance phone lines, she seemed happy. She, I realized, had successfully moved on.

I believed I had as well. Her next birthday came and went and I didn't call. My birthday passed without contact. Her friendship had lost its importance to me.

Soon Anita was again pregnant, and this time we had twins. Considered high risk, she spent most of the pregnancy in bed and did everything in her power to assure the delivery of healthy babies. She ingested lots of water, orange juice, folic acid, and organic greens she grew in her solarium. At her doctor's order, her only exercise was getting out of bed each day to water and prune the plants. I took care of Michael and took him to day care. I made sure the house was clean and everyone was fed.

Anita grew enormous, but she glowed with life. To me, she was the picture of heath.

David and Daniel, named for her father and brother, were each nearly six pounds.

When they were born, I decided to leave the trading floor. I had made enough money to last for a long, long time. Having promised my mother I'd do so, I toyed with the idea of finishing my degree; however, staying home with Anita and the boys was more than a full-time job. Our relatively serene home with one child turned into a house of chaos, and having three boys underfoot was like living inside a live volcano with action constantly bubbling.

Someone was always crying, in need or in bed with us.

Anita was back in full force, reveling in her role as a mother and even joking that twins were the current punishment for the abortion. She took up running and religiously performed a rigorous exercise program to get back to her pre-pregnancy weight. When she reached her goal, 130 pounds, she announced that she was through having babies and asked me to have a vasectomy. I didn't hesitate.

After the twin's third birthday, I went back to work as a private financial consultant. My office was in downtown Chicago, and at first I drove to work and stored my car in the building's parking facility. But I hated sitting in stagnant expressway traffic and missed reading on the train. So I joined the ranks of the suit-wearing, train-riding commuters. I became one of those guys whose ties I wanted to cut off back when I first started commuting from my mother's house. One of those guys I swore I'd never be.

* * * * * * * *

Since I hadn't given Noelle my home phone number or address and I hadn't written to her, we had been out of touch
for nearly three years. As far as I knew, she didn't make an attempt to contact me. Once I had a new office, however, I gave
into fatalism and sent her a business card along with pictures
of the boys.

She responded immediately. It was Christmastime and Noelle
had always been big on Christmas cards. *"How wonderful to
hear from you,"* she wrote. *"Congratulations on the news of
your twins. It must be exhausting. Marc and I have some news
too. We're leaving California. We're moving to his hometown in
Wisconsin, some six hours north of Chicago."* She wrote further
that they hoped to have children and didn't want to raise them
in California, especially since the public schools weren't to their
liking. *"By the way,"* she continued, *"I know exactly where your
office is because Marc's aunt lives across the street. Don't be
surprised if we drop in and see you sometime."*

I laughed and cast aside the card, feeling it would never
happen.

But it did happen. It was a dreary spring day—more than a
year later—when they showed up.

"Mr. Rolland you have visitors," said Gina, my secretary.

"Who is it?"

"They said it's a surprise."

"They? How many?"

"Just two."

As I leaned forward and looked past Gina, I glimpsed what I
thought was red hair and for a brief, almost panicked moment,
thought it might be Noelle. No. No way. It was impossible. Why
would she come to my office?

I rose, brushed off the front of my pants and out of habit,
straightened my tie. My face felt hot. I stepped into the office
lobby and saw at once that it was Noelle.

It felt like an electric shock. I couldn't look her in the face
and couldn't find my voice. Again, I straightened my tie and
focused on the face of the man, her husband, Marc Andersen.
I recognized him from the pictures she had sent. "Hi Marc," I
managed, reaching out to shake his hand.

"Do you two know each other?" Noelle asked, shaking her
head a little. The light played off the tendrils of her red hair,
and she frowned.

"No. No," I said quickly. "I just know your picture. I mean, I
recognize it from Christmas cards."

"Yes," he laughed, shaking my hand vigorously. "Noelle and
her Christmas cards."

Marc was tall. Big. And I don't say this often about other men, but really good-looking. I felt small and stupid—like I had just been caught in the act of doing something wrong. Finally, I dropped Marc's hand and looked at her.

She was beautiful—as beautiful as I remembered. "Noelle Moncada," I said. Saying her name made me feel more relaxed. I took hold of her cold hands. "What are you doing here?"

"It's Noelle Andersen, thank you very much. I told you we would drop by someday when we were in the neighborhood," she said. "Well, we were in the neighborhood. Is this a bad time?"

"Oh, no," I said. "No, no. I was just about to go to lunch. Why don't we all go to lunch?"

We ate lunch at a restaurant near my office and afterwards they left abruptly, saying they were going across the street to visit Marc's aunt. I watched them make their way across the busy street arm-in-arm, trotting to the median. She turned around, saw me watching, and waved. Her smile, big as ever, sparkled in a triangle of sunlight that had managed to penetrate the clouds.

I sighed and jammed my hands inside my coat pockets. Looking up to the gray, Chicago sky, the sun had once again disappeared. Mechanically, I walked back to my office and pulled open the heavy door. A wind tunnel sucked me inside—forced me to step back into my life.

As I rode the elevator, I felt empty—even used. Did she bring Marc to show him off? Or was she showing off me to Marc? I didn't know. It was all so strange.

Watching the elevator light blink up the scale, *nine, ten, eleven, twelve* . . . I replayed the lunch. At one point, when Marc left for the men's room, Noelle grabbed my hand, looked at me earnestly and claimed she didn't want to "lose me."

Lose me? What was she talking about?

That night I made a huge mistake. I told Anita I had seen her. It had been so long—years—since we had spoken of Noelle. I was positive her name—her presence—would have little effect on my wife. I even hoped—albeit somewhat foolishly—that Anita had forgotten about her. To my knowledge she had never known about my true relationship with Noelle. I never told her that we started seeing each other while she was back in New Jersey over the holiday break when she discovered she was pregnant. And I, of course, never mentioned that Noelle and I had slept together.  But now I needed to expose my secret. I needed to tell Anita who I really was. I needed her to know me, and Noelle was a part of me.

As I uttered the second syllable of Noelle's name, I witnessed a change in my wife's expression. I saw her eyes grow hard as black granite and watched as she exploded with rage.

"You saw her?" she screamed. "You actually saw her? How could you?"

"She was with her husband, Anita."

"Do you think that matters to me? It doesn't matter. You were supposed to be rid of her. How did she even know how to find you?"

It didn't matter to her that Noelle was happily married. That she knew how to find me, and that we had kept in touch for years, *years!* after my trip to California—long after she had asked me to rid her from my system, was too much for her to take.

"She's your addiction," Anita shouted. "Can't you see there's no room for her in our life?"

"It's not like I'm having an affair with her, Anita. I don't understand why she's such a threat to you."

"It's not because you *are* having an affair with her," she said. "It's much worse."

"What do you mean, worse?"

"It's because you *want* to." She marched to our bedroom and slammed the door.

What followed were long, poisonous periods of silence between us. One minute she giggled and sang to the boys and another, when I walked into the room, she grew cold and silent. Oh, if only I had kept my mouth shut. Why had I finally elected to expose my secret relationship—to blurt it out like a confession? Did I think my wife, the woman who had harbored animosity toward Noelle since college, would grant me penance? Forgive me?

She would never forgive me where Noelle Moncada was concerned. She insisted that the two of us could not be friends. Not if I wanted to stay married to her.

There was only one thing for me to do.

I didn't call Noelle again and I didn't hear from her until she sent a Christmas card to my office. When I saw the return address, I almost threw it away. But I didn't. For a long moment I held it in my hands.

Anita had been right. I was like an alcoholic staring at a bottle of wine, willing himself not to pop the cork.

My phone rang and I ignored it. I got up and closed the door, then walked to the windows and looked down on the bustling city. There were no answers coming to me from the streets of Chicago.

I picked up the card and held it up to the light. Seeing that it contained a photo, I couldn't help myself. I opened it. I couldn't resist one last look.

# 27.
# Noelle. 1995.

I married Marc Andersen on my thirtieth birthday. It was a small, civil ceremony at the Claremont Hotel, an elegant white, Victorian landmark in the Berkeley hills. For the ceremony we had two rules: Nothing religious. Nothing sexist. I wanted as far away from Nick and the Catholic Church as I could get. My mother was the first to know about the engagement and Janette was my only bridesmaid. I had gotten that part right. And everything about the wedding was right and perfect. Marc and I made each decision together.

Even though I had met Marc while I was still engaged to Nick, it had been nearly two years after I returned Nick's ring before Marc and I saw each other again. We met by accident. It was at a Greek Theater Dead Show—a place surreal and smoky—a concrete carnival of the unwashed, filled with old hippies, new hippies, and babies with cotton taped to their ears. There were mingling scents of patchouli oil, clove cigarettes, and marijuana. In spite of the concrete amphitheater, cement thrones, and staid pillars, the place had a certain sway when the music began. The colorful crowd, faithful attendees of every show, knew every line of every song. They penetrated the air with harmony. Even the nearby trees waved dreamily in time.

I saw him first. Actually, I saw his eyes. And in them I recognized a feeling. In a blur of tie-dyed color, this man stood alone. He smiled, acknowledging me immediately. Without words, we joined together in a dance as though the moment were perfectly choreographed. The feel of his hand gently clasping mine, the way our fingers fit together, the electric tingle that shot through my body when he touched the small of my back, made the moment timeless and dizzying as I spun in circles. "Noelle," he finally whispered. "Where have you been?"

Allowing myself to plunge into a relationship with Marc was a gift. It was like a reward for wading through the chapters of my identity and finding a girl—a woman—whom I finally liked and even loved. For two years I had been a solitary person, working hard and learning the ins and outs of the small publishing company for which I worked. I had come to love my job and my coworkers, along with my outdoor adventures with Lara. I loved the freedom of making my own decisions—decisions as simple as what to wear in the morning, when to pull over to fill my gas tank, and what wine to order with dinner. I learned to cast aside a book without finishing it when I realized I didn't like the characters or felt the story was dull. I learned to quit doing what I didn't like doing. And I learned that it was okay. The sun would rise the next day, the fog would roll in during the afternoon, and somewhere, stars would sparkle at night.

The world became more beautiful to me outside myself—outside the constant self-scrutiny and self-loathing I'd heaped upon my being for as long as I could recall. I suppose it's what Janette always meant when she told me to *lighten up!*

When I lightened the ponderous load of my own self-interest, I allowed room for Marc to move inside—to fill me with his world, his brilliance, and his happy, positive attitude. We talked endlessly, comparing careers in law and publishing and how we saw our futures. He discussed his cases and his desire for a private practice. I discussed the manuscripts at work and my goal of writing and publishing something of my own. We spoke of our families—our siblings, mothers and fathers. When I spoke of my father, it was of the man that really existed. He was no longer a fantasy or a childlike dream. I admitted that losing him so early in my life left me feeling unresolved about boys, boyfriends, men, and potential husbands.

We spoke freely of past relationships without teasing or jealousy. He had had one serious girlfriend and several not-so-serious girlfriends, but gave me every indication that when he was with me, he was mine—and mine alone. I spoke of Nick and why I waited so long to start a new relationship after we broke up. I said I needed time on my own to learn to make decisions for myself.

Marc and Lara got along well, and he made it a point to meet and get to know my family and the friends I spoke of so often—Ruby, working hard to earn her Ph.D. in psychology, Lisa, married and living back in Springfield with her husband

and two daughters, and Cleo King, a Colorado forest ranger, still lusting after hairy men. He wanted to explore every inch of what had shaped me.

I dated Marc for a year before I finally told him about Joel Rolland—my soulful friend, whom I had promised to stay in touch with forever. Marc was unfazed. While Nick had been adamantly opposed to my having any kind of relationship with another man and viewed Joel as a threat, Marc didn't require an explanation.

"I have friends of the opposite sex too," he said. "I may have lusted after them at some point, but I didn't choose them. At least not the way I choose you."

Shortly after that we found a small house to rent where we lived together for two more years before getting married.

I stayed in touch with Joel, just as I had promised, although I only had his office address and office phone number. He never elevated my status to friend-of-the-family. He did, however, send birth announcements for his boys, first a son named Michael and then three years later, twin boys named David and Daniel. Their mother's name was rarely, if ever mentioned.

It occurred to me that I was his secret—the other woman dwelling in some kind of emotional passageway of his mind. But I didn't care. I had Marc, and I talked endlessly of him and our life together. On my birthday Joel called me either at home or at work and sent Christmas cards. And that became our pattern. Birthdays and Christmas. It went on for years—ten years since we made the friendship pact, five years into my marriage, and two years after Marc and I moved to Wisconsin and expected our first child.

Then I received a letter from him telling me to stop writing and calling.

* * * * * * * *

The crumpled letter sat between us, the subject of discussion. It was the case of Rolland v. Moncada.

"He's in love with you," said Marc after reading Joel's letter for the second time. "He's having difficulty in his marriage and he and his wife both know why. It's you."

"That's *wrong*," I said. "Whatever was between us sexually was left back in college. He knows it and I know it."

"Did you write something in the Christmas card to offend him?"

"I sent over a hundred cards that day, counselor. It didn't mean anything more than an annual holiday greeting to an old friend. Or at least I thought he was a friend. This is a guy I've known for almost twenty years."

"People change, Noelle," said Marc.

"People don't change," I said. "They simply reveal themselves."

"Well, you have a point. You told me he'd never given you his home address or phone number. Doesn't that tell you something?"

"Anita never liked me."

"I thought you said his wife didn't remember you."

I shook my head. *"He* said that during a phone conversation. I assured him she'd remember me if he brought up my name."

"You are rather unforgettable, my gorgeous wife," said Marc, pulling me close. He lifted my shirt and rubbed his warm hand back and forth across my belly, like he was petting the baby. "Maybe he finally brought up your name. Or maybe she busted him with the Christmas card under his pillow."

"Marc!"

"Well?" he said defensively. "I'm just trying to help you make sense of this."

"Whatever," I said. "Obviously he's got things going on that I don't understand."

"I'll say."

I picked up the letter. By this point, I had it memorized. "This really isn't about me, is it?"

"Listen Noelle, you slept with this guy, right? And when you did your relationship was no longer about friendship. He knows it, his wife knows it, and it's high time you know it too. You and Joel crossed the line. And once you cross it. . . ."

"But. . . ."

"No buts," he said, taking the letter from me and setting it back down. He squeezed my hands. "Let me tell you something about guys. For guys it's always about sex. *Always.* We're just a bunch of hounds always thinking about sex and always considering the possibility of sex with any woman we meet. It's this female *fuckability* factor that goes into action every time we come face to face with a woman. And just like you'll never know the feeling of getting kicked in the balls and I'll never know the feeling of giving birth, it's just something you'll have to learn to understand. So instead of trying to read more into this letter and getting yourself all worked up about it, the question for you should simply be what you're going to do about it."

After a long pause, thinking about pending labor pains and getting kicked in the crotch, I said I'd do what Joel had asked of me. "I'll honor his request," I said. "I'll leave him alone." And with that I got up and threw the letter back in the garbage can and tried to clear my mind of Joel Rolland—of Joel and Anita and Joel and me.

I wanted to believe my own words: *It wasn't about me.*

Shortly after dinner, Marc went to bed and I stayed up for a while and watched the snow fall silently onto a built-up pile outside our kitchen window. Marc had shoveled the roof and it left an outside curtain of snow, obscuring the view and insulating us like an igloo.

*Two beings ignoring the cold. . . .*

I couldn't sleep. With my bladder threatening to explode every hour and the bulkiness of my stomach keeping me from my favorite sleep positions, I got up, used the bathroom, and found my way through the dark, my arms stretched before me like a blind person. I strode through the kitchen past the curtain of snow and into the living room, and approached the Franklin stove where glowing red embers remained from the evening. Picking up a poker, I stirred the remains and a small, hopeful flame ignited. I reached for the last log and set it on top. Dog tags jingled like sleigh bells in the basement where Luna and Stella spent the nights, snuggling together in a cardboard refrigerator box. They knew I was awake and nearby.

As the lone log burst into flame, I closed the stove doors part way and sat in an oversized chair near the fire's warmth. The picture windows were clear, yet frosted like miniature ice rinks and through them, the fallen snow glistened in the moonlight. The outside world remained frozen. Hulking, black pine trees stood and stared back, silent observers. Leafless oaks and maples formed a complex labyrinth of black lace.

A cloud of smoke from the chimney swirled into view.

I thought of the first time I saw Joel—a night in a high school gymnasium—he with his curly hair and I in my loathsome cheerleading uniform. I thought of Lara, whom I hadn't seen since Marc and I moved from California. Still unmarried, she remained a spiky-haired student, still taking her hiking trips and searching for eagles and perfect love. She had had such long hair in high school and she was so smart. I remember how she encouraged me to take more challenging classes and insisted that I didn't give myself enough credit. But even her compliments felt like insults. She was so much like my sister. And as with my sister, I wanted to please her and make her proud. I couldn't grow up until I had achieved that goal.

I rarely heard from Janette since she got married and had a child—a son she named Earl after our father. She lived in eastern Tennessee, and with her husband ran a school for the deaf. She faithfully phoned on my birthday, but mostly I heard of her accomplishments and activities through my mother, also happily married and living in Florida. Her husband, an investment banker, was ten years younger than she. He worshipped my mother. We made annual visits to see them in Florida, usually during the holidays. But this year, because of the baby, we wouldn't make the trip.

I placed my hands atop my stomach and took comfort in the baby's steady hiccoughs—little explosions, taps from the inside, reminders that I would never again be alone.

The log shifted and a few sparks popped like a Fourth of July sparkler. Hints of orange ember appeared in the smoke cloud outside my window. I wondered how long the fire would last. Would it stay strong through the night and fulfill its purpose of keeping me warm? Or if I turned my back, ignored the fading flames and allowed it to die, how long would it take to become nothing more than a pile of ash—something to clean up?

The fire needed intermittent yet constant attention to stay alive. Just like a friendship.

Joel had been in my first college class, Oral Interpretation. What a surprise to hear him—anyone—say my name as I walked in the classroom. And to see him sitting there with a warm and inviting smile, I knew I had chosen the right school. He became Soulful Joel and I became Noble Noelle. We all had such silly yet fitting names in that class. I wondered, did Daphne still call herself Daphne Duck?

My mind moved to thoughts of Joel's roommate Don Juan— Donny the Moax—who became the man with whom I'd compare each subsequent lover. I remembered Cleo King, Ruby Pappas, Lisa Leigh, and the veranda where we spent spring afternoons at the dorm. I remembered when Joel stumbled outside my door with a bottle of Tanqueray, screaming my name for all to hear.

As the fire simmered and popped like bacon frying, I recalled the details of my college life. I wavered between the feeling of it being a long time ago or like yesterday. It's funny how memories do that—how they replay in our dreams, meld together and confuse.

I thought of the night Joel and I stole the glass from the pool hall and called it our "well-insulated goblet." That was another snowy night—the night he kissed me in the middle of Illinois Avenue. It was only a moment and yet I touched my lips and could still feel the memory. How lucky I was to have experienced it and to have known it was a moment I would never forget. Weeks later I saw Anita wearing his "NO!" shirt. That moment, too, etched in my brain and recorded a message telling me I didn't deserve that kiss in the middle of the street. I didn't deserve to be loved like that. And yet months later, I slept with him. I—we—crossed the line from friendship to that mysterious place from where you can never turn back.

It was a stolen moment and the moment that made it ultimately impossible for us to be friends.

Just before I became pregnant with Marc's child—about eight months earlier—I had seen Joel in Chicago. As Marc and I rode the elevator in the tall building to his office on the twenty-eighth floor, he had asked if I knew whether or not Joel would be in his office. I didn't know. I just wanted to take a chance—to surprise him—to see his face and have him finally meet not only my husband, but also the woman I had become. If I had called first I would have given him the opportunity to say no, not today.

Joel was indeed surprised to see us. I can't say he was delighted, but he immediately offered to take us to lunch at one of his regular haunts around the corner. An awkward trio, we sat at a table by the window on a chilly spring day, and Marc at once excused himself to use the bathroom. Joel said he couldn't believe we just dropped in like that.

"I don't want to lose you," I had said, gently tapping his hand.

His hair was short. Corporate. It exposed a high and expression-prone forehead. A small furrow appeared between his brows—knitting an almost vacuous look that masked his usually clear eyes. *I don't want to lose you.* It was as though he turned the sentence around in his head, interpreting it. I think it scared him and he knew as well as I that whatever was between us had already been lost.

The rest of the lunch was filled with small talk. Joel asked about our new home, our dogs, and how we liked the cold climate after so many years in California. We asked about his children and he dutifully pulled photos from the wallet in his back pocket.

He insisted on paying the bill and then offered to walk us to our car. We said we planned to visit Marc's aunt who lived across the street from his office, and we bid him farewell. Marc shook his hand and I hugged him, unable to feel anything through his thick, wool coat.

I didn't know it would be the last time we'd ever come face to face.

Did he?

He didn't call on my birthday, and, of course, he didn't send a Christmas card. Instead he sent three sentences asking me to stay out of his life.

* * * * * * * *

I descended the bare, wooden steps to the basement, petted the dogs and collected a hand-full of soft, lanolin fur. Tufts of white follicles danced in the air like snowflakes as both dogs rolled on their backs and basked in the late night massage. I gave them each a final pat and then approached the firewood pile, a neat stack piled as high as my forehead. The oak logs were heavy and square. I chose them for my bucket over the scrappy birch and poplar scattered between them with bark falling off like loose-fitting clothes. But I filled the bucket with too much weight and succumbed to the warnings of my obstetrician and removed three logs. The state of pregnancy, the condition, was beyond my control, and it was essential that I respect the limitations it placed on my body. As I slowly hauled the load of wood up the steps to the steady beat of Luna and Stella's panting, I approached the stove and wished I could slow down the demands of my thoughts as well.

Accepting the separation—the loss of my friend—was not an easy task.

The fire crackled as it happily accepted the fresh logs. And as I fed them to the flames like sacrificial lambs, I recalled a line from a novel I had recently read that claimed the only stories worth telling were those about separation.

And then I knew the truth. As much as I needed to separate from Joel and to end our friendship, I wasn't quite ready to let him go.

From Marc's briefcase, I took a yellow legal pad and hunted for the fine tip marker I usually reserved for crossword puzzles. Left inside the *New York Times Crossword Puzzle Dictionary,* marking the place where I had last looked up another word for "drench," I grabbed it like the prized gold ring and started writing.

I began with Joel's letter and then continued with the story of the boy I had met and the man I grew to know and love. I meant to tell the story of our friendship.

After the first page, however, and maybe even the first few paragraphs, the characters became other people. They were no longer Joel and Noelle or Anita and Marc. They, in a way, were all I—all products of my imagination whom I bent and twisted and formed into a story about love and relationships—about boys and girls becoming men and women and whether or not a friendship could exist after two people crossed the line into unfamiliar territories.

For me it became a lesson on how to let go.

For the next several weeks, Marc was busy preparing for a trial. I worked during the day. I worked late at night, next to the fire, while he and then soon, our daughter, Emily, slept peacefully upstairs. Through writing and through endless moments of connection with my daughter, I grew to understand an entirely new degree of love. The utter ache I experienced when looking into the perfect, full-moon face of my precious baby girl, and the need to drop all when I heard her cries, was to truly know the meaning of selflessness. Comparing this emotion along with my love for Marc, illustrated the differences in the more possessive passion I had felt for Joel.

I had used him and his feelings to justify my own, and I now believed that loving him was a vague rehearsal for first learning to love myself and finally, for loving Marc. What came through on full volume was my immaturity in that relationship—the need to have it, to hold it, and to show it off.

What I thought was soulful was in reality, only selfish.

I put aside the legal pad and worked on my laptop computer, and as the pages churned from my fingertips—thoughts recorded as quickly as I imagined them—I finally realized that my friendship with Joel was no longer important to me and I could let him go. I could honor his request, withhold any needs I thought were once tantamount to my existence, and release him from any so-called obligation or friendship pact. I could even release him from his memories.

At the very least, I owed him that much.

# 28.
# Joel. Present Day.

I finally heard from my father. Actually, I heard from his son, my half-brother. William, Will, wrote on his twenty-first birthday, the day he learned of my existence. He was about to finish his liberal arts degree and, still not sure what he wanted to do, hoped to attend graduate school at Northwestern. Maybe go to law school? He wanted to move to Chicago, and he wanted to meet me. To be friends.

He wrote that our father was well and that he sent his regards.

"Ha!" I spit, reading that last line of his letter.

All I knew of this enigmatic brother was in this letter. That he was old enough to legally drink, knew about me and wanted to move to Chicago. The disingenuous flavor punctuating this letter by sending me my father's regards made me wonder whether this kid was simply being kind or if he was just a bold-faced liar. I supposed there was only one way to find out. I had to meet him, to welcome him into my life. And more importantly, I had let go of my need for my father's acknowledgment.

But the morning after his letter arrived, I learned once again how unresolved issues have a way of creeping up when you least expect them.

I sat at my kitchen table. A roll, making its uncomfortable presence known at the top of my pants, had formed in the last few weeks, and for the first time in my life I thought about dieting. I sucked in my stomach and sat up straight, lamenting the thought of having to give up the nights when I could eat an entire batch of Tollhouse cookies and not think about running three miles in the morning to work off the calories. I sipped my coffee and removed the rubber band from the morning paper. Stained with black ink, the green rubber projectile shot across the table with a snap. Glancing through the headlines in the first section and then the Business section, I flipped to the Lifestyle section. It was Monday. The day they published my favorite column, "News of the Weird." Paging to it, I suddenly stopped.

"Oh my God," I said. "I don't believe it."

There she was. A grainy set of half-tone eyes staring at me, watching me drink my coffee and boring into my thoughts.

*Noelle Moncada Andersen to sign copies of her new novel,* A College Affair.

A thud came from the ceiling above me and I nearly dropped my cup. At once a sense of guilt caught in my throat like a thick piece of meat. I quickly closed the paper and rose to my feet. Listening, there was nothing more than the steady ticking of the second hand on the kitchen clock above the sink, keeping pace with my rapid and culpable heartbeat. I took a deep breath. No one was up yet and the house still belonged to me. Michael, I reasoned, must have dropped his book again. He always fell asleep with a book in his hand. He was like me. He loved words. And just as my mother had taught me, I taught him to mark each word he had looked up in the dictionary. His choice was to use an orange highlighter.

I refilled my cup with as much coffee as cream and returned to the table. Again opening the paper to the article about Noelle, I stared at her photo. I'd recognize her anywhere. Reading further, I discovered where the book-signing event would take place. The House of Books, a popular chain store now occupying the retail space that I first knew as Troves of Treasures, and then later It's A Beautiful Day record store. The newspaper ad felt like a personal invitation into my past—into my neighborhood and into my life.

I pushed aside a piece of toast, leaving pepper-like crumbs on the table, and wondered if I would look the same to her. Now in my mid-forties, my hair was thin and receding, and with a hint of half-moon circles beneath my eyes, I barely recognized myself in recent photographs. Beer guts and jowls and whether or not it was time to join a gym were subjects creeping into idle moments at the office, and each time one of my colleagues spoke of buying a new sports car or Harley, I shook my head and told myself I wasn't quite ready for a middle-age crisis.

Having adolescent and teenaged kids would send anyone into a midlife crisis, I reasoned. The minute I got home each night, I left myself in the seat of my car and entered their chaotic world of homework, baths, and stories. Each night Anita and I passed each other in the hallway between the boys' rooms like mere acquaintances brushing shoulders on city side streets. She'd give me the finger and call it "hallway sex." It was her funniest joke, and some nights it enabled us to laugh through the "witching hour." We dragged through that last daily hour of parenthood, and then finally crawled into bed, too tired to read, to talk, or even to watch a program on television let alone share the intimacies we once deemed so important to our marriage.

The days were filled with impossible schedules and calendars overflowing with basketball and soccer games, practices and birthday parties—the telephone answering machine asking would I coach the Little League ball team again this summer? School Board meetings, classroom volunteerism, fund-raising committees and Anita's Bunco group, which once a month kept her out well past midnight. And last night as the kids cleared their dishes and rummaged for dessert in disgustingly old Halloween candy collections, the twins enthused about taking karate. Would it ever end?

I'd had enough coffee. Leaving a one-inch puddle in the bottom of the cup, I looked at the clock and knew it was time to leave for work. I didn't want to go. I wanted to go back to bed, pull the covers over my face, and snooze away the morning. I couldn't help but think of the freedom of late night kisses and mornings without alarms. I thought of snowball fights, baseball gloves, and stingray bicycles. I remembered Maria, now happily married with three children of her own, and a game of Five-hundred. I thought of kissing her on a park bench and each of us believing we'd done something wrong. *Oh, how innocent we were!* I thought of college and a world where everyone I met was an intellectual. I thought of Noelle, of the poem she wrote for me, which I was sure I still had somewhere, in some forgotten box in some corner of my life. I thought of the night we made love and the afternoon in California when she told me it had been the most important sexual experience of her life.

*I was the best she'd ever had,* I told myself with a great feeling of satisfaction.

I got up and dropped my cup into the sink, adding it to the pile of last night's unwashed dishes. Anita had asked me to do them. I forgot. I had promised my mother I'd finish school. I guess I forgot to do that as well. Who had time between dealing with the kids and work and the foibles of the neighbors? Who could even think clearly when living in the crowded suburbs where people drove around in their minivans and SUVs filled with children, with one hand on the wheel and the other flipping the bird at every passing driver? When, I wondered, did everyone around me become so exceedingly insipid?

I bought a copy of Noelle's book, *A College Affair,* during my lunch hour. It was a self-torture I couldn't avoid and, with Carly Simon's song "You're So Vain," playing inside my head like a number one tune on AM-radio, I hoped that this so-called "college affair" would be about me.

Opening the book, the first words I read were my own:

*Dear Claire,*
*I don't think it's fair that you keep in touch with me. It's not fair to me and it's not fair to my wife Joanna. Please don't write to me or call me anymore.*
*Jack*

"Who the fuck is Jack?" I asked, flipping to the back cover, looking for something—anything to assure me that my insides weren't about to be mangled. A knot formed in my gut. It was a familiar feeling—like the way it felt when I read letters from dissatisfied clients who blamed me for stock market losses.

Reading on, I soon discovered she had changed all the names. She put a mask on my life and called it fiction. What was this? Some kind of revenge? The hope I had felt five minutes earlier while whistling, *"You probably think this book is about you. Don't you? Don't you?"* had turned to dread.

Fatalistic by nature, I couldn't help myself. I sucked in the pages, turning them quickly, reading as though breathing. My hands shook a little and a stirring inside my stomach evolved into a sexual, almost orgasmic feeling. Was it flattery?

I raced ahead, careful to read each word, and I let them flow through me like the sweet pleasure of ice cream. But within a few pages, a mouthful became a brain freeze. This wasn't I.

I was not Jack.

Noelle was inside the mind of a stranger, imagining, staging, and supplying answers to questions that were either never posed or had no need of an answer. The character may have been based on me, but it wasn't the man who looked back at me in the morning mirror.

She had rewritten herself as well. Claire. Where did she get that name? She wasn't as tall or as beautiful, but she was smart and self-assured. Unlike Noelle, she had confidence in her decisions—like she knew what she was doing all along.

I cancelled the one appointment I had that afternoon and remained in my office reading until I finished her book. Closing it, finally, and looking at her photo on the book jacket—the same photo that had appeared in the paper, I felt that she may have changed the characters: The names, the faces, the places, and the events, but in what was left of my invaded soul, I knew the subject was *us*.

It was a rejected future. The *us* that never was.

I'd have to keep this book at my office and hope Anita didn't learn of it. I know I couldn't risk bringing up Noelle's name again. Why should I dredge up all those old, painful feelings? Just as Noelle and I never talked about Anita in the early days, ever since I wrote the letter asking her to stop all contact, Anita and I had learned not to talk about Noelle.

I intended to keep Noelle Moncada as dead and buried as I once kept the memories of my father.

Unfortunately, this book, coupled with my brother's letter, proved to me that false burials were an impossible task. Even Noelle wrote of this impossibility in her story: *"Memories cannot die. They are our burden, our pleasure, and our constant reminder of who we are."*

I knew even before I finished reading it that two nights later I wouldn't resist driving my car along the railroad tracks near my old neighborhood on the night of her book signing. It had been a long time since I was in that neighborhood. Since we sold my mother's house, the only reason I ever returned was to drive past my childhood home and show the boys where their daddy grew up.

"Cool!" they always said, like tourists seeing the home of a celebrity from a bus.

Once or twice we got together with Joe and Carol and their kids for backyard barbecues or softball games in the forest preserves. But for the most part, I had become a visitor to my hometown. I had outgrown it—moved on.

On Wednesday night, however, my old hometown still looked the same. The same brick bungalows stood silently and evenly spaced in neat rectangle lots with square patches of matted lawn, just recovering from a winter snow blanket. Daffodils and tulips in front of evergreen bushes, oak, elm, maple, the occasional crab apple or redbud punctuated and individualized the properties with vivid color. The same high-speed trains filled

with earnest city workers traveling home, slowed and stopped at
the many stations along the route. Passengers exited with their
heads down and bee-lined toward their cars.

Headlights. Taillights. Car horns. Train whistles. The occasional
child yelling, "Hey, wait up!"

I was a block away from the bookstore. Would I go inside?

I recalled the last time I was in that store. It had been
a record store, and the indifferent sounds pumping from the
speakers issued a message: It was not Noelle who I wanted. It
was Anita.

Anita was my first choice. Yes, Anita. My wife, the mother of
my children, the love of my life. She had been right all along.
Noelle *was* like a drug addiction. She was the cigarette that for
a time, I couldn't quit smoking. And even though I'd gone cold
turkey for years, I had the sneaky, unpredictable urge just to hold
that cigarette between my fingers, just for a little while, without
striking a match. Indeed it was a true addiction—a red snake, a
constant temptress gnawing and reminding—hovering as pesky
as a gnat and as monumental as a death in the family. And this
book, this event and the advertisement in my newspaper, was
one more reminder that I would never quite be rid of her.

*  *  *  *  *  *  *

It was 7:30 p.m. Dark. Chilly for late spring. I rolled up the
window and turned the heater on low. The crossing gates at the
railroad track began to blink—a rhythmic red warning. I stopped,
first in line, and the zebra-striped gates lumbered downward. My
heart beat a little faster and my palms tingled. I gripped the
steering wheel tightly and asked myself what I was doing. Anita
was home with the boys, going through the routine without
me. I told her I had a dinner meeting.

It was the lie of an addict.

A train whistle sounded in the distance, soft as a mourning
dove, but grew in intensity as the silver cars came into focus.
The train slowed and stopped and passengers disembarked and
scattered. The whistle blew again and the giant metal monster
slowly chugged forth. The gates went up in slow motion. *Ding-
ding-ding-ding-ding.* Red lights blinked, alternate winking eyes,
and I followed the blinks like a patient guided into hypnosis. A
car behind me honked. It snapped me to attention, prompting
me to ease my car over the tracks. I barely felt the ripple in
the tires.

My fix grew closer and closer.

At last the store came into view. Bright fluorescent lights burst from the large bookstore windows, the focal point of activity on the street. While trying to keep focused on the busy road before me, through quick, sharp glances, it appeared that a sizeable crowd was inside. Would I go inside? Talk, laugh, shake hands? Was she expecting me to come—to take credit as the man in her story?

I continued forward to the next corner, turned, and found a parallel spot. There was no need for coins in the sidewalk parking meter after six o'clock, and yet I looked inside the ashtray for spare quarters and dimes.

My son's Eminem CD played softly through the speakers. Had it been on all along?

Stepping outside the car, I jammed my hands into my coat pockets, rounded the corner, and walked toward the store. A young couple, arm in arm and smiling, passed and looked at me as though they knew me. Did I know them? Another train whistled in the distance. The late commuter train from the Loop, I thought. Or maybe it was a slow moving freight.

I came up behind a young woman walking a small dog on a leash. It was a beagle with its mouth open slightly, exposing small, sharp teeth and a tired tongue. The dog turned its head and looked up at me, panting.

I felt exposed.

The store grew closer. The lights grew brighter. The door handle was nearly within reach. I stopped and fixed my shoulder to the glass. Peering inside, I watched people mill about and heard the sound of my own breath channeling in and out. The aroma of my past—of Noelle—grew so strong I could taste it. I was too nervous.

I couldn't do it. I couldn't go inside.

Leaning forward, peeking like the seeker who was supposed to hide his eyes and count to fifty—cheating—I saw her in profile. She was seated in the midsection of the store at a card table that held a colorful flower arrangement with a yellow bow and two neat stacks of books. Behind her stood an easel holding a poster with her name and picture. "Meet the Author," it read. Same red mane, although shorter and styled, same luminous skin and small, slightly turned-up nose. The same straight, noble posture.

The same Noelle Moncada.

Always friendly, she smiled and spoke with a certain familiarity to a solicitous fan, eager to meet her and have her sign the book.

Seated next to her was Marc, handsome and proud. A bit of gray touched around his temples. He looked distinguished—an ideal complement to his wife.

A young girl with a riot of curls as full and red as Little Orphan Annie shared his chair. Their daughter. A beautiful child. I wondered what they had named her.

As I continued to spy, to watch this happy family, my stomach calmed and my palms no longer sweated. Distant train whistles persisted, people walked and laughed and made their way toward home. All around me, life rushed by. People brushed past me on the sidewalk without noticing or caring that I was there. I was nearly invisible. I was just Joel Rolland. A husband, a father, a brother.

I was no one's son, but I was a happy man, and I believed both Noelle and I had each gotten what we wanted.

I straightened, stepped in front of the window and for a moment imagined she saw me. Then I returned to my car and pulled my cell phone from my coat pocket.

## Acknowledgements

Many thanks to Ric Bollinger for encouraging me to enter this manuscript in the McKenna Publishing Group Fiction Contest, and for consistently supporting my writing career.

Thanks to my writing friends and authors at thenextbigwriter.com, especially Kirk Ort, Selah Cooper-Holl, Diana Methot, and Jerry R. Travis.

Thanks to my editor, Hope Hollenbeck, and my friend and careful reader, Carol J. Craig. Thanks to Jeanine Ertel for her constant support… "sing loud Louise!" I also thank my sisters, Gayle VanLehman, Mary Beth Urbanek, and Debra VanOrt for reading the story in many different stages.

Thanks to everyone at McKenna Publishing Group, particularly Leslie Parker for her design expertise.

Finally, thanks to my kind and patient husband, Mike, for *everything*. Without question, you are my best friend. BBPL.

Printed in the United States
92051LV00004B/15/A